W9-DAO-089

tangled up
in daydreams

also by
rebecca bloom

girl anatomy

rebecca bloom

𝓌𝓂 William Morrow *An Imprint of* HarperCollins*Publishers*

tangled up
in daydreams

TANGLED UP IN DAYDREAMS. Copyright © 2003 by Rebecca Bloom. All rights reserved. Printed in the United States of America. No part of this book may be reproduced in any manner whatsoever without written permission except in the case of brief quotations embodied in critical articles and reviews. For information address HarperCollins Publishers Inc., 10 East 53rd Street, New York, NY 10022.

HarperCollins books may be purchased for educational, business, or sales promotional use. For information please write: Special Markets Department, HarperCollins Publishers Inc., 10 East 53rd Street, New York, NY 10022.

FIRST EDITION

Book design by Shubhani Sarkar
Illustrations by Philip Puleo

Printed on acid-free paper

Library of Congress Cataloging-in-Publication Data

Bloom, Rebecca, 1975–
    Tangled up in daydreams : a novel / Rebecca Bloom.—1st ed.
      p. cm.
    ISBN 0-06-621258-8
    1. Young women—Fiction.   2. Sun Valley (Idaho)—Fiction.   3. Los Angeles (Calif.)—Fiction.   I. Title.

PS3602.L66T36   2003
813'.6—dc21

2003056237

03 04 05 06 07 WBC/RRD 10 9 8 7 6 5 4 3 2 1

For my family

tangled up
in daydreams

Her hair would just not cooperate. No amount of Green Tea shine extract or crushed bamboo Bed Head spread was going to tame the cherry-stained poof. Molly stared at her reflection and tried to smooth the frizz that was only getting slicker and stiffer with each layer. However, if not for the fro, she could focus on the scaly patch of skin just below her left eye that was beginning to sprout tiny red bumps. How come facials created freakish post-visit breakouts in spots that, even in the past, never succumbed to the hellish wrath of teenage acne? Molly hastily dabbed on some cover-up lotion and grabbed a polka-dot scarf from the drawer. She could only focus on one flaw at a time. If she dwelled on them and two or three managed to squeak by, her full self-conscious body chorus, which can usually drown out one off-key harmony, would get all worked up into a tizzy of wrong notes and caterwaul too loud to ignore. Molly had no time for the self-doubting symphony tonight. She was already late, and Jaycee was going to arrive in seconds to pick her up.

Molly rummaged through the pile of semi-clean clothing draped on the side of her dresser. She grabbed a pair of worn-in cargo pants, a red studded belt, and a black partially wrinkled but passable tank. With a few jeweled cat collars fastened to her wrists, a spritz of Trapeze, her favorite new perfume that she had just picked up from a little store in Venice, a black vintage band uniform blazer, a black suede bag, and a pair of Costume National boots, she was put together and perfectly timed to the first car honk. She got in and threw her coat in the back of Jaycee's car. Her friend had also paper-dolled it quite well. In her tight cropped jeans, yellow one-sleeved ruffled sweater, strands of fake pearls, camo kitten heels, and short spiked hair, which still had pink tinges, Jaycee had fashioned herself into a pint-sized, punk country club girl.

"Nice look." Jaycee gestured to Molly's head scarf. "Very Ali MacGraw."

"Thanks." Checking in the mirror to see if it was tight enough. "You don't even want to know what's under here. I think 'nest' is not even an adequate adjective."

"Who cares? It's just me and you tonight, baby. You have no need to impress." Flipping on the radio. "This is Alison. The girl we are hearing tonight."

"Is this what you played the other night when we made dinner?" Picking up the CD case and turning it over. "Like the pearls by the way."

"Yeah, I was going for a debauched debutante thing. This . . ." skipping tracks, "is my favorite song."

"Nice." Leaning back and enjoying the music. "She sounds a bit like early Natalie Merchant. Very throaty."

"But, not so round, and a little more punk rock. It should be a good show."

The girls gabbed and listened all the way to the bar. They parked in front of Goldfinger's and walked in. The show had yet to begin, so they pulled up two bar stools and ordered martinis from the cute Australian whom Jaycee used to sleep with.

"Hey, Mark," Jaycee said as she kissed the tall, burly bartender on the cheek. "How's it going?"

"Terrible since you dumped me, love," he answered as he winked at Jaycee. "What would you two like?"

"Martinis and my friend Molly here likes hers very dirty."

Mark went to the other end of the bar to make their drinks, and Molly and Jaycee settled onto their perches. Goldfinger's was dark in that perfect bar way. You could see everyone clearly enough to know whom you were talking to, but they fortunately couldn't see all the flaws you carefully masked behind the carefully spackled foundation and last-minute accessories. With the focus blurred in just the right way, everyone looked somewhat attractive. Besides being dark, the bar had gold, padded walls and a cool go-go-girl cage set up in the corner. Very James Bond. Very LA. There were about twenty other patrons there, milling, checking, and scanning about. No one looked familiar, so Molly and Jaycee continued in their own little world of conversation.

"Jay, I'm so pissed at you for introducing me to John."

"What's wrong now?" Pulling up the back of her jeans. "I knew I should have worn a belt."

"It's fine. I only see a peek of thong." Checking her friend's ass. "Anyway, it's the same shit. He overtalks everything! I'm just so sick of him calling to order these summit meetings every friggin' week on the state of our relationship," Molly complained while she sipped her cocktail. "It's exhausting."

"Isn't that, like, your fourth 'relationship' talk in what, a month? And, what's the deal? He's being more of a chick than you ever could!"

"Yep. He needs me to be aware of all the nuances of his feelings about us, and how close we are, and what he wants, and what I want, and how we can get to the next level. After an hour we figure out some steps to take and for a short time things are great, but then it's another talk and we're back to square one. It's so annoying."

"I'm sorry I tried to play cupid," Jay apologized as she chugged her drink. "I thought you guys would be a good match. You have so much in common, and he fits right into your whole struggling artiste thing."

"Mentally we are, and I love that he is so communicative because usually guys flee the minute anything resembling feelings comes up, but everything is so cerebral all the time. It's sort of stopped being fun and sexy. And, because of all this serious head stuff, the guy for some insane reason just won't let us get intimate."

"Intimate how?"

"Intimate, intimate."

"No way?!"

"Yes, way."

"You guys have been dating for, like, two months!" Jaycee exclaimed. "I know that you like to wait a while before you do the deed but that's a long time even for you!"

"No kidding," Molly responded as she took another sip. "I finally meet a smart, cool guy who I feel safe with and want to sleep with, a guy who is open and honest, yet even when I'm practically naked in his bed splayed out like a porn star, he won't jump me! I'm beginning to think maybe he is gay, or completely unattracted."

"I don't think so, but what is this world coming to when a girl can't get laid when she wants to?" Jay stated as she began to laugh at Molly.

"It's going to hell is what's happening." Molly laughed with her.

"What are you going to do?"

"Well, I think it might be time to extricate. According to his schedule, we're about due for another chat and I think if I can't get him to understand that sometimes we need to be a little more free, I'm probably going to break up with him. It's not what I really want to do because I just dig him, and he's so smart and he kind of makes me all fluttery, but this pseudo relationship isn't working for me."

"Will you do me a favor? Don't say anything yet and just drop the ball a little."

"What do you mean?" Molly asked and then turned to the bartender. "Mark, can I get another? Jay?"

"Yeah, I will have one too, thanks. I mean, don't call, and don't make plans, ignore him for a while and see what he does. Let him miss you."

"Okay, but what if he just bails?"

"Then fuck him." Answering matter-of-factly. "I have this strong premonition that once he senses you straying, he'll jump to attention and give you what you want, which right now is a lit-tle nookie."

"Hope you're right because I'm about ready to give up."

"Of course I'm right. I am always right."

"Bullshit, but tonight you can have your little ego trip."

"Thanks." Batting her eyes. "I need a smoke, let's go outside."

"You lead, I follow."

The two girls picked up their new drinks and headed to the back of the bar.

"Oh, I forgot to tell you, I put one of the new Marc Jacobs jackets on hold for you. You need to come in and try it on tomorrow," Molly told Jay.

"Is it cute?"

"Yeah, I think they will look great on you. They're cropped and the cotton is really soft."

"I love that you work at a cool clothing store. I feel so in the fashion know."

"Glad to be of service, but I am so sick of peddling other people's wares. I can't wait to do something on my own."

"So do it." Pausing near the dance floor. "What are you waiting for?"

"It's expensive to start a line, to start anything really, and I don't even know yet what I want to really make. Sometimes I still think I want to paint, or I don't know."

"I'm sure your parents would be more than happy to help you out."

"I know, but I want to do it myself."

"Just because you ask for help does not make you less independent."

"I guess, when the time is right, it will all come together, and until then I will keep myself and my nearest and dearest clad in today's freshest styles." Pulling Jay along.

"Fine, fine. I get the point."

Just outside there was a patio set with red lights, black vinyl banquettes, and leopard upholstery. A canopy of smoke hung above despite the open ceiling, and the air was damp with perspiration and fading perfume. More people had arrived and the two girls couldn't find a place to sit or lean anywhere. Jaycee took the lead and tried to find them a place to settle, but bodies and faces began to crowd the view. Then out of nowhere, a voice erupted behind them.

"You guys look a little lost—wanna join us?"

Molly and Jaycee turned around and there stood the most magnificent man they had ever seen. His eyes glowed from within, almost as if he were wearing some new Halloween-appropriate contacts. The girls literally stumbled. Sounds disappeared, the lights dimmed, and Molly lost her breath. She could actually feel her heart beating through her skin. It wasn't that he was so perfectly pretty. His dark hair was messy and in need of a cut, his Pac-man shirt was moth worn and ill fitting, his nose was slightly crooked, and his cheeks were ruddy, flushed, and sprinkled with freckles. There was just something about him. Molly felt electric, fluorescent, feverish. She couldn't decide whether it was those haunting gray eyes or the curl of his brown hair, or how his voice sounded familiar that sucked her in. It didn't matter because he was magic, and Molly fell in love with him at first sight. It was immediate and scary, like someone knocked the wind out of her.

"Uhh," Molly stuttered, and somehow simultaneously spilled her entire drink down the front of her black tank top.

"Sorry, didn't mean to startle you." Apologizing. "Let me get you a napkin."

He quickly walked back into the bar.

"Nice move, butterfingers." Jaycee dissed her. "You're so smooth."

"Fuck, why am I such a loser? I can't believe I just did that in front of such a god." Molly tried to wipe the liquid off her chest. "I mean . . . guy."

"So I take it this one is yours?" Jaycee asked as she winked at Molly.

"What do you mean, mine? I don't even know him," Molly deflected and started to get flustered. "He's fair game."

"Whatever. I know you, and you only pull the klutz routine when your pheromones start synapsing."

"Am I that obvious?"

"Yes, but it's cute and he must think so too because here he comes with like a ream of paper napkins."

"Here, will these work?" Thrusting about twenty napkins at her.

"I think so." Molly laughed while holding the many napkins. "But I didn't fall into a pool."

"I guess I got a little carried away." He laughed with her. "My name is Liam."

"Molly, and this is Jaycee." Molly gestured next to her, but Jaycee wasn't there. "Well, that was Jaycee."

"Nice to meet you. And her." He smiled. "Sit down?"

"Sure."

"I'll be right back. I'm going to go get you another drink. Martini?"

"Please."

Liam vanished so Molly had to sit down alone at the small table. Two other guys and a tall, thin blond girl were sitting there already and as soon as Molly's butt touched the bench, they all cast this "What the fuck are you doing here at our table?" look at her. The attitude they shot at her could have laid the queen of confidence, Miss J.Lo herself, out on her ass'ets.

Molly wondered if people woke up in the morning and just decided to be mean for the hell of it. Like "Hey, it's Wednesday and I'm going to be a total asshole today just because." Was it more fun to be nasty and cruel or was it just easier? Anyway, the guys leered and the girl sneered, and Molly began to shrink under their bitchiness. Before she totally melted into the seat and fell victim to these wannabes, Molly gave herself a little "You're cool, you're swell, you're the bomb" pep talk and decided not to cower. Instead, she sat up straighter, smiled, and then quickly looked for a cigarette in her bag. She had a cute guy coming back to talk to her and that was all that mattered. She pulled a Camel out, lit it, and inhaled. Nothing like the taste of nicotine to cover up the taste of nerves.

"Here you go, Molly." Liam handed her a drink and then sat down. "Have you met my friends?"

"No, can't say that I have." She smirked at them.

"This is Elena, Zander, and Elliot. Guys, this is Molly."

"Hey." The collective grunted. "Got any more smokes?"

"Sure." Molly threw a pack down on the table and as soon as it landed, they lunged at it like wild animals.

"Easy there, kids," Liam scolded his friends. "They aren't usually so misbehaved. It's just one of those nights." Redirecting his attention back to Molly.

"It's okay. Sometimes when you're jonesing, etiquette flies right out of the proverbial window."

"Exactly. So, Molly, should we have one of those bullshit conversations that people usually have when they meet at a bar?"

"You mean the ones that include the standard what do you do, where are you from, are you married type questions?"

"Yep. That would be it."

"I don't know. That seems too mundane." Molly, smiling.

"I agree. Why is it that people always resort to talking about the most meaningless subjects when they are trying to make a good first impression?"

"Probably because they are nervous and are just looking for common ground. It's not like you can randomly meet someone and start talking about Camus."

"You've read him?" Liam's eyes widened.

"Sure, but just *The Stranger.*"

"I loved that book, all about man's identity and existentialism."

"What are you reading now?" Molly asked.

"Well, I've forced myself to go a little more modern and at the suggestion of my sister-in-law, Anita, I'm reading this book, *High Fidelity,* by some British guy. I saw the movie, but she says the book is much better."

"Well, I did like the movie, but I absolutely loved that book. This guy I met when I was traveling abroad recommended it as the quintessential book on a guy's psyche."

"I'm only halfway through it, but so far it depicts exactly how guys think about relationships and love."

"Every girl should read it then and get the insider's perspective. We need all the help we can get when it comes to men."

"We aren't so complicated."

"Yeah, right!" Molly laughed out loud. "Tell that to my girlfriends."

"You just haven't met the right guy." He smiled.

"Now you sound like my grandmother."

"Sorry, but it's true. Not all guys have these whacked-out theories about coupling with someone."

"Maybe, but I'm hesitant to believe that these days. I'm really an optimist, but that's getting tiring. You always face too much disappointment."

"True, but you live a fuller life. Expecting the best from people and situations is always the way to go," Liam continued.

"But a lot of times you live it alone because most people look at the downside of things and avoid emotional connections. Most expect to be hurt and alienated, so they bail before anything at all happens."

"I can't imagine doing that. Sure, it is hard to be vulnerable and let yourself be open, yet that is the only way you get all the good stuff."

"Most people are afraid to do that," Molly pointed out.

"I don't know, Molly. I just don't believe in shying away from strong feelings whether they are good or bad. It's only through pain that you can live better."

"That sounds a bit morbid."

"I don't mean that only suffering and a doom-and-gloom attitude get you anywhere. I mean that all emotions, fear, pain, passion, love, are scary, but they are what make you alive."

"Like if you let yourself get involved, get torn to pieces, and get your heart broken, you wind up better for the trip?" Molly asked.

"Exactly. I can't live a safe life, a life blanketed to make everything balanced and boring. It's a waste of time to live with okay and fine. Why bother?"

"I agree with you, Liam, but it's hard to always pick yourself up. Defeat is not an easy thing to rouse yourself from because when and if you do live this super-charged give me pain, give me heartache, give me love type of life, you constantly get fucked because most people aren't doing the same thing."

"Well, maybe then it's time for you to win a little," Liam said.

"That would be nice for a change."

"So, Molly, this is definitely not one of those bullshit conversations."

"No, it certainly isn't." Grinning at him.

They both smiled at each other and Molly knew that her troubles with men were over. For about five minutes they just stared and grinned and drank each other in. Nothing could interrupt the twirl between them. It was just Molly and Liam and they had just fallen for each other.

"By the way . . . are you?" Liam, breaking the silence.

"Am I what?" Molly looked at him funny.

"Married?"

"No! Are you?"

"Nope."

"Good."

"Ditto."

"Last name?"

"McGuire. Yours?"

"Stern. And you are . . . ?" Molly asked.

"A musician."

"Ahh, perfect."

"Do I detect a note of sarcasm?" Liam asked.

"Not yet." Smiling at him. "But, I'll get back to you later on that one."

"Cute. You?"

"An artist trapped in the body of a salesgirl."

"Painting? Sculpture?"

"A little of everything right now. I haven't found my niche just yet."

"You will, one day it will hit you and then you'll be golden."

"I'd like that. So, now what?" Molly wondered as she played with an olive in her drink. "Shall we continue?"

"No, I think now that we know each other so well, you should find Jaycee, say good-bye to her, and leave with me."

"Right now?"

"Right now."

"Okay."

"I'll meet you outside."

With that Molly stood up and headed back into the bar to find Jaycee. She had no idea what she was doing or why, but it really didn't matter. Her mind was swimming and she loved every minute of the dip. This was one of those once-in-a-lifetime moments that she just had to grab. It was scary, potentially dangerous, and completely irrational, but it was also a must do. Even if he turned out to be a psycho, which was pretty much even odds at this point, she had to follow her gut and follow him out the door. Molly spotted Jaycee at the end of the bar talking to Mark and rushed over to her.

"I'm leaving."

"What?"

"I'm leaving."

"How?" Jay asked. "The band hasn't even gone on yet."

"With Liam."

"Who's Liam?"

"The god."

"You're joking, right?"

"Nope. Is that cool?"

"No, but does it matter what I think?"

"Not really," Molly answered. "And I know how bitchy and lame that sounds, but I just have to go."

"What about John?"

"Wasn't it you who told me to drop the ball a little?"

"This is not dropping it a little, this is pretty much popping it and watching it shrivel up and blow right out of the stadium."

"Don't be so dramatic."

"Okay, okay, go, but leave your cell on because I'm going to call and check on you."

"Thanks, babe." Molly kissed her cheek. "Wish me luck."

"Just get out of here, Mark will keep me company."

Molly grabbed her coat from behind the bar and bolted for the door. She swung it open with such force that she almost took Liam out with the corner of the shiny edge.

"You are dangerous!" he exclaimed as he stepped backward to avoid the injury.

"I'm so sorry." Molly blushed. "I'm having coordination problems tonight."

"Couldn't tell," Liam said with a straight face.

"Liam, I'm really sorry," Molly repeated as she started freaking out. "I'm not usually such a disaster. I swear . . ."

"Relax," Liam interrupted. "I'm just giving you a hard time."

"Thanks. Not like I'm not nervous enough," she muttered under her breath.

"Why are you nervous?"

"You weren't supposed to hear that." She blushed again.

"But I did."

"Let's just get out of here before I change my mind."

"Sounds good. I wouldn't want to lose you now."

Liam offered Molly his arm, and the two of them walked together to the parking lot, their streetlamp shadows blending into one. They made their way to his perfectly restored vintage muscle car and started driving.

"Where to?" Liam asked, pulling onto Sunset.

"Wherever. I got no plans." Checking the side-view mirror to see if her scarf was secured. "Well, I had plans, but this tornado sort of swept through and turned them on their head." Looking at him.

"I kind of like being a force of nature."

"I bet you do." Bantering.

Liam leaned his head out the window at the next stoplight and looked toward the sky.

"How about the beach? We can pick up some beers."

"Sure." Not knowing why she was so casually agreeing to drive to a deserted beach with a total stranger. Maybe it was the way Sunset Boulevard's neon lights framed his cheekbones.

"So, what's under there?" Tugging at the edge of her scarf.

"You don't want to know. My hair sometimes acts like a very stubborn two-year-old. It refuses to cooperate no matter how tender I am with my coaxing."

"Let me see." Trying to pull it off.

"I don't think so." Dodging his hands. "The interior of your car is not big enough to handle it."

"Please?" Grinning at her. "Now I have to see."

"Nope, patience is a virtue, dear boy." Grinning back.

"Okay, okay." Grabbing and holding on to her hand instead. Molly could swear she felt sparks.

As Molly and Liam drove all the way down Sunset Boulevard to the beach, they didn't really talk much more. Both of them settled into silence, nestled in their own little fantasies of what was beginning between them. Even when they stopped at 7-Eleven to get some beer, they barely uttered a sound, quietly picking, paying, and pocketing the change. Already they felt familiar, like they had done all these tasks a hundred times before. Already they were dancing. It wasn't until they had parked, ditched their shoes, and walked onto the cool sand that their tongues loosened.

"Beaches at night with a guy always make me laugh a little," Molly shared as she kicked the sand at her feet.

"Why?" Lifting the beers under his arm.

"Something about the romantic potential they're supposed to have. You know, with the 'moon on the water casting this lovey-dovey halo of light on the cute couple' and how for me, the reality never came close."

"How so?"

"When I was sixteen, I went to Hawaii with a friend of mine and this one night we went to the beach with these two hot valet parkers. I thought, 'This is my moment. The stars are all in line,' " Molly stated as she walked to the water. "It was supposed to be my romance-novel kiss."

"Supposed to be?" Liam asked as he walked next to her. "What does that mean?"

"Well, this surfer guy, who I think said he was related to Keanu Reeves, and I pair off. We are sitting on the sand and he's nonstop talking to me about surfing, which I thought was so fascinating because every time he said the word 'wave' his lips kind of curled and his right eye twinkled. He kept talking and talking, and I kept swooning and willing him to plant one on me."

Molly swallowed and willed herself to shut up. Any guy could see right through her subtle song and dance around the whole kissing issue.

"Somehow hours pass and I hear my friend start calling my name, yelling that it's time to leave. So I look at him really hard and bat my eyes, all the while thinking this is going to be the best kiss of my young life if he would only just do it. He leans in and shoves what must be a tongue the size of a cow's in my mouth, poking it in and out like an iguana!"

Molly said another small prayer to her God that she could just close her yap.

"It felt like he was checking my molars for leftovers from dinner. And, to make it worse, he tasted like beer and cigarettes. Here I was on the most beautiful beach in Hawaii, with a gorgeous Hawaiian surfer, and instead of being in heaven, I was a bit player in a Roger Corman T and A movie."

Molly took another deep breath and waited. Her face was flaming and her palms were coated with a slick layer of sweat. She could feel her tight black tank sticking to the underside of her breasts as perspiration dripped and pooled on her stomach. Why had she revealed such a silly and stupid anecdote!

"Poor girl, it's a shame that guy ruined your perfect moment. Usually that happens when you have one of those romance novel/romantic comedy scenarios staring you in the face."

"Yeah." Molly thanking God that he was going with it.

"I actually sneezed all over some girl once. Shelby Harrington, the hottest girl in the eighth grade finally liked me, and back then I was not the cool rock-star guy I am now."

"Who said you were cool?" Winking at him as she walked to a spot and sat down.

"Nice." Walking toward her and sitting down next to her. "We went to this dance together and we snuck outside. I'm just about to lay one on her when this volcanic sneeze erupted all over her rosy cheeks. I could see the snot glisten."

"That is so gross! Yours is way worse."

"She screamed and for a year no other girl would come within fifteen feet of me and my lips."

"They must have gotten lonely." Staring at him.

"Who?"

"Your lips."

"Is that a subtle hint that I should swoop in and create a new beachfront memory?"

"I thought telling you my kissing story was a pretty blatant hint."

"Nah." Grinning.

"So?"

"So?"

"Are you going to swoop or not?" Molly asked.

"Definitely." Liam leaned in and began to fake a sneeze. "I . . . I . . . I . . ."

"Don't even!" Molly giggled.

"Never."

And Liam kissed her. She did not notice the broken beer bottles around them, nor the trash washed up onshore. She didn't hear the yells from a bonfire down the way, nor the hum of the Pacific Coast Highway behind her. It was priceless. All the sweeter because of how off-kilter the night had been. They kissed and kissed until the sun rose, and when they were done, they drove all the way back to Hollywood and grabbed breakfast at Swinger's. Molly's hair was free and disheveled and Liam's lips were puffy, but they were still in their lovely, perfect moment. It wasn't until he dropped her off at home and kissed her one last time that the moment ended, and for them, it would be the first of many.

one

The cab driver must have thought she was a hooker. Black eyes bruised with make-up and a jagged tear running down the length of her fishnet-clad thigh. A maroon ribbon hand-knit scarf hung limp and sweaty around her neck, its threads sticking to the under-side of her chin. The thin white tank and rumpled patch-work denim skirt draped over her body like hand-me-downs. Chipped metallic-blue nails clutched a shredded tissue in one fist and a small leopard-print purse in the other. Lying in her lap was a dark red suede coat smudged and stained with God knows what. Blood or sweat or maybe tears. The air around her smelled sour, like the sheets of an eight-year-old just waking from a monster-in-the-closet nightmare. She was a walking zombie, *Night of the Living Dead* part twelve—the postmodern version. Her face was swollen like a prizefighter after a third-round knockout, her long reddish hair twisted, tumbling down her back like dirty rope, and her lips puckered like a bad collagen injection. A giant kewpie doll minus the gleeful grin and coy demeanor.

The fact that Molly was exiting Cedar Sinai hospital probably didn't help in defending her honor. Looking so ragged and torn, she could easily be walking away from being salved and bandaged from wounds left by an oversexed john. It wasn't the case of course, but since there was nothing sweet or innocent about her ragged appearance, people could jump to the wrong conclusion. And, that doesn't leave much wiggle room when the stares present themselves at exactly the wrong time. She wanted to crawl into a dank, moldy hole and die.

"Where to?" asks the cab driver.

"Beverly and Sycamore."

"Rough night?"

She couldn't bring herself to respond. Putting words together to make a sentence seemed like an alien concept. She couldn't think straight. All she could do was just stare in front of her with a gaze a hypnotist would love. A cold, vacant gaze trained on the back of the doily-covered headrest. Slowly, she swiveled her head toward the window and sighed. It was the first time in hours that she was aware that she was actually still breathing. As her breath fogged the passenger window, she began drawing on the glass, tracing shapes and patterns in the damp frost. Mindlessly, Molly played tic-tac-toe and doodled as the cab inched along Beverly toward her house. Her home. What is home now?

As she swallowed and shifted her weight, the springs along the cab seat creaked and whined. Suddenly bored with her picture

game, her eyes settled back in front of her and tears slowly fell
onto her freckled cheeks. At first, she let them fall and hang on
her face like the crystals of a chandelier gracing the White House
foyer. They seemed to cool her hot skin and she almost liked how
they streamed down, tickled her neck, and pooled into her lap.
As they began falling faster, she vainly attempted to wipe them
away with the distressed Kleenex. The futile gesture left her
worse for wear as huge rings of black mascara smeared into her
blotchy complexion. The tears were relentless and pounded
her into submission. Her body convulsed. She frantically wiped
and wiped her face, trying to free it from grief. She only suc-
ceeded in rubbing it in.

She could tell the cab driver was checking her out the whole
time from his rearview mirror. She could feel his eyes wandering
over her. She could hear the echoes, the questions rattling in his
brain. He was front row, privileged with a prime ticket for watching a girl crumble into the pleather interior of his taxi. How
fragile and fucked up she seemed.

"Are you okay?" Asking as he handed her a new tissue.

"Thank you." Accepting his gesture and then blowing her
nose.

"Here." Handing her the entire box. "Just keep them back
there."

"I don't think I'm going to be okay." Startling herself with the
admission.

He was surprised too. He wasn't counting on a response. It
was more just a rhetorical question to ease his discomfort of having someone so lost and distressed in his cab. Molly looked so
awful that silence seemed worse then polite chitchat. He cleared
his throat and looked at her again in the rearview mirror.

"Nothing can be that terrible. A little time always sets things
right."

"How cliché. Thanks for that brilliant bit of Hallmark wisdom." Sneering, sniping at him.

The driver paused, surprised again. "No need to be so hostile."

"Sorry," she softly apologized as she continued to cry. "I didn't mean to be rude. It isn't like me to do that."

"It's okay. But sometimes Hallmark makes a strong showing. Even cliché affirmations can be comforting."

"Whatever." Halfheartedly. "I just don't look to Shoebox greeting cards for wisdom. And besides, there is no card anywhere to make me feel better."

"Things can't be so terrible now that they can't get easier later."

"Everything is terrible and nothing's ever easy."

"I can't imagine a girl like you has it that bad." Eyeing her through the mirror. "You look like a pretty together person."

"Yeah, right." She almost laughed, pushing a lock of hair out of her face and tucking it behind her ears. "I'm not as together as you think." Mumbling.

Molly took a deep breath and turned back to the window. He sighed and flipped on the radio. He'd done what he could, and they were almost at her stop. Tina Turner's "Private Dancer" filled the cab and easily buffered the uncomfortable silence.

Finally he arrived on her block and pulled the cab to a slow stop. She handed him back his Kleenex box and a twenty she found in her purse.

"Thanks for the ride." Collecting her stuff and opening the door.

"Your change . . ." Trying to hand her back the money

"Keep it. Payment for your words of wisdom," she said, quietly.

And with that she was gone, leaving the idling cab on the corner. The cab driver wondered if she was going to make it inside safely or if she was safe to herself. He waited a little while, feeling some sort of paternal protection. Eventually, he slowly drove away.

Molly trudged toward the building, her feet clad in lead-soled boots. Every step was heavy and labored. She tried to shrink smaller and smaller, crawling into herself as she approached the door. Maybe the tinier she was, the less this was going to hurt. Less surface area equaled less volume of pain. She stood in front of the door frame for a minute trying to catch what was left of her breath. God, how was she going to walk in there? Walk back into their home? It was just an ordinary building with a few units, a couple of cats, and a testy landlord. After a long minute, she adjusted her strap, threw the dark coat over her shoulder, and picked her underwear from out of her butt; she was readying herself for battle like all those action stars do in all those action movies. Trying to commune with Rambo, he would be her strength.

The building was just as worn as she was. The eggshell paint cracked and peeled along tiny earthquake fissures. The lawn was balding and brown, dying in the summer heat. Mismatched green and blue tiles lined the pathway to the door and bougainvillea vines twisted all around the wrought-iron balcony on the second floor. This gingerbread house was somewhat moldy and stale. No Hansel nor Gretel for whom to spiff up the place. Dew ran down the windows like tears. They were both crying.

She began to wonder where was worse: out in the cool brisk morning freezing her tits off or inside where mourning had literally settled in. After another long hesitation, she stuck her key into the door and pushed it open. Walking into a dark hallway scattered with beer bottles and plastic cups, cigarette butts and used matches, she tread timidly. Everything smelled like mildew and fermented alcohol. The stench pinched her nose and she let out a little yelp. Wiping her face and covering her nose with her palm, she began to wind her way upstairs. Maybe it was the overwhelming odor, or the hallway's intense darkness despite the new day's light that made her hallucinate, but in an instant, bodies began to shift into focus. Molly's eyes played tricks. Last night's memories came flooding back, and without warning the staircase filled with people pushing and jostling for position. Molly's own limbs became coated as a slick layer of sweat attached to her torso. She was walking through her own box of Cosby-endorsed Jell-O pudding. A Chemical Brothers tune filtered into the hallway and arms flailed into high intensity techno dancing.

Molly struggled to move through the crowd, the fluidity of her transit constantly jarred. A flying elbow connected with her rib cage, and a shoulder jutted into her back. Molly's breath was knocked from her chest. In trying to find those tiny passageways between bodies and backs, her feet were lifted off the ground. She surfed through a sea of perpetual motion handed back and forth in a rhythmic symphony. Molly was redeposited onto the sullied floor, littered with ashes and memories. A bottle cap wedged itself into her shoe. She leaned down to extract it, smearing her dampened fingers onto her already dirty jacket. Her hands now tainted with someone else's spit.

She began shoving her way through the leather-pantsed party girls with Crayola-colored alternative hair, tube tops, and nose rings, but Molly hit roadblocks everywhere. Bouncing through the crowd like the old version of Atari Pong, she was starting to lose her balance. The flow was overwhelming. Just as she began to slip, people began nodding and smiling at her, softening the blows of the careless elbows. Out of nowhere, a short girl with cat-eye glasses, green camo army pants, Nike sneakers, and tight light blue lace tank linked arms with Molly and kissed her cheek. Jaycee grabbed her with the authority of a best friend and although she was smaller than most in that petite, waify want-to-hate-her way, she forcefully led Molly through a black door frame.

"Hey, babe. Where have you been?" Squeezing her arm and looking more closely. "Molly, you look like shit."

"Thanks, J." Rolling her eyes. "I was just downstairs, entertaining the troops."

"Who would have thought so many people were going to

show." Looking at the crowd. "Liam must be happy his party is so rocking."

"Our party, missy."

"Sorry, it just seems like he was more into it than you."

"That's not surprising. Where is he by the way? I lost him a little while ago."

"I saw him in the back about a half hour ago with Zander."

"Fuck! Liam knows I didn't want him here anymore. I can't believe he invited him."

"Well, he's here. So is you know who."

"How fabulous." Getting upset. "Elena just can't seem to help herself. You would think that by now she would just give up. Disappear."

"Relax. It's a party." Giving her another squeeze. "Besides, they are probably just sitting around playing music or something. They know better than to mess with the wrath of Miss Stern."

"Maybe." Unconvinced. "Who are all these people anyway?" Changing the subject.

"I thought they were friends of yours." Laughing. "You are so popular."

"Like totally." Smiling back. "You are, like, so lucky to know me!"

Inside Molly's apartment there were even more people. Two couples sat entwined on the red velvet love seat, whispering into each other's pierced ears and laughing. Along the windowsill, a series of similar hipster guys with wallet chains and tattoos downed Heinekens and passed a joint around. In the corner, sitting around the dining room table, a group of girls looked like they were bobbing for apples as each leaned down to snort lines of coke. First one, then another, arising with the all-too-familiar nose wipe and brief bug-eyed stare. Maybe this party hadn't been such a good idea. Molly blinked hard to focus on the images before her. She knew her house was empty, so why was she still seeing people mill about? She blinked again and as quickly as they appeared, they vanished.

She was standing inside her vacant apartment feeling like a stranger in a strange land, wondering what was real. Trapped inside her memory, Molly was reliving last night down to the smallest nuance. It was so vivid, the colors were saturated, almost liquid, and the sounds vibrated like a tuning fork. Last night was almost tangible; she was living inside her own personal postcard, although this one she would assuredly not sign "wish you were here." Every conversation was replaying, every face was smiling the same smile.

Molly took a deep breath and sat down. She ran her hands over the new burn mark on her red couch and traced the edges with her finger. She opened her little bag and pulled out a pack of cigarettes and a lighter. Inhaling, a large cloud of black smoke billowed above her. So much for six months cigarette free. She brought her Camel down to the soft fabric and watched as it sizzled and burned beneath. Now there were two neat black rings on the cushion. They looked better together. Things always look better in twos. Just as Molly brought the cigarette back to her mouth a hand touched the back of her neck. Molly jumped and dropped the cigarette in her lap. A piece of fringe fizzled. She grabbed the butt and turned. Suddenly, she wasn't alone anymore. The room was once again occupied with those from before. Music again played, laughter echoed, and conversations ricocheted. The scene only changed slightly. Now there were two girls at the table talking like Chatty Cathy dolls instead of three, and the wallet-chained men had wandered into the kitchen. Molly swung her head around the other direction to see where the hand had originated and there was Liam. He leaned down and gave her a long kiss.

"Hi."

"Hi." Kissing him back.

"I missed you, Molly."

"I didn't go anywhere." Getting up and moving closer to him. "What have you been doing?"

"Nothing special, just chilling." Grabbing her by the waist.

"Really?" She nuzzled into his arm. "Jaycee told me Zander and Elena were here." Trying not to sound too bitchy.

"So?"

"So, I thought that after our past run-ins, they were going to stay away from things having to do with me. You promised me. I don't care if you see them sometimes, but I just don't need them circulating around our house. Bad karma."

"I know, but I ran into him yesterday and he already knew about the party. I couldn't tell him not to come. And Elena always follows Zander. Besides, I didn't do anything with them, we were just hanging. He's my friend even if he is a fuck-up, and she's totally harmless. It's all good, baby, don't freak out."

"I know and I want to believe you. But . . ."

"Then believe me. Don't do this now." Kissing her again. "Do you want something to drink?" Changing the subject.

"I don't know." Sighing.

"I don't care if you do, have fun."

"Okay, then. But just a beer."

"Love you."

"Me too, Liam."

Liam walked toward the kitchen and Molly watched him. His lanky body moved with the grace of a gazelle and as he gently pushed his dark wavy hair back from his face, the subtle gesture sent chills down Molly's spine. Just watching him move made her fall all over again. The way his body effortlessly curled and weaved through the air made Molly weak. It was like Liam lingered just above the sidewalk like an angel. Otherworldly and weightless, he traversed the distance in his own unbreakable bubble. Who knew what buoyed him, but it was this quality that drew Molly in.

He was so unaffected by the world at large. He beat to his own drum and followed his own patterns. It wasn't as if he was making some big statement like the rules didn't apply to him, they just didn't. He was one of those rare creatures who always wound up in exactly the right place, knew exactly the right things to say, and made everyone else in the room feel like a million dollars. Molly knew she wasn't the only one he touched with this power— everyone respected and watched him as he moved through life. Girls wanted him for themselves, guys wanted to be him, and even small children and parents were enraptured by his calm confidence. It was why she fell for him in the first place. He was marked with this sparkle that Molly had never encountered before and wondered if she ever would again.

She remembered the night they met like it was yesterday, even though at least two years had passed. She would never forget talking about books and music and how life needs to be lived passionately. Drinking beer on the beach, watching the waves, and kissing and kissing until she couldn't tell whose lips and tongue were whose. How salty and crispy and perfect the six A.M. fries were, and how when he pulled away she turned and watched him blow her a kiss. The tears began falling freely. Molly's apartment was empty, again. The place that once radiated the warmth of a good home now echoed and hummed with the sounds of disappointment. Molly looked toward the kitchen hoping to see Liam, hoping he was still real. There was nothing there; she was alone.

The tissue still clenched in her hand from the cab had disintegrated into lace. The rag was not strong enough to hold even an Evian spritz. Molly got off the couch and headed down the hallway toward the bathroom to retrieve a roll of toilet paper. Maybe that would be enough to mop up her face full of tears. As she walked, hearing her boots clack against the wood floors, a cacophony of new noise bellowed. Music and laughter reverberated along the walls. The party was back in swing and voices filled the void. She ran smack into Liam.

"Hey, there." Juggling the drinks. "Molly, you must get over this need to clobber me."

"I'm sorry, I spaced." Smiling at him. "Did I get you wet?"

"No, but this crashing drink thing has always been our theme."

"How could I forget the night we met?"

"Here you go, sweetheart." Handing her a drink. "A beer for my girl."

"Thanks." Taking a long sip and eyeing his bottle of water. "Is all this okay?"

"Yep, it's really fine. Where did you just go by the way?"

"I don't know. It was one of those daydreamy things. I guess watching you walk away and shake your butt made me fantasize." Kissing him slowly.

"So, you like my butt, huh?" Kissing her back and pulling her into a hug.

"Yep. I fancy it."

"I fancy you." Kissing her again. "Am I alone in wishing all these people left so we could do it right here, right now?"

"I'm so with you. I've got an idea. Come with me." Pulling him toward the back of the apartment.

"I knew I liked how your mind worked."

Molly pulled Liam through the crowd and to the back bathroom they kept secret during parties so only one toilet got fucked up. They quickly rushed inside and locked the door behind them. Liam pulled up Molly's skirt and she unbuttoned his pants. He lifted her onto the counter and pulled off her underwear. He kissed her hard on the mouth and ran his tongue along the edges of her lips. Molly slipped her hand up his shirt and around his back. Soon they were having sex. They had this new thing that they did every time they messed around. They kept their eyes wide open and stared at each other the whole time. The results were incredible intimacy and kicking orgasms. Even though this little bathroom tryst was a quickie, it was worth it.

"You're so beautiful," Liam whispered. "I love you."

"God, Liam," Molly breathed. "I love you too."

"Don't ever leave me, Molly."

"I won't. Without you . . ."

"Nothing seems right." Finishing her sentence.

"Nothing tastes right."

"Nothing smells right."

"Nothing sounds right." Molly, starting to giggle. "We are so lame!"

"No shit. Least we both are."

"True."

"Will you . . ."

Before Liam could finish his sentence, someone pounded on the door. Molly snapped back into reality and found herself alone, sitting on the toilet, holding an entire uncoiled roll of toilet paper. Molly felt the nausea attack her stomach. She turned and violently threw up into the bathtub next to her. Her body convulsed with dry heaves and tears and snot began running down her face. The putrid mess dripped onto the white porcelain. Molly reached for a crumpled towel and tried to wipe off her face. She reached over, turned on the faucet, and tipped her head into the basin, letting the cool water lap over her and rinse away the mess. She wiped it off again and left the water running as she walked to a knock at the door, where Jaycee stood in the doorway, her short hair sticking up and her face red and swollen. Without a word, she pulled Molly into a hug, and fresh tears sprang into Molly's eyes.

"Are you okay?" Jaycee asked as she pulled their intermingled bodies back onto the couch.

"No. Not really." Molly, wiping her nose.

"Molly!" Bursting into fresh tears too.

"Jay, please."

"I know, I'm sorry, I just can't . . ."

"Me neither." Molly, taking a deep breath. "What now? What am I going to do?"

"I don't know, Mol." Hugging her again. "I can't believe it. Again?"

"God."

"Have you spoken to his family?"

"Yeah, earlier." Wiping her nose. "Elizabeth and Teddy will be here tonight."

"What exactly happened this time?" Jay, wondering.

Molly rose from the couch and walked into the kitchen. Jaycee's voice and questions had become background humdrum like elevator music: persistent, ever present, and unneeded.

"Do you want some coffee?" Molly asked.

"What?" Following Molly to the kitchen. "Coffee? Now?"

"It seems like a good idea." Opening the fridge and retrieving the grounds.

"Molly, what are you doing?" Trying to get Molly to look her in the eye. "Just stop a minute and talk to me."

"Milk?" Fiddling with the coffeepot. "Sugar?"

"Molly, come on. Stop with the fucking coffee!" Jay, yelling.

As Jaycee reached for Molly, Molly reached into the cupboard and brought down two mugs. Their arms' collision was a minor train wreck and both mugs came to a crashing accident on the floor.

"Fuck!" Molly screamed as she leaned down to clean up the broken shards of pottery. "Fuck me." Starting to cry again.

"Shush, here let me help." Leaning down to help her friend. "Molly, maybe you should go lie down for a while. I'll deal with all this. I'll have this place spick and span in no time. You need to just chill."

"Thanks, but I don't have time to lie down. I'm leaving as soon as I can. I have to get out of here."

"Where are you going?"

"Home. I want to get on the road as soon as possible."

"You should really wait and get some sleep. You're in no shape to drive, what, like sixteen hours? And besides, what about . . ."

"I'm going. I have to go pack."

With that Molly left the kitchen and walked into her bedroom leaving Jaycee holding a broken handle. In her room, Molly carefully folded and packed her things. There was something soothing in the methodical motion. Perhaps order and neatness could come to replace the chaos even if it was only in color coding her thongs and tank tops. Not really knowing how long she would be gone, she overstuffed two bags with her cream cashmere sweater with the moth hole on the left sleeve, her brown flat-front pants that looked better than all her black ones, her favorite five pairs of jeans, and her collection of rock T-shirts from concerts she had never been to. The bags barely zipped, but Molly did not want to leave anything else behind that she thought she would need. She was already leaving him behind. That was enough. She peeled off her clothes, fell into a clean T-shirt and sweats, and dragged the bags into the living room. Jaycee then helped Molly bring them to the car, and they carefully packed the trunk of her beat-up black Land Rover.

"Are you sure this is the right move?" Staring at her friend. "You really think just picking up and leaving is a good idea? I don't really get this. It's not going to all go away just because you bail."

"Well, I already told his mom that I had to go for a while. Elizabeth understood." Throwing her purse into the backseat along with her suede coat. "I have to get the fuck out of here. I can't breathe." Running her hand over her back.

"You shouldn't. You need to deal with all this."

"Maybe not." Looking at her friend. "Jay, I'm holding on by a thread."

"But," biting her lip, "I don't want you to go. I . . ."

"Look, I have to." Getting into the car. "You know something? Last night, I think he was going to ask me to marry him."

"Oh, God, Molly."

"Today I should have been sleeping in, feeding him the fresh baked scones I was going to whip up, and staying in bed all day making love. Best day of my life."

"Molly, all of that could . . ."

"Nope, it's done, over. He broke it all. Smashed everything to bits. He promised me."

"How do you know he broke the promise? You told me on the phone that Zander was driving. What aren't you telling me?"

"Jay, I gotta go."

"Molly." Touching Molly's arm. "What's really going on here? There's something else. I was there before, don't shut me out now."

"Look, please just let it go." Staring Jaycee right in the eye. "I will call you and we can talk, but right now I just can't."

"Okay, fine." Letting go of Molly's arm.

Molly stared back at her apartment.

"We were going to be a family." Taking a deep breath. "But I refuse to be some long-suffering wife of a magical guy who may or may not come home every night. I can't do it anymore, pick him up, and fix everything. I don't want to have four kids artfully named after beat poets running around the yard who only know their dad because I play them some song he wrote for me before they learned to walk."

"Okay, Molly, okay. I love you. Go, but just come back." Approaching Molly and hugging her. "But I thought you wanted to name your kids after Jane Austen characters?"

"Cute." Molly, squeezing Jaycee back. "What can I bribe you with to clean up?"

"Nothing. I'll do it now."

"Will you also watch the place? Get mail, et cetera?" Handing her a spare key.

"Now you are pushing it." Smiling at her friend, trying to lighten the situation. "Call me when you get there, and give your sister-in-law a special pat on the tummy for me."

"I will." Shutting the door and turning the ignition. "Thanks."

"Hey!" Jaycee banged on the window. "What should I tell him?"

"I don't care."

As she drove away, Molly didn't look back even though she could feel Jay's eyes on her as she drove down the block. Thank goodness at least Liam's mom had understood her need to vacate the premises since Jay really didn't. Molly was relieved not to have to really explain. She felt grateful to have Elizabeth in her life, that she had gotten to know such a unique woman was a bonus to dating Liam. Not only was she smart and vibrant, she was also the kind of woman who'd been there, done that, and never judged. It was always easy to talk with her about anything. Elizabeth McGuire was a woman much like her own mother, which is why Molly felt so comfortable around her. Put together, accessible, and eager to be better, do better, and make the world better.

Elizabeth and Liam's dad had split up when he and Teddy were young and she had charted her own defiant path. Liam's father went on to remarry and have another family, but Elizabeth dedicated herself to her sons and her constant need to create instead. Elizabeth was able to make a living from her sculptures, and that, coupled with a sizable inheritance from her parents, allowed her boys to explore whatever struck their fancy. She never placed importance on making money and being a buttoned-up, well-suited professional; all she wanted from her boys was a faithful striving for beauty and truth. Part hippie, part intellectual snob, and part earth mother. Molly felt instantly at home with her, and was probably also partly why she immediately felt at home with Liam. Unlike Teddy, who rebelled from his mother's modernized sixties artist commune ideology and became a lawyer, Liam embraced Elizabeth's ideals and passions. He acted, painted, and of course played music. All the people who filtered into his life through his mother, he quizzed, collected, and catalogued. Liam ravaged other artists or writers or chefs for their knowledge and incorporated all he learned into his own creativity.

Molly remembered the first time she went up north to meet and visit with Elizabeth. Liam and Teddy had planned a sixtieth birthday surprise for their mother, who had just moved to a new house in Napa. She was living in this old Craftsman with a large back studio. Her new boyfriend was an acclaimed chef at one of Napa's most celebrated restaurants. With his help, the boys organized a multicourse small dinner party in the restaurant. There would be ten guests, and Molly was nervous that her first meeting with her boyfriend's mother would be at such an important special event. It had taken Molly an entire afternoon to even pack. When Liam came over to get Molly for dinner the night before they were leaving, Molly was barely visible under a mountain of shoes and clothing.

"Molly, we are only going away for a few days." Liam, eyeing the piles. "What are you doing?"

"Don't ask." Grabbing another dress from the closet and holding it against her body in front of the mirror. "What do you think?"

"It's pretty," Liam responded.

"Pretty? That's it?" Tossing it on her bed.

"I don't know. I like it, it's fine."

"I can't be just fine." Half disappearing into the back of her small but overstuffed closet. "I have to be fabulous."

"You are." Shoving everything aside and sitting on the bed.

"What are you doing?" Yelling at him.

"What do you mean?"

"All of that had an order, a system, and you just fucked it up!" Refolding.

"Molly, you must chill."

"Easy for you to say." Getting more hyped up. "I can't go to dinner. Go without me."

"Molly, Elliot is meeting us with his new girlfriend, Maggie. You promised. You are being a little dramatic." Starting to laugh.

"No, I am not!" Glaring at him.

"Watch out, you may give Joan Crawford a run for her money."

"Stop!" Trying to glare through her now forming grin. "You're not helping."

"NO MORE WIRE HANGERS!" Grabbing one off the bed and leaping up. "NO MORE WIRE HANGERS!"

Liam began chasing Molly all over the bedroom while Molly bobbed and weaved through the maze of accessories.

"Stop!" Molly shouted, laughing. "I mean it."

"NO MORE!" Getting louder. "Come here, my pretty, I won't hurt ya!!"

"Liam!" Molly shrieked.

Then he pounced. Everything fell to a large mound on the floor, and Liam began tickling Molly. They wrestled and soon Liam had Molly pinned.

"Say uncle."

"Never!" Trying to wiggle from his grasp.

"Say it!" Pinning her hands with one of his and tickling her with the other.

"No way!"

"Uncle, easy enough word." Letting his free hand roam up the hem of her skirt.

"Nope, do what you may, but I will never give in. Alex trained me well."

"Really?" Moving his body off hers and moving slowly down her torso, all the while still keeping her hands pinned. "I have my ways."

Soon enough Molly caved under his kisses, and they made love on top of the mess.

"You don't play fair." Molly sighed.

"I never much liked playing by the rules." Rolling off her.

"I'm still not close to being packed."

"How about this?" Dislodging a turquoise Chloe print chiffon dress from beneath Molly's elbow. "I always liked this on you."

"Where did you find that?"

Liam shrugged.

"Will your mom like it?" Sitting up and readjusting herself.

"Molly." Pulling her back down to him. "She's going to love you."

"You think?" Looking at him.

"I know." Kissing her slowly.

After that it took Molly all of about five minutes to throw her stuff into a bag. They were out the door fifteen minutes later to meet their friends.

When Molly and Liam finally arrived at Elizabeth's house, Molly started to feel seasick again. Her stomach swelled and her lip was tender from where she had been biting. This was the very first time she was meeting a boyfriend's parent. Molly had never done the meet and greet before. All the rest of her boyfriends had been briefish affairs or they were from places on the East Coast. This would be a first, and luckily for Molly she couldn't have had better. Elizabeth immediately swept Molly into a hug. She could smell the gardenias on Elizabeth's clothes and her large turquoise necklace pressed against Molly's chest.

"I'm so glad to meet you, Molly. I've heard such wonderful things." Pulling Molly into the house.

"Me too." Letting Elizabeth lead her.

"Liam." Turning to her son. "You never mentioned how lovely she was." Winking at Molly.

"That's just a bonus, Mom." Looping himself through his mother's free arm. "Are Teddy, Anita, and Paige here yet?"

Anita was Teddy's wife, a poet and teacher, and Paige was their two-and-a-half-year-old daughter.

"Yeah. I put them to work in the kitchen making snacks. Paige is taking a little nap on the sunporch. Come on, we may need some extra hands."

The rest of the weekend went as smoothly, and Molly felt right at home. Things only got better after Molly gave Elizabeth the gift she had brought. Molly had deliberated long and hard about what to give her. She wanted it to be unique and thoughtful, but that was difficult when you didn't really know someone. Initially she thought about an art book or candles, but all of that seemed impersonal. Then Molly found this gorgeous leather-bound journal with heavy handmade cream-colored paper at an Italian paper store in Beverly Hills. The front was embossed with small flowers and had a long leather tie to keep it carefully closed. It was something Molly would have loved to receive. Molly also bought a set of sketching pencils and wrapped everything together in a piece of vintage silk fabric and tied it with a large satin bow garnished with a cluster of felt rosettes. The gift itself was a little piece of art and Molly's fingers were crossed that Elizabeth would enjoy it.

"Happy birthday, Ms. McGuire." Molly handed the package to Elizabeth.

"Elizabeth, please. And thank you. This is almost too beautiful to open." Untying the ribbon. "You shouldn't have."

"I wanted to."

"Oh, Molly, it is wonderful." Tracing her hand over the cover. "I love it. Thank you so much." Giving Molly a kiss on the cheek. "It's really perfect."

"You're welcome. I never can have enough journals."

"Me too. I am going to go put it next to my bed. I am about to run out of room in my sketchbook, so this will be immediately used. I am so happy you came up with Liam and shared this birthday with me. My son is a lucky man."

Molly instantly felt lighter from the inside out. From that moment on, the two of them became friends. Elizabeth would send Molly articles she thought she would like to read, little trinkets she thought Molly would like, and after Molly began her jewelry business, beads from various trips abroad for Molly to use. Molly loved this woman, loved that she had this friendship. Molly panicked that while Elizabeth was understanding now, would it last? Would she still be there for Molly? Would this whole life she and Liam created above and beyond the two of them vanish? It wasn't just about their connection and the bonds and promises they had made to each other. It was the friends and the family and the memories of a tight-knit group that could easily unravel. Molly's stomach turned and she pressed her foot a little harder on the gas. She could not drive fast enough, but she should have known she couldn't really just ride off into the sunset.

Liam was still everywhere. He was in her mind, her car. Whether it was the CDs in the changer or the pair of teal fuzzy dice slung over the rearview mirror he won for her at the street fair in Los Feliz last summer. He was everywhere, in everything. A half empty pack of light blue American Spirits, a five-year-old brown sweatshirt on the seat, dirty Nike sneakers in the back well, set lists and sheet music from his last gig, a box of Altoids, and three unread *LA Weekly*'s. His mess in her car was something she used to love. It made her feel attached and part of something, not just alone and floating. The first time she found something of Liam's in her car was just a few weeks after they had met at Goldfinger's. She was looking for a pen between the seats and came across a mint-green skinny hair elastic. As she rolled it between her thumb and forefinger, she remembered how it had flown from his hands on their first real date. They had just shared a pepperoni pizza and a few beers and were heading to a movie.

"Are you sure you want to see it again?" he asked. "We can go to a different flick or rent one."

"No, I loved it. If a movie hits that sweet, romantic but not cheesy nerve I can see it over and over again," Molly answered while pulling the car out.

"Well then, it will be my treat."

"Thanks."

"I'm not really a repeater myself. At least not in the theater. Renting is a whole other ball game though."

"And I'm not really a renter."

"Really? Molly, how can you not? What about the classics?" Asking in amazement.

"I know, I know. I have this huge list in my journal."

"Well, my dear, plans have changed. Name one movie on that list and we're going to go watch it at my place."

"Let's see. How about *Raging Bull*?"

"Done. Drive on."

"You have a rental card, right?"

"What are we going to do with you?" Liam, laughing.

He then adjusted his tiny ponytail, and the elastic went flying. He couldn't find it and it remained wedged until Molly retrieved it. When she put it in her hair, she actually felt a spark. Thank God she wasn't wearing hairspray. She was turned on just thinking about the fact that she was wearing him, touching him. It was her little secret; he could now go with her everywhere. Her own Thumbelina small enough to fit in her pocket. When it finally broke, Molly stashed it in the change pocket of her toffee-colored wallet.

Now the spark had turned into an electrical fire, Molly was burning, and his stench had to go. The sweet scent of his spell had soured, contaminated by a truth Molly could not shake. Molly drove straight to the car wash. She dumped everything into the metal trash can sitting under the handheld vacuums. The sweater, the smokes, the half-written lyrics, even the broken rubber band. She wanted nothing left to let her linger. If she had had a match she would have lit the clichéd "burn your boy-friend's stuff bonfire" despite the gas pumps nearby. She riffled through her Case Logic of CDs and searched for something that was just hers. That was a hard task. Liam had become part of her blood, coursing through her, replenishing her like water, and now she was choking. Tears welled up again and Molly barely managed to get out of the car wash in one piece. She really didn't want to throw him away, but what could she do? He promised he would stop all the bullshit, he promised he wouldn't leave her. It wasn't until a few months into their relationship, when they had hit that spend-every-single-solitary-moment-together, that she really realized he even had a problem. Liam would always have one more drink than everyone else, one more hit, one more line. He was always a little fuzzier, like a Van Gogh painting.

Molly loved it at first. He was dangerous and creative. Molly always did the right thing, said the right thing. She followed the rules. Molly had one of those great relationships with her par-ents where she could tell them when she experimented with drugs and they would talk about them intellectually. They would ask her questions, not grill her over an open pit of hot-tongued moralism. She had proven herself responsible and they trusted her. Liam brought out all that smoldering rebellion dormant within her. Initially, before she realized how symptomatic it was, they would occasionally stay up for days doing coke and talking about the most interesting things Molly had forgotten. It was as if they needed all those extra hours of awake time just to share and catch each other up on everything they had been and done before they met.

"Who was the first person you knew you hurt?" Liam asking her while wiping his nose.

"What do you mean?" Reaching for the tightly rolled bill.

"What was the first knowingly mean thing you did to someone else? The worst thing you ever said?"

"Why do you want to know? I don't think I want to tell you."

"Molly, I love you. Nothing you can say will change that. I want to know everything about you."

"What did you just say?" Sputtering out the water she just drank.

"I want to know everything because I am falling in love with you."

"Really?"

"Yeah, really."

"You are the first guy to say that to me without prompting."

"Well, I'm glad."

"I think I love you too." Leaning over and kissing him.

"You think?" Looking at her in mock horror. Or maybe it was real horror, and that made Molly sure.

"I know I love you." Kissing him again. "Worst thing, huh? I don't know if I have one."

"Molly, you *are* sweet but everyone has one."

"Fine." Snorting another line. "I kissed my boyfriend's brother at the junior prom."

"You naughty thing, you." Laughing. "Did he ever find out?"

"No, we did break up shortly after, but I never told him. Why bother if it was already ending."

"Why did you do it?"

"I think I was just excited about being wanted. Kevin was my first sort of high school boyfriend and it was a shock to me that he actually wanted to be with me." Getting up and getting another glass of water. "I was such a nerd, you know, braces, no boobs. I had a guy into me and when another, even if it was his brother, dug me too, I just went with it. I was overwhelmed by my own need to be wanted. Very egocentric, I know."

"And now?"

"Now what?" Sitting back down. "Did I make out with Teddy when he was visiting?"

"Very funny. No, are you still that girl?"

"Boobless?" Eyeing her chest. "Don't think so, thank God."

"Stop." Liam laughed. "Seriously."

"Yeah." Getting a little quiet. "Sometimes."

"Do I ever make you feel insecure?" Putting his arms around her.

"No, I just sometimes am that sixteen-year-old nerd who feels awkward and lame, and I wonder how in the hell I got lucky and got you."

"I don't see it that way. I don't see you that way. I got lucky and got you."

He paused a minute and took her in. Molly shivered, overwhelmed by his gaze. "Molly, your honesty blows me away every day," he said quietly.

Molly pulled the car over, flipped open the door, and threw up. How was she supposed to move on, move past this? Even as she remembered an example of how drugs snaked through their lives, she put a romantic spin on it. Would she be permanently under some emotional voodoo curse? Under the influence of something? It was as if Liam were a stomach parasite, and Molly couldn't completely purge him. He was her phantom limb. The ache that constantly throbs. The thing you miss even when you think you have everything you need.

All the guys before Liam had always had parts and pieces of what she wanted. Things that would compliment her and make her feel whole. She always fell fast and frantically for those who offered a smidgeon of what she lacked, what she missed inside. The high was in what they made her see in herself. Their wanting was her mirror. Lucca wanted passion and spontaneity, while John wanted consistency and stability. But when Liam walked toward her that night in the bar, it was the first time she felt whole within her own skin. He was his own man, and he loved her because she was her own woman. They made a bigger whole. They looked into the mirror together. Now Molly felt like a half for the first time in a long time.

The only way to get through this was to keep going. Molly looked into her rearview and pulled herself back onto the high-way. She had a long way to go. Her cell phone beeped. Molly looked down and saw she had voice mail. She pulled over again and dialed her code. Amid laughter and music Molly could barely make out the message.

Baby, it's me. I'm looking at you right now talking to Jay. You're so cute. Anyway, I didn't want to interrupt. I'm going with Zander to go grab his guitar from his pad and come back. We just worked out this great tune. *Yeah, Molly, it is hot.* Dude, give me the phone back. And, Mol, I wanted to ask you if you would marry me before we were so rudely interrupted. For-ever me and you, mon petite cheese ball.

Molly stared at the phone. Why did everything have to get so fucked up? Molly kept hitting one on the cell, repeating and repeating and repeating the message. Every word a tiny stab, killing her softly, but unfortunately not in a Roberta Flack kind of way. Molly sat in her car on the shoulder of the highway for hours, just listening to Liam. She was completely unaware of the traffic around her, the subtle changes of the sun, the sounds of a living, breathing city. Molly was entombed within her car: its frame, her coffin; the message, her eulogy. Listening to her dream come true, the words she thought she would never hear, her sixteen-year-old knight on a white horse romance-novel fantasy, her every single eyelash wish, Molly's heart broke.

two

Night descended and Molly pulled into a gas station/diner outside Ely, Nevada. Bobbie's Café looked soft and safe through the dusky haze. Molly filled her tank and pulled into a small parking space at the end of the lot. She grabbed her coat and purse, and walked into the restaurant. The quiet din of lipstick-covered coffee cups, cherry pie plates, and egg-stained silverware was actually a welcome change to the melancholy dirges Molly was playing in the car. She picked up an old *USA Today,* a plastic

menu from the counter, and slid into an orange vinyl booth. She flipped off her flops, folded her legs under her, and pondered the traditional fare as she wrapped her hair into a bun. As she read, she realized that she hadn't eaten in more than twenty-four hours.

"Hey, sweetie. I'm Rose," a flaxen-haired older woman stated. "Can I start you with a cup of coffee?"

"Yeah, that would be great. Can I get some skim milk with that?" Looking up from the menu.

"Sorry, all we have is two percent. Will that be all right?"

"Fine."

Molly returned to her menu. Usually it wasn't in her genes to lose her appetite when she was depressed. Her whole family chowed down at the first glimpse of sorrow. Maybe it is a Jewish thing to stuff oneself to stave off sadness, filling the belly with something comforting like mashed potatoes or ice cream to ease the situation. Molly's mom, Helen, even made her a big ol' chocolate cake when her first goldfish, Finger, died. She let Molly eat it without a fork, frosting first, until there was more chocolate on Molly than ever was on the cake. As Molly's eyes fixated on fries, a grilled cheese, and a black-and-white shake, she knew the tradition would not be broken as her appetite returned with vengeance. There would be no grief diet for Molly.

Liam was really good at feeding Molly whenever she felt blue. He had this knack for sensing her moods and knowing exactly what would draw her out. Whether it was a box of Kraft macaroni and cheese or imported foie gras from this little market in Beverly Hills, he knew just how to indulge her. Once Liam learned of her sugar cereal deprivation as a small child (only Kix and Cheerios were allowed), he came home from the market with twenty boxes and two gallons of milk.

"What are you doing?" Molly exclaimed when she saw the buffet laid out on their dining room table. "You are a nut!"

"Well, my girlfriend here has never known the true pleasure of slurping up Alpha-Bits or Lucky Charms." Shaking the assorted boxes. "One cannot go through life without experiencing the insane sugar rush that they provide."

"There's enough cereal here to feed a small nation. How much am I supposed to eat?"

"All of it." Liam grinned as he walked to the fridge and pulled out the first gallon of milk. "That's the plan."

"A bite of each, right?" Pulling out the wooden chair and sitting down.

"No, no, no, my dear. You must have a bowl. That is the only way to experience it fully. The Day-Glo sugar stained milk is the best part." Pulling out his chair. "I will join you of course."

"Okay." Taking a deep breath. "This is going to be a long night. Where shall I start, chef?"

"My personal favorite circa 1979ish. Cookie Crisp." He poured her a bowl. "Note the crunchy cookie. It stays relatively crisp."

"How poetic." Molly laughed.

Before she dug in she raised her spoon. "A toast."

Liam raised his spoon. "To?"

"You, for taking care of me later and holding my hair when I puke from all this milk."

"Cheers!" Liam planted a big kiss on Molly's lips. "I will always hold your hair."

Molly licked her lips and blinked. Before her lay the plastic menu and a steaming cup of coffee. With a shaky hand, she poured the milk and stirred in the sugar. How long would it take for her to be able to exist only in the present instead of somewhere in her memory, especially if the memories felt more real, more vivid, more vital, than the reality before her?

"You're back," Rose stated.

"Back?" Molly, clearing her throat.

"You seemed a little lost, and I didn't want to interrupt. You okay?"

"Not really, but I am starving." Looking back down at the menu. "I would like a grilled cheese with cheddar, fries extra crispy with a side of ranch, and a shake. Hummm, chocolate."

"Will do, honey." Writing down her order. "You take care of yourself."

"Thanks."

Molly opened her bag and pulled out a small mirror. She dipped the edge of her napkin in her water glass and wiped around her eyes, trying to get rid of the last layer of the mascara. She really needed a shower. Last night's glitter was looking like a disco queen limping into the eighties. Molly opened the paper and searched for the crossword puzzle. Something to keep her mind occupied and reading the front page's tragedies were not going to soothe her mood. Before she could fish for a pen and begin, her dinner arrived. Molly looked at the greasy feast and dove in, headfirst. The melted cheese and ice cream expanded in her mouth, swirled on her tongue, and coated her insides with a thick layer of fatty consolation. Soft and round, she swallowed, and tried to forget.

Molly finished and paid the check. Rose came over with a large cup of coffee to go. A small bag with grease stains was clutched in her other hand.

"Here." Rose handed everything to Molly. "To keep your energy up while you drive."

"Thanks. What do I owe you for them?" Looking in the bag and peering at a few doughnuts.

"On the house. Just make sure you get to where you are going in one piece." Smiling at Molly.

"That's really nice of you. Good night." Molly pushed open the door with her hip.

" 'Bye." Rose waved.

Molly slowly walked to her car, the heaviness of the food weighing on her step. After grabbing a sweater from the trunk, she settled behind the wheel and readied herself for the long haul ahead of her. Already feeling car-neck creep upon her, she wondered if she would be able to make it all the way home without anymore unnecessary pit stops. She also wondered if she was doing the right thing. All that intense girl power she raged earlier was beginning to wear off, and her anger was sinking into something that was feeling like forgiveness. Molly redialed her messages and played them again. Liam and marriage and hating him and leaving him and loving him all twisted together into a sickening stew. Here was the queen of solid decision making, sucking at sticking to her guns.

Molly should have had waffles; they would have more represented her mood. It wasn't like her to be so wishy-washy. Whether it was her major in college, American history, or her senior prom dress, señorita red with a tulle underskirt, she always could directly channel her gut instinct. Even if the choices were trying and both potential options lent themselves to tears and trauma, Molly was not a waffler, a shifter, a should-she-do-this-or-thater. She knew it was something that had attracted Liam to her, and Jaycee also loved that in her. It was why she trusted Molly with everything, from the minute they met at a backyard barbeque shortly after Molly moved to LA, and made sure Molly was her nearest and dearest. About a year after they met, Jay sealed their friendship with a really lovely sentimental exchange, which happened to occur in a dingy bathroom with beige tiles and a wobbly toilet seat.

"Okay, I have something to tell you." Jaycee, pulling her into the tiny bathroom of Mako's, their favorite karaoke bar.

"That sounds a little scary." Molly, looking at her best friend. "Are you feeling okay?"

"Yeah, I just need to share this big epiphany with you. Come on." Dragging Molly behind her.

The two of them smushed into the small stall, and Molly perched as best she could on the khaki-colored toilet seat, her red leather pants squeaking as she moved.

"Spill it, baby." Retying the lace on her Adidas sneaker. "My pants refuse to let me hold this position for too long."

"I just wanted to tell you how much I value our friendship and that I thank you for everything you do for me all the time."

"What?" Looking up at her friend.

"I just want to thank you."

"How many cocktails have you had? You're not usually so mushy." Staring at her. "I feel like we are in that Natalie Merchant song."

"One beer, and Molly, stop joking. I just know that I would not be who I am today without you. You've really been an amazing example, and I just felt like telling you."

"Me? Really?" Starting to blush. "Okay, what did you do?"

"What do you mean?"

"What did you do that I am going to be really pissed at you for because all this is a little odd."

"Can't you just take a compliment for fuck's sake?!" Getting riled. "I just felt like being nice."

"Okay, no need for expletives." Looking at Jaycee. "Wow. I don't know what to say."

"You don't have to say anything. Just listen."

"Okay."

"You're like the strongest person I know. You always follow your instincts and are totally honest with your emotions. You have taught me to be truer to my own sense of self. So much of who I am is related to all the model qualities I see in you."

"Uhh." Molly blushing. "Thanks, but, uh."

"No buts and don't try to deflect."

"Thanks." Still blushing. "I don't do well with compliments."

"I know, that's why I wanted to tell you." Pulling Molly into a hug.

"I may start to cry." Molly, tearing up. "I hate you. Now I am going to look like Joan Jett the morning after."

"I know. But she's a badass."

Then Molly was saved from this praise-a-thon by a loud knock on the door.

"Shall we?" Grabbing Jaycee's hand.

"Yeah."

"I love you." Kissing Jay on the cheek. "This made my night."

"Me too."

Molly went on to give the best karaoke performance of her life. Pat Benatar watch out!!

That night Jaycee gave her this incredible gift by naming something Molly always sort of knew. Sometimes having a friend point out something remarkable and good is all one needs to reconfirm a dedication to living as one's best self by following gut instincts. After remembering this tender moment, Molly swallowed hard and promised not to let this life decision throw her. She wasn't going to let Jay, nor herself, down. She was strong and true and determined, and even if she was nauseated, she would get through this without any Pepto. She started the car, but before she pulled out, she erased Liam's proposal. For a girl who used to save all his messages for weeks at a time, this was a major step forward. Although her fingers did shake as she pressed the buttons, and a few more tears eased down her cheeks, she finished the task and began the last leg of her journey.

It was much easier for Molly now that she was driving at night. The cool darkness seemed to comfort her, wrap her in a patch-work security blanket of blindness. What she could not see, she could not fear. When she was a little girl, her parents used to drive her around late in the evening when she couldn't sleep or had a nightmare. The slow rumble of the engine, the lights, the brisk air, all soothed her. They put her back to sleep, or at least into a calm awake state that resembled sleep and eased Molly's four-year-old nerves. Unlike some, even when she was that little girl with nightmares, Molly was never afraid of the dark, afraid some heinous monster would leap from behind her pink closet drawer and whisk her away to some rotting, moldy underworld. It was the clear details of day that frightened her. The trash, the traffic, and the throngs of rash, disgruntled people everywhere were more threatening than what was invisible or covered by blackness.

When she was twelve, Molly went on her first school camping trip. Unlike the rest of her girlfriends, Molly jumped at the chance to do a solo and spread her sleeping bag under the stars: she was all alone, at night, in the middle of the desert, and she was in heaven. While the rest huddled in tents somehow reassured by the thinnest layer of plastic, Molly was barefaced, staring at the stars. It was in the dark sky that her imagination flourished. With the obvious obscured, the facts cloaked by shadow, Molly was free to create her world her own way. It was at night that she evolved and grew into herself.

As she drove, the sky deepened into an impenetrable black. It looked like the saucers of a tripping raver's eyes in the midst of an Ecstasy peak during a perfect Paul Oakenfold set. It was hallow, and dead. Molly shivered and reached into the backseat for a scarf. The chill kept her alert and awake. Tonight, and pretty much all of today, was a black day. Devoid of warmth and tone, it was flat and even and unforgiving. Molly always used to color code her days. A sign would be sent, maybe it was the color of her toothpaste, or of the first sock she glanced at in the drawer, and that would be her theme. It wasn't as if she dressed the part, only wearing green from underpinnings to headband, it was more of what the aura, the energy, of the day would be. It had been so long since Molly had had a murky, dingy day with Liam. Not since the last promise. She touched her back, rolled her wrist out of habit, remembering. Since that night and his grand turn around, she tended to the more radiating, prismatic, incandescent hues when they were together. She felt like her entire body was on fire when she was with him, flames flickering from the tips of her hair and a faint smell of smoke rising off her skin. She was her very own X-Man character. Everything she experienced or tasted or smelled seemed twice what it had been before. She was pulsing, alive. She was a beating heart.

On their twenty-first date, Molly knew she loved him, really loved him, and not in that schoolgirl crush obsession way that she had felt after the first five minutes, nor in an enhanced, drug-induced way she had felt in those first few weeks. She loved him as a woman, whole and round and earthy. She had woken up next to him, staring at a freckle on the back of his left shoulder. It was the warmest shade of brown, hazelnut. That was her color. She kissed it along with all the others ringing the top of his back and he rolled over to meet her mouth. Morning breath was not even a thought. It was then that Molly could not tell where she began and he ended. They were this stalk of hands and fingers growing and moving in harmony, fitting together like LEGOs. Everything clicked and ratcheted into the right holes and notches. After they made love, they showered together. He washed her long red hair carefully and then combed it, detangling all her knots. They dressed and headed off in her car.

"Wanna see a movie?" Liam asked as he flipped through the *LA Weekly* she had on the floor.

"Sure. What's playing?"

"I'm kind of in the romantic mode myself."

"Really? Well there's that one with John Cusack and Gwyneth Paltrow that just opened."

"Cool. Let's see. . . . It's at four-fifteen at the Grove."

"Usually I have to beg and plead with my guy to get him to see a chick flick." Turning to look at him and feeling all fuzzy inside. "John would only see political movies with subtitles."

"Your guy?" Grinning at Molly.

"Uh, I meant, the guy I am dating . . ." Starting to blush. "Not that you are my guy, I mean . . ."

"I'm not?"

"Well, I don't . . ."

Liam leaned over and gave Molly a long kiss just below her ear, inhaling her before he pulled away.

"I better be, or I am going to spend the rest of my days looking for a girl who tastes and smells exactly like you."

Molly smiled and took his hand. They rode the rest of the way to lunch in silence, both relishing their togetherness. Molly could feel the chocolate-flavored coziness spread like frosting inside her. Her heart and lungs, a pool of hot fudge. Nothing could be better than feeling like you are inside a mug of cocoa.

At lunch, Molly ordered a tuna sandwich and a cup of coffee.

"Excuse me." Getting up. "Pit stop."

Molly peed with a shit-eating grin on her face like she was three and using a big girl's potty for the first time. She walked back and slid into the booth, facing him.

"Babe, come sit next to me."

"What?"

"Sit next to me over here."

"But, Liam, then we can't look at each other and beam across the table."

"You're too far away over there."

Molly got up and snuggled next to him. She had never sat on the same side before. Sideways talking had not been her thing, except if she was at a sushi bar.

"Much better. See, we can still look at each other." He lifted her chin to meet his gaze. "It's just closer."

"Almost too close. I feel like you can see every pore on my face!" Molly laughed. "Thank God I happen to have great skin this week."

"Except for that little zit on your . . ."

Molly's hand flew up to her face and she turned crimson.

"Really!?"

"Relax, I was kidding." Pulling her hands away.

"Asshole." Pretending to pout as she reached for her coffee. She took a sip and it tasted perfect. "Did you do my coffee?"

"That's something no one has ever accused me of, but yes, I did it. Quarter of an inch skim milk, half a sugar, and a dash of cream, right?"

"Yeah." Taking another sip. "How did you know?"

"Paid attention."

"I love you."

"I love you, too."

It had become that easy to say it. Her certainty came down to him knowing how she liked her coffee. It was always those small things that sucked Molly in. Not the grand gestures of love and romance, but the little things that make up a boring life. Buying her shampoo to keep at his house, her kind of toothpaste. Stocking the fridge with things she liked, or bringing her magazines when she was sick. All the tiny details that made the biggest statement of all: "Hey, I am listening, I am watching, I am remembering all of you, I see you."

Molly blinked hard and screamed at herself for remembering yet another instance that made her fall in love with Liam. She stuffed a piece of the doughnut in her mouth and vowed to keep her mind as still as possible for the duration of the drive. Molly looked at the clock in the car and estimated that she had about two more hours to go. She surprised herself by getting this far without stopping. She couldn't believe she was still awake. Molly rolled her neck and rubbed her shoulders, trying to squeeze the tension from them. The knots were impenetrable, like small stones imbedded in her muscles. Pretty soon she would be the Thing from the *Fantastic Four*, her body coated in an armor of stress. Everything was so tight that one wrong move and she would snap both mentally and physically. She prayed she would arrive in one piece. Molly flipped to the last CD in her changer and began singing along to No Doubt. Molly's head bopped to the beat. It was easy to get lost in the rhythm, easy to get lost in ambient noise that didn't recall some moment, some memory. If she could focus just on the sound inside her car, she knew she would make it home.

three

It was four A.M. when Molly pulled into the familiar driveway. She smiled when she saw her mom's old-school, navy Mercedes sedan parked under the port-korshere. She was finally home and the much-needed comfort of a parental embrace was minutes away. Molly raced to the door and fumbled for her house key. She slipped it into the lock and quickly turned the metal handle, every step pulling her closer and closer to the moment of coveted release. In her haste, Molly forgot to turn off the alarm and within

thirty seconds of her early morning entry, the shrill bleating of Alert One disrupted the quiet. Molly's fingers slipped on the small buttons as she tried to shut it down. Lights flicked on and feet pattered down the stairs two at a time.

"Who's there!?!?" Molly's dad, Henry, shouted. "Helen, grab the phone! Hurry!!!"

"Dad, easy," Molly yelled over the siren. "It's me."

"Molly?" Henry looked around the corner and saw her standing there.

"Yeah, I forgot the code." Staring at the key panel. "I'm so sorry for scaring you."

"I got it." Henry walked over to her and shut the system down. "You always did know how to make an entrance."

"Hi, Dad."

"My girl." Pulling her into a hug.

"Henry, I got the alarm company on the phone," Helen called from the staircase. "Is everything all right?"

Helen rounded the corner and broke into a big smile when she saw her somewhat bedraggled daughter standing before her.

"Everything's fine here. My daughter set it off by accident. The code word is Baxter. Okay, thanks." Helen hung up. "Molly, what on earth?"

Before Helen could pull her into another hug, Molly burst into tears.

"Baby, what's wrong? Henry?" Looking to him. "Molly, what is it?"

"I . . . I . . . Mom . . ." Molly choked on her tongue and her tears.

"Shush, come on, let's go sit down. Henry, go get her some water."

Helen led Molly to the sofa in the family room and sat with her. No matter how big Molly got, she always seemed to fit into her mother's lap like it was made just for her. It was probably an embryonic connection that allowed every curve to perfectly suit

Molly. Helen always told Molly the story of *Thumbelina,* the young girl who was so tiny that her mother had to carry her around inside her pocket. Molly was her little pocket-sized doll. Molly felt that way about her mom too—she loved tucking into her. Helen was the puzzle, and Molly was one of two perfect pieces, the other being her older brother, Alex.

When they were children they used to fight over this precious lap time and tried to work out some operating system that didn't leave Helen with dead legs permanently imprinted with her children's tushies. Actually, they used to get into tussles about everything. With four and a half years between them, common ground was something fertilized only after Molly grew up a bit and age difference shrunk. So until Molly turned sixteen, and Alex twenty, their parents would have to negotiate with them over every single activity. If a random McDonald's trip occurred with Dad and Alex, Molly would schedule in her own McMuffin fix. If Molly got the shiny new red shoes she wanted after reading *The Wizard of Oz,* there would have to be a quick stop at Kazam, for satisfactory comic compensation. A give and take, a constant competition. Alex inevitably won most of their skirmishes. How can a little girl compete with age, brawn, and wily coyoteness? No matter how clever or tough Molly tried to be, she ultimately fell short. What could she really do? Tell on him? Like that worked. Alex then would hang her stuffed animals from ceiling fans or lock her in her room when their parents were out to dinner, or he would creep in her room at night with this twisted gorilla monster mask, jump on her bed, and growl in her ear. It took Molly years of reading *Curious George* and watching *Project X* before she could even look at a monkey in the zoo without crying. Eventually Molly, overwhelmed by the repercussions of being a tattle-tale, learned to stop telling on her brother, and Alex had no need to mastermind new ways to torture her. They learned to coexist almost peacefully.

But Alex wouldn't rest until he won the ultimate contest: the car. Sometimes it was about the armrest, sometimes the front seat, or who would get to pump the gas and wash the windows. If Molly and Alex were pro wrestlers, the car was their ring. Elbows were thrown, knees buckled, pinches flew at backs and butts. No ride was taken without a slew of new bruises and teary snot. Helen managed to solve the front-seat round when she told the kids that they would alternate days of the week. One would be odd days, one would be even. Well, smarty-pants Alex, of course, calculated in his eight-year-old brain that there were more odd days in the year, so he called it first. Molly didn't know to complain, so she just went with it. Besides, she would soon learn that she held ownership of the front seat on October twentieth, Alex's birthday. Apparently, he wasn't that smart after all. It was a serious bartering chip that Molly wielded with extreme vigor.

Helen and Henry, though, did not have much success with the rest of the car quarrels. The bickering came to a head when Molly was five and Alex nine. The family was on their first trip to Europe, a brief driving stint around Paris, England, and Scotland. Well, driving meant a lot of time spent within an automobile. Once out of London, Helen and Henry relaxed into the plushness of their automotive interior, chatting about routes and maps and pastures, while Molly and Alex mutually decided it was a good time to begin sparring. Whatever they could fight over, the hump where they laid their feet, the gum they were supposed to share, became a full-on attack. Every ten minutes, Molly and Alex would scrimmage, yell, and pinch until Henry decided to become dictator of the car castle.

"Enough—if I hear one more word from back there you are both in serious trouble!" Henry yelled.

Henry was really scary when he yelled, so for a short spell they were under control. Molly played with her doll, and Alex played with his pocket Donkey Kong. Then he had to go and try to unhinge Molly's new claim of the armrest. First Alex flicked his hand and scattered Molly's imaginary tea party, then there was the silent poke, a little shove to dislodge her tiny arm. Her response was a scowl and a reshove. His, a pinch and a push, and then all hell broke loose.

"I was here first." Molly, whining.

"No. I was, *move!*"

"*No!* I hate you!" Molly yelled, starting to cry.

"*Move!*" Alex growled between clenched teeth.

"*What did I say!?*" Henry's voice erupted from the front seat like Mount Vesuvius. "Didn't I tell you two to be quiet?" he continued, pulling the car over to the side of the road.

"He started it." Molly sobbed.

"I did not, you're such a baby." Pushing her again.

"That's it! If you two don't shut your mouths and leave each other alone, Alex, I am sending you to military school, and Molly, you are going to boarding school. No more fighting, no more talking, not a peep from either of you until we get to the hotel!" Henry demanded, pulling the car back onto the road.

Alex and Molly went silent. That is until Molly's five-year-old curiosity got the best of her. Little Molly was a glutton for punishment.

"What's boarding school?" she asked in a loud stage whisper.

"It's where parents send really bad kids."

"Send them where?"

"To sleep away school."

"Do you get to see anybody?"

"No, just the teachers."

"What about Mom and Dad, and you and Baxter?" Trembling.

"Nope, no one, you get locked up far, far away with no parents, no dog, no nothing."

An hysterical, dying animal sob came roaring from Molly's mouth. Tears streaked down the apples of her cheeks. Helen tried to comfort her as Henry pulled the car over again. He got out, came around to her door, and picked her up, trying to undo the damage. From that moment on, Molly and Alex tried to maintain peace. "Tried" is the key word. They at least managed to make it through the rest of the countryside, and that was a major accomplishment. Henry and Helen just learned to get used to the raised level of noise, and the volume they had to preserve on the radio to drown it out. One day their kids would be grown, and silence would pervail. One day . . .

Henry returned to his daughter and handed her a glass. Molly sat up and choked down a few sips. She wiped her face on her sleeve and drank a bit more.

"Honey, what happened?" Helen asked.

"It's over."

"What is?"

"Liam."

Molly took another sip, and lifted her head up to her mother. She watched concern begin to crinkle on Helen's brow.

"Baby, what happened? I thought you guys were doing really well lately."

"We were, but now it's just all fucked up." Molly eyes brimmed with tears. "It's all ruined. It's . . ." Crying harder.

"Oh, my sweet girl." Wiping off Molly's face. "Shush."

Helen rocked Molly on the couch until the crying eased.

"Let's get you into bed and we can talk about all this later."

"Mom, I can't move." Blinking back tears. "I can't."

"Here we go, lean on me."

Helen carefully guided her daughter from the living room. With Henry's help, they both walked her upstairs. Along the wall were images of a shinier Molly. Happy-go-lucky in bangs and braces, a red rose corsage tucked on her wrist, a graduation hat shielding a smile from a perfect May day.

Molly's room was still pink. Every one of her rooms wherever they had lived was pink. Even though the family moved to Sun Valley long after Molly played with dolls and pinned up posters of Rob Lowe, Helen could not resist. Molly was twelve, about to begin middle school, and Alex was in high school when Henry decided to move his law practice from Los Angeles to Sun Valley. Henry was trying to pull his family tighter together and a smaller, more easy-going lifestyle was something that he thought would do the trick. Things had been too distracting in LA. Always more work, more business to keep his mind and time occupied. The move was sudden and lots of teenage bellyaching echoed through the house the months before, but once they arrived to blue skies and sports galore, Alex and Helen settled in. Molly, on the other hand, was still drawing navy-and-black tear-stained landscapes of LA.

It wasn't until school began and Molly met Renee that she embraced her new town. Henry remembered coming home that night and seeing Molly with the first real smile on her face since they had moved.

"Hey, kiddo." Kissing her head. "I've missed that grin."

"I met the coolest girl today, Dad!" Molly burst. "Her name's Renee and she came and sat with me at lunch, which was really nice because no one ever sits with the new girl on the first day. And we even swapped lunches!"

"What was wrong with yours?" Henry asked, thinking back to his carefully made lamb sandwich and couscous salad.

"Lamb?" Molly plugged her nose. "I didn't eat it last night either."

"Sorry."

"Don't be, Renee practically drooled over it! Her mom never cooks and always has Renee on some crazy diet. She had yogurt and carrots, which I thought was a perfect lunch, so we both eyed the other's for, like, ever and then we traded!"

"Do you want yogurt tomorrow?"

"Earth to Dad!" Molly laughed. "I have my first new friend. You better keep up those fancy lunches because I promised her I would bring something even better tomorrow."

Henry laughed and hugged his daughter. "I am at your service."
"Thanks, Dad." Running out of the room.

It was at that moment, when all his family felt happy to be in
Sun Valley, that he knew the move would help. There was more
time for baseball games and weekend hikes, but as time passed
and more good memories were made, work was still there, still
all-encompassing, and Henry felt like he was the one looking in
on the three other Sterns, trying to catch a glimpse of who and
what they had become. Molly and Alex would walk on eggshells
with him, not bother him with silly childish things like home-
work help or rides to and from friends' houses. They had put
him on a pedestal. He sometimes liked the view, liked that he was
only needed to swoop in and save the day, but he was isolated and
alone. He missed the day-to-day, the routines, the messy faces.
Once the kids left for college, and Helen curled even more into
herself, he knew he had to make an even bigger change. With his
wife on her own little platform, and him still cemented to his, all
they could do was try to reach out but never quite touch. Their
arms open, yet frozen. Henry closed his part of the practice,
reconnected with his lonely wife, and followed his true childhood passion—cooking. The restaurant he subsequently opened
was a perfect blend of Henry's readiness to feed and Helen's
uncanny ability to nurture. Helen was thrilled by their new-
found love for each other and finally Henry was living in the
center of his life and not on the fringe. Their lives kept improv-
ing the older they got and they knew they were lucky.

Molly complained to Henry when Helen painted her room
pink. Molly had wanted something tougher, but it comforted
Helen to have something constant, something remain just as it
was when Alex and Molly romped around in onesies with bunny
ears and feet. The color of cotton candy and Bonnie Bell lipstick
would suffice, and Helen ignored Molly's protestations. Molly
would always be her rosy baby despite a big move to Los Angeles
and a life whose pulse Helen could not really put her finger on.

It wasn't that she couldn't relate to her daughter, it was just that it was so alien, so independent. In their phone calls, which thankfully had remained daily despite the distance, Molly would relate stories of music, bars, and parties decked out with the trappings of young Hollywood. Helen could only imagine how her once awkward, gangly, full of braces daughter managed to squeeze into her fifth pair of leather pants and strut.

Molly's outward confidence was something that Helen had always admired in her daughter. When Molly was born, after one look, Helen was hooked. Her baby's skin was an addiction. It radiated this inherent goodness, and the minute she touched Molly's little hand, she felt a sense of calm. Molly always had this serenity about her, an inner balance. Whenever Helen had a bad day, a smile from Molly would make her feel instantly at ease. Molly's innate sweetness was a comfort. They say that children learn from their parents, but Molly could always teach Helen something: how to be still in a moment, how to be herself more often. Helen tried to incorporate Molly's independence and lust for life into her own. Seeing her literally in a heap, snuggling ferociously into her rose-hued comforter searching for respite, made Helen choke. How did her fearless female get here? How did a girl so set on her path, so sure of herself, devolve so quickly? How could she help?

"Do you want me to rub your back?"

"Yeah."

Molly rolled over and lifted up her tank top. Her mother's cool fingers on her back tracing tic-tac-toe felt good. It gave Molly something else to concentrate on. After about five minutes, Helen could see her daughter's body beginning to unravel, uncoil itself.

"You know, when you were a little girl, a baby really, you never liked to be touched?"

"Really?" Molly whispered, even though she knew this story well.

"Every night I would sit by your crib and rub your back just like this. Initially you would squirm away, but eventually your breathing would steady and you would fall asleep."

Helen looked down and saw that Molly was out cold. She pulled down her shirt and tucked in the blanket tightly around her. No matter how old Molly got, in certain moments, she would always be Helen's baby.

Molly was walking on a beach. It was twilight, the magic hour. Everything was frosted, the air alabaster. At first she was alone, casually tracing her name in the sand with a stick. As the water danced alongside, Molly kept rewriting, trying to imprint herself onto the beach. She looked up and saw a pelican dip over the water. The sun was setting. She returned to her canvas, methodically drawing her L's.

"Molly, Molly, Molly."

"Hi, Liam."

"Nice name."

"My favorite name is Charlotte."

"Like the spider. I remember you told me that night you were sick and I sat with you by the bathtub for hours."

"She taught Wilbur how to be a proud pig."

"You taught me how to be a proud man."

"Why did you leave me?"

"You left."

"You promised."

"I tried. I am trying."

Liam took hold of her stick and quickly fashioned something in the ground beneath her. It was dark. Molly turned and he was gone. She tried to read what he wrote but the tide had already washed it away. She fell to her knees, stabbing at the sand with her glittery nails, trying to decipher the words. She kept grabbing and poking, her fingers becoming numb and raw, scraped clean by nature's pumice. Soon she would hit China.

Molly awoke with her hands balled into fists, clutching the blush blanket swathed around her. Her face was hot. She rolled over. The clock read one-thirty P.M. She hadn't slept this late since college, and those early afternoon wake-ups were usually preordained by large amounts of beer, sex, and marijuana. A sliver of light shone around the edge of her patchwork curtains, nudging her left foot with its rooster call. Molly disentangled herself from her covers and sat up. She grabbed a hair elastic from the nightstand and stood. Gingerly, she opened the curtain, slowly letting her eyes adjust to the brightness. Outside, she could see in the corner of the yard a patch of sunflowers. Their yellow smiles hung low and swayed in the light breeze. Molly twisted her hair into a ponytail and made a mental note to pick some later to sketch. Maybe doing some of the little things she always did would help her regain her center. She pulled out her journal, but set it back down on her bed. There was just too much to write and she was just too tired.

When she walked downstairs into the kitchen, smells of garlic, thyme, and apples tickled her nose. That was something she could always count on, the very particular, special aroma of the Stern family kitchen. It was always warm and luscious, damp with the odor of earthy mushrooms or just-picked potatoes. Spicy with cinnamon and nutmeg, crisp with the freshness of sweet peas and honeydew melons. Their safe little cave housed a cornucopia of treats every day of every year. All of the Sterns were fabulous cooks. Henry handed down tradition after tradition, mirroring all the teaching he received from his mother, grandmother, and handful of aunts. While other little boys were out on their bicycles or climbing trees, Henry clambered around his mother's ankles, watching and stirring when told. His mother used to say that when he was a baby, the only place he would quiet down was under the kitchen table. The moment she wrapped him up and placed him in an old vegetable box, this little smile would wash over his tiny face. Somehow his body chemistry boiled at the same time as the chicken soup on the stove.

Molly too loved the kitchen, yet it was something that came to her later in life. When she moved back to LA for college and had her first apartment, she was grateful for her father's skill in the kitchen. She learned to appreciate food on his terms and whenever she screwed up some perfectly simple dish, she called her father for the remedy. Now she loved taking random raw ingredients and dicing, dashing, and dispersing them into something complete, a new entity entirely formed from her imagination. The unprepared food, her tabula rasa. She grabbed a glass from the cupboard and went to the fridge for some juice. Pinned in place with a princess teddy bear magnet Molly had fashioned in second grade for a Chanukah present was a note from her mother.

> *Honey, had to go help Dad at the restaurant. Didn't want to wake you. Wasn't sure what you would want so there is some squash soup on the stove and fruit in the fridge. Come by when you want. I will call later to check in. Mom. Oh, also, Jaycee called to check on you.*

Molly took the note down and sky-hooked it Kareem Abdul-Jabbar–style into the trash. She pondered her breakfast/lunch decision. Tossing a glance in either direction, Molly headed for the stove and lifted off the copper lid. The smell of ginger and onions pricked her senses and she ladled herself a big helping. After tearing off a big piece of crusty sourdough, she took her meal to the table. From the window she could still see the patch of flowers. It would be a yellow day. Unlike yesterday in all its unflinching blackness, today she would try to focus on a more cheery shade. Yellow, heat, sunlight, Labrador puppies, yet also the color of jaundice and three-day-old bruises. Molly would try to stay with the puppies.

Molly returned to her soup, but it just didn't taste right to her. She went over to the sink, dumped it down the drain, and watched the golden liquid swirl. Maybe now that grief diet would kick in. She washed out the bowl and left it facedown on the blue-checked towel beside her. Molly went over to the phone and dialed. It wasn't until she heard the message on his cell that she realized she had called Liam. She hung up quickly and took a deep breath. How long would he be instinct and the thing that she thought about when she wasn't trying to think about anything? She needed to train her mind on something or someone else, but who could become breath overnight?

Molly looked back to the phone and this time placed the call she was attempting in the first place. Jaycee picked it up on the third ring.

"Hi. It's me."

"Molly! How are you? Your mom said you were still sleeping when I called earlier," Jay answered.

"Okay, I guess." Halfheartedly. "How's the place?"

"Clean, finally. I think I lit most of your candles trying to get the beer smell out."

"Thanks. By the way, I forgot to deal with work stuff. Do you think you can go by the studio and send out the order for Barneys? All of the necklaces are laying right in the middle of my desk and the order form is next to it. You would just need to check all the tags and make sure the right ones get in the box. There should be packing stuff, and send it COD insured for the amount of the order. You can use my UPS account, and the number is in the Rolodex."

"Done. I'll call when I get there to make sure. Will you be around later?"

"I'll have my cell on. Also, you might as well send me some finished pieces and my workbox too. Maybe I can design while I am up here."

"How long are you staying?"

"Don't know yet."

"You know he called me today wondering where you were. He told me what really happened."

"Yeah." Swallowing hard. "And?"

"And, I get it, but you can't just run away. You're supposed to be the grown-up here."

"Whatever, I can for now. I just can't talk to him. You didn't tell him where I was, did you?"

"No, but he's not an idiot. He figured it out."

"I hope he doesn't call." Breathing hard. "Look." Starting to tear up again. "Jay, I got to go. Thanks for everything."

"Molly, you need to talk about all this. Stop cutting me off! Please, just stop for a second and focus."

"I just can't. I don't want to focus and think and deal! I just want everything to fucking go away!"

"That's exactly why you need to talk about it." Getting upset. "It's not going to go away by you shutting your eyes real tight and clicking your fucking heels three times!"

"That's all well and good, Toto, but I'm hanging up."

"Molly, come on."

"Gotta go. Love you." Interrupting and hanging up.

Molly went back to the sink and splashed water all over her face. The cool liquid eased the temperature of her overheated cheeks. Her yellow day was beginning to dull and look like congealed turkey fat the day after Thanksgiving.

four

After showering long and hard, and crawling into a pair of dirty gray cords and a pink Abercrombie fake-aged T-shirt, Molly grabbed her hobo bag and headed outside where her car stood shiny and newly washed. This was one tradition Molly missed desperately in Los Angeles. While she barely managed a bath once a month for her Land Rover, Henry was a twice a weeker. Molly smiled and climbed into her spit-shined chariot. She flicked on the radio and drove into town. Exactly eight minutes later,

at 3:12, she pulled in front of Helen's, their family restaurant. She saw her mom's, dad's, and brother's cars parked and spaced evenly down the street. Determined not to fall into another weepfest, Molly pulled a Mr. Potato Head and plugged a big fat smile on her face.

She pushed open the walnut wood door. The restaurant was empty except for her mother carefully sipping a cappuccino and going over the reservation book at the end of the bar. Her mother's silvery blond bob hung over her eyes as she bent her head down while working. Her faded khakis and pale green cashmere short-sleeved sweater contrasted with the dark wood of the restaurant.

"Hi." Giving her mom a kiss on the cheek. "Make me one?" Taking a sip from Helen's cup.

"Hi, baby. Sure." Looking up at her daughter with her green eyes. "Double?"

"Yes, I need the caffeine."

Helen got up from her seat and went around the bar. She resteamed the milk and hit the espresso machine. Soon, a perfect latté was walking back to Molly.

"How are you doing?" Handing it to Molly.

"Fair." Taking a sip. "I slept forever."

"I didn't want to wake you, you looked like you needed the rest." Sitting back down. "Ready to talk?"

"Let me go get something to eat from Dad, and then we'll see what springs forth."

"What about the soup?"

"It just didn't sit right."

Molly got up and took her cup with her as she traipsed back into the kitchen. Her flip-flops slapped against the cool certainty of the waxed cranberry-colored concrete floor. The aromas tickled her nose immediately, their delicate web of fragrance warming her senses. Angel, the line cook, stood next to Henry behind the big stove, stirring large stockpots and preparing sauces. Alex sat on a little stool by the counter, trimming and portioning the meat. And Charlie, the prep chef, worked feverishly whisking oils, preparing his dressings. Renee, now conveniently Alex's wife, walked in from the back holding a tray of apples sprinkled with butter and brown sugar. She popped them into one of the ovens. She was the first to see Molly.

"I know that girl." Coming over and giving Molly a big hug. "Your parents said you made quite an entrance this morning."

"Yeah. You know me. I am all about big productions." Squeezing back. "Is that your belly I feel?"

"Yeah." Rubbing her hand over her tummy. "It just really popped out. I'm starting to look like a house."

"How far along are you now? Five months?"

"Almost six."

Molly leaned down and talked to Renee's stomach.

"Hi, little one. I'm your aunt and can't wait to meet you." Standing back up. "You look great by the way. Where did those boobs come from?"

"Pretty amazing, right? One of the only perks." Winking at Molly. "How are you doing?"

Molly was about to answer but was swooped into a Stern bear hug. Her dad and brother smothered her with their arms. The smell of raw meat and vegetables wafted around her.

"Hi, fellas."

"So what's going on, sister?" Alex asked while sitting back down. He nudged the back of his wrist through his curly brown hair, going back to his task.

"Hungry?" her dad asked. "I can make you some pasta."

"Sounds good, Dad. Thanks."

"I asked you a question, Molly," her brother restated, ditching the pleasantry.

"Jeez, I heard you. We can talk later when you aren't bearing sharp steel."

"After work, I'm coming for you." Pointing a knife at her.

"Fine." Cutting him off with a reluctant agreement. "Renee, how much longer are you planning on working?"

"A few more weeks. I have been training this new girl, Ashley. I think she's going to work out fine."

"Great." Swallowing the last of her coffee. "Oh, are you still doing yoga classes, with the baby and all?"

"Saturdays at the Sacred Cow."

"Count me in." Heading for the door. "Dad, I'll be outside with Mom."

"I'll bring the pasta out when it's ready."

Molly went back into the front room and sat down next to her mother.

"Mom, I just don't think I'm ready to talk about it."

"That's okay." Patting Molly's hand. "Did you see Renee?"

"Her tummy is so cute! I can't wait for that baby to get here."

"I know, I went with them to their first sonogram and it was amazing. I think I have the picture in my purse. I was going to mail you a Xerox, but I forgot." Getting up and walking to the coatrack in the corner. "Here. My first grandchild. I'm so proud."

"Wow, it looks like a peanut. Our very own Goober."

Molly's mom, instead of sitting back down, went over and began folding a stack of napkins laying on one of the tables. They were all different French Provençal patterns based in gold, coral, and red tones.

"What do you think of these? We just got them in. I ordered them when Dad and I were in Saint-Tropez."

"I like them. They look good on the tables." Getting up to help. "I like the flowers too." Gesturing to the sunflowers.

"I brought them from home. We have tons in the backyard."

"I saw them when I woke up. They inspired me to try to have a yellow day."

"Glad it's not blue."

"Glad you are not a poet." Winking at her mom.

Molly and Helen quietly folded and placed napkins for a while, their actions mimicking each other like a well-rehearsed ballet. It seemed as if each were listening to the same song, singing in the silence.

"How's the business going?" Helen asked.

"Good. Jay is sending off that big order I got from Barneys and I just got some pieces in the October issue of *Elle*. I went kind of crazy the last few weeks and made a ton of pieces so I can fill orders right away if need be, which looks like it was a good idea because I'm not sure when I'm going home. Jay's still trying to persuade me into the store thing."

"What do you think about it?"

"Definitely not at the top of my list of things to think about right now."

"Okay. By the way, I think that Susan wants some more for the store here. Your jewelry has been a big hit up here with all the summer tourists."

"Cool. I'll go see her. Jay's sending some up with my materials."

"Good. Maybe you want to help out here a bit? While you sort out whatever it is that you are going through?"

"Sure, and I will tell you when I can, Mom."

"I know, I know. I'm just worried."

"So am I."

Molly walked over to her mother and gave her a kiss on the cheek.

"What a picture. My two girls," Henry called out while walking in. "Molly, here you go."

"Thanks, Dad."

Molly went back to the bar and sat down behind her plate of steaming pasta. Her appetite immediately returned. Molly forked her plate with the ferocity of a scavenging dog feasting on a half-eaten McDonald's burger lying limp in a dark alleyway. She barely swallowed between mouthfuls.

"Slow down, kid." Henry chuckled, his round, ruddy cheeks glinting. "Alex isn't here to hijack your meal."

Molly's stuffing her face ended with the ring of a phone. From within her purse on top of the bar, Molly's cell sang. Thinking it was Jay, she ran over and flipped it on.

"Hello," she answered.

"Hey," a sleepy voice purred.

Molly could feel the hairs on the back of her neck stand up on end and she felt her pulse beating in her ears. She gulped.

"Molly, are you there?" Liam asked.

"Yeah." Choking out the word.

"Hey."

"You said that already." Still trying to catch her breath.

"I guess. So . . ." Liam searched for words. "You're home?"

"Yeah. I pretty much left from the hospital."

"Jay told me and so did my mom when she got in a little while ago. How are you?"

"How do you think?" Stifling a large sob.

"I know."

"No, you don't!" Raising her voice.

"You're right. Molly, I'm so . . ."

"Don't even! Don't even let the words fall from your mouth." Starting to yell. "It's all bullshit!"

Henry and Helen looked at each other and back at their daughter. Helplessly they watched her entire body react.

"Molly, I'm sorry. I am."

"I told you not to bother. I can't do this."

"I fucked up." Liam starting to cry into the phone.

Molly put her hand on the receiver and dry-heaved. Her body convulsed and hot tears fell on her cheeks.

"I really fucked up. Fuck." Crying harder. "I'd do anything to take it back."

"Well, you can't, and I can't do this anymore. Liam, it's over." Crying with him.

"Just like that?"

"You're kidding, right?" Getting her wits about her. "You broke the promise, the one fucking thing I asked of you ever."

"I know, but give me another chance. It won't happen again, ever. I'm going to get help. My mom is taking me to a place right after they let me out of the hospital. I know I can't do it alone and I am going to get clean. I am going to this time. I have a problem, and I'm going to fix it."

"I'm glad, but I just . . ." Molly let out a giant sigh. "I'm all out of get-out-of-jail-free cards."

"Molly, please," Liam begged her. "I love you so much."

"I love you too, but I just can't go down this road with you anymore. I'm so scared, too scared. This is so much more than I bargained for. I'm becoming this road map of scars."

"At least wait until I get home."

"Take care of yourself. I gotta go." Molly hung up the phone.

Molly held the cell in her hot hand, and she stared at the smooth buttons. Her knuckles were white. Helen came over and put her arms around her daughter's waist. She pulled her into a hug and Molly broke down. Tighter and tighter she clung to her mother until the floor and ceiling dropped away.

It was dark when Molly woke up. Somehow she was wrapped in a black blanket, tucked into the couch in the family room of their home. She had no recollection of coming home, or of falling asleep. The only thing to tell her she had been crying was the dull throb of her sinuses and a thin crust on her lashes. The clock on the TV read eight-thirty. How long had she been asleep?

Molly went into the kitchen and poured herself a glass of juice from the fridge. Every muscle in her body ached whenever she moved. Everything was clenched, trying to form a skin shield. Too bad it was too late for the blow not to punch a hole right through her. Maybe Molly was being too harsh, but her and Liam's do-or-die dance had begun months and months ago.

Various issues began piling themselves up on her balance the closer they got and the more time they spent together.

Molly had this theory that often in relationships, the thing that attracts you the most to a person is ultimately the thing that repels. Like with her coffee and how he remembered and watched every little nuance, Liam was capable of this insane level of attention. When Molly was around him, nothing got past him, no twist of her hair went ignored. He ate her up with his eyes and drank her in with his words. His attentiveness was a third person in the room with them whenever they made love or counted sheep. It made Molly more aware of herself than she had ever been, how she carried herself, how she fidgeted when she was nervous, and when she was horny how she would tug at her left earlobe. Their relationship was a finely tuned mechanism, all the bolts were in place and complemented each other.

But, as time went on, Molly came to realize that Liam's ability to focus so intently on something or someone was not just special to Molly. It was how he was with everything in his life. He was all about details and delineating each and every environment he was in. Every person he came in contact with fell under this gaze. This level of concentration was given to everyone, but as easy as Molly could be with him and feel the most seen she had ever been in her life, she could also just as easily slide to the fringes and feel invisible. She could cease to exist.

Molly began to understand this quality about Liam on her twenty-seventh birthday. She planned this shindig at a bowling alley deep in Hollywood. Since Molly wanted things to be a little dramatic, she requested that everyone dress up, slicked back hair, high ponytails, etc. Twenty-five of her nearest and dearest donned their best bowling shirts and jeans and threw down their best strikes. Molly had on this tight pink snap-front shirt that Jaycee had bought her with BUNNY embroidered in red cursive letters. ("Bunny" was Molly's bowling alter ego.) Jay had a green shirt with JOANIE sewn in black near her breast. Drinks, cigarettes, and balls flowed, and the only thing missing besides a DJ who played something other than Top Forty boy-band beats was Liam. Molly had spoken with him at six, laid his shirt on her bed (they weren't living together at this point but he had a key), and left to get a quick bite with Jay without seeing him. Liam had mentioned a few things he needed to get done and instead of getting dinner he would have to meet her there. No biggie. But it was eleven and he was still nowhere to be found.

"Where's Liam?" Jay asked as she handed Molly yet another Jack and Coke.

"Good question, Joanie." Checking her cell in her bag to see if he had called. "No messages."

"What is he doing?"

"No idea. Some errand." Looking to the door.

"On your birthday?"

"Yeah, whatever." Still looking at the door.

"Think if you look hard enough he will materialize?"

"Maybe." Smiling a weak smile.

"He'll be here." Sensing Molly's deflating spirit. "Cheers!"

The girls clinked glasses and Molly chugged down the sweet liquid. Her clear pink day was getting a bit muddier. It was becoming more mauve. Molly tried to throw herself into her own party, dancing to 'N Sync, bowling a string of gutter balls, and drinking heavily. By midnight, Molly was drunk and had a mild case of whiplash from scanning the door too frequently.

"Jay, I need cake." Stumbling slightly as she made her way to her friend.

"I thought you wanted to wait until he got here."

"Fuck it. Let's do it."

Jaycee went over to the Ralph's box resting on the counter behind the group. She undid the top and pulled a lighter out of her pocket. With the cake ablaze, Molly sidled up next to her and everyone sang "Happy Birthday." Molly made a wish everyone

could easily guess and blew. Cake was cut and passed around, and
the party continued. At about one-thirty, Molly found a chair,
and instead of flitting back and forth among her friends, she
held court, high on sugar and whiskey. The party was winding
down when finally, a familiar voice caught the edge of her ear,
and she turned around with a face full of drunken elation. Her
smile soon faded when she saw that Liam was not alone. Wrapped
around him like last year's pashmina was Elena, the girl she had
met at Goldfinger's the night she first met Liam. A girl who
never stopped casting Molly the evil eye despite the six months
that had passed, Elena tossed Molly her special look and grinned
like a Cheshire cat, holding her arms tighter around Liam.
Molly's stomach began to roll.

"You've got to be kidding me?!" Molly stated.

"Molly." Untangling himself from Elena. "Happy Birthday!"

"Yeah, Happy Birthday, Molly." Elena slithered.

Liam came over to Molly and leaned down to give her a kiss.
Molly turned her head and his lips met with the edge of her hair-
line.

"What?" Liam asked. "What's wrong?"

"What time is it?" she asked him.

"It's like ten-thirty." Looking at his watch. "Oh . . ."

"Yeah." Starting to feel even more nauseated.

"I'm sorry."

"There might be some cake left over there and if you guys
want to bowl, I think you are going to be playing each other
because we were just about to leave." Getting up from her perch.

"Molly, I'm sorry. The time just got away from me."

Molly looked up and got a good look at his face. His eyes were
saucers, spinning like the teacup ride. He was flying.

"You are so high."

"No, we just were hanging out." Blinking hard, trying to
merge the two Mollys he was seeing into one.

"Whatever. Have fun." Molly grabbed her one shoe and purse
and headed to the cashier.

Jaycee and Liam followed after her. Molly paid and retrieved her other shoe. She sat down on the floor and began slipping on her sneakers.

"Molly, where are you going?" Liam asked squatting down next to her on the carpet. "I'll come."

"Home, and no thanks. I wouldn't want your little friend to get lonely." Standing up. Molly swayed slightly and fell into him. She could smell Elena's perfume everywhere. "Shit."

Molly raced into the women's room and threw open a stall. She fell on her knees and heaved. God damn her weak stomach. Frosting and Coca-Cola sloshed in the bowl. She felt hands on her hair as Jay held it while she continued emptying her system. Molly was a total mess. Liam poked his head in as Molly was splashing water on her face.

"Are you all right?" Coming over to her with a paper towel.

"Just dandy." Snatching it out of his hand. "You're in the girls' room."

"So?"

"So, go!" Molly glared at him.

Liam blanched, and turned on his heels. Molly wiped off her face and hands.

"I need to get out of here as fast as possible."

"No problem. Just hold on to me," Jay answered.

Jay and Molly swept past Liam, Elena, and the remnants of the party. When Molly was finally belted into Jay's pickup, she burst into tears. Still tasting bile on her tongue she reached into Jay's glove compartment and retrieved an Altoid.

"What a fucking dick!" Jay exclaimed pulling out of the drive-way. "He strolls in super late with *it* and expects all to be fine."

"*It*?" Starting to grin despite herself.

"Yeah, *it*." Grinning. "You cannot call that evil thing a her. It devalues the entire female race."

"I wish she looked like Cousin Itt." Wiping off her face again.

"I used to think Elena was hot, but soon I realized she had no soul. Every time I see her, it's like she morphs into Medusa circa

Clash of the Titans. You, on the other hand, are like Aphrodite reincarnate."

"Thanks." Leaning over and giving Jay a kiss on the cheek. "Great fucking birthday!"

"It was. Don't let him ruin it."

"Too late." Getting teary again.

"Stop. I command you!"

"Command me?"

"Yes, I'm giving you specific important orders to not dwell on what your lame-ass stupid boyfriend has just done until tomorrow."

"It is tomorrow."

"Tomorrow, tomorrow. We are going to call the rest of our friends, go to my house, drink more, get super stoned, and celebrate the perfectness of you until the sun comes up!"

"Fine. I always do as I am told."

"Can I get that on tape?"

"Just drive." Turning up the radio.

Molly and Jay rallied a small group and hung out dancing and singing karaoke off Jay's machine until dawn. Molly was numbed by liquor and weed and soundly fell asleep in Jay's bed. What truly was celebrated was the perfectness of Molly's best friend. Jay had an uncanny ability to boost Molly's immune system and get her through the night.

The morning after though was a whole other enchilada. Molly woke up at about noon with a throbbing headache and stomach cramps racking her torso. Half twisted in Jay's blue duvet, she struggled to untangle without rousing her friend. Molly gingerly inched out of bed, came to a standing position, took two steps to the bathroom tripped on a random stiletto, knocked over a glass of water, screamed, fell back into the bed, and landed on Jay.

"Fuck!" Jay exclaimed.

"Sorry," Molly replied, rubbing her foot and readjusting her tush so it wasn't directly on top of her friend.

"Your ass in my face is not what I usually like to wake up to."

"I know, sorry again." Wiping the sleep from her eyes. "I tried to be quiet."

"Something you are never good at." Rolling over. "What time is it?"

"Twelvish. I'm going to get in the shower. Where are the extra towels?"

"Hall closet. Wake me again when you are all done."

"I'm going to borrow clothes."

"Whatever."

Molly made her second attempt for the bathroom and this time she was successful. She rummaged around in the drawers, searching for Advil and a rubber band for her hair. She flipped on the hot water and slipped off her underwear and tank top. Under the spray, she took a deep breath and replayed the scattered images she could recollect from last night. There was a party full of friendly faces, a boyfriend who showed up wrapped around the girl she hated most in the world, a close-up of some sketchy toilet, her horrible rendition of "I Love Rock 'n' Roll" karaoke style, and a best friend who did her best to make everything all right. Molly took another deep breath and let the water massage the back of her neck.

This was the first time Liam had really disappointed her. As simple as that. An event that could only have brought them closer had turned into a sour little pill of reality. Molly felt a bit woozy. How could he have managed to fuck this one up? It was so easy. Show up for your girlfriend's birthday party, mingle with her friends, and make her feel like a million trillion dollars. A no-brainer. Molly wondered what the excuses would be, what line of defense he would take. Molly knew she would forgive him, her resolve would turn to mush the minute he showed up, but in the pit of her stomach she had this nagging sensation that this wouldn't be the last time.

Molly dried off and threw on her dirty underwear, a pair of

Jay's red Juicy track pants, and a wife-beater she found in the drawer. She went back to her Sleeping Beauty and nudged her gently.

"Hi."

"Still sleeping."

"I'm going to call Bozo and get him to pick me up."

"I'll drive you." Not moving an inch.

"It's cool. I have to deal anyway. Thanks again. Call you later."

"You know I want those pants back." Still not moving.

"Of course, I would never." Patting her head.

"Sure you would."

Jay grunted and pulled the blanket around her tightly. Molly retrieved her clothing and shoes from the floor and walked into the living room. Beer bottles, cigarettes, and burned-out candles littered the coffee table. Molly tossed everything into the garbage and found the phone. She dialed.

"Did I wake you?" Asking after he picked up on the third ring.

"No, not really. Been up for a while. Molly, I'm so sorry about last night."

"I know. Look, let's talk about it later. Will you come get me?"

"Jay's?"

"Yeah."

"Be there in ten."

"Can you bring my flip-flops I left at your place?"

"See you in a minute."

Liam arrived and sheepish was an understatement. He was more wimpy than Mary's dumb lamb. Eye contact was minimal, and a slight rosy tint remained on his cheek well after she had gotten into his car. It was very quiet except for the radio.

"Molly, I really don't know what happened."

"What does that mean?"

"I went over to Elena's to help her set up her computer, and then she was showing me her new artwork, and we drank some wine and did some blow, and Zander came over and we were all just hanging out. Then, I was at your party, and well . . ."

"Do you know on how many levels this upsets me?"

"I know." Liam pulled the car over and turned off the ignition. "I wanted your birthday to be special for you, and I messed it all up."

"Did you hook up with her?"

"Are you insane?"

"Did you?"

"Molly." Glaring at her. "She does nothing for me."

"But you do everything for her. You know how much she hates me and wants you. Fuck!"

"She doesn't hate you." Saying earnestly. "She thinks you're great."

Molly burst out laughing.

"Are you kidding?" Laughing harder. "They both wish we had never met."

"They are my best friends, Molly."

"I know, and that's fine. But don't you see that last night you let them totally screw me over? They sucked you into their little vibe and you instantly forgot about me just like that." Molly snapped her fingers. "Because I was waiting for you and feeling all mopey, I drank way too much and puked cake in some nasty-ass bathroom! It was my birthday for God's sake!"

"I'm sorry. Look, what else can I do? It won't happen again. I promise."

Molly looked at him and saw in his eyes how serious he was. He leaned over and kissed her.

"Here, give me your watch." Grabbing her hand.

"What?"

"Okay." Taking it off her wrist. "It's officially February eleventh again. Today is your birthday. You are one lucky lady because you get to celebrate twice." Refastening it. "All day is Molly day. How may I do you?"

"Food and coffee would be a good start."

"As you wish, Buttercup."

He leaned over and kissed her again. Molly softened under his lips.

"Before we adjourn to the grease pit, I have something for you. I meant to give it to you last night, but, well, here."

He reached in the backseat and produced a shoe box wrapped in newspaper tied with a red piece of yarn. He placed it in Molly's lap. She ripped it open. Inside was a letter-sized envelope and a tape. Molly opened the letter and inside was sheet music. She began reading the words as Liam pushed the tape into the player. Soon, gentle guitar chords filled the car and Liam's melodious voice echoed. He sounded like mittens, mashed potatoes, the best broken-in boots. He was part Whiskeytown, part Jackson Browne, with a dash of Jeff Buckley thrown into the mix. Familiar and comfortable. Molly sat back and listened.

When she wakes, she brushes the stars from her hair
Tangled up in daydreams,
She yawns and tugs at her sleeve.
She thinks she's all alone
But I watch her when she's unaware,
She doesn't always notice me
But sometimes all I can do is stare.

I knew it when I met her
I could never forget her,
The warmth of her smile
Was going to last for a while.
Forever and always
The near and the far days,
With all the words she speaks
I'm slowly swept off my feet.

I want to touch her skin
Tattoo her onto my tongue with a taste
She is a photograph not yet taken,
A drawing I long to trace.
There's more to remember with every glance,
Even with eyes closed I see her
A meeting by chance becomes my do-or-die dance.

> I knew it when I met her
> I could never forget her,
> The warmth of her smile
> Was going to last for a while.
> Forever and always
> The near and the far days,
> With all the words she speaks
> I'm slowly swept off my feet.

I am under her spell,
Left in the midst of her magic
I'm lost without it
Just the thought of her overwhelms.
There is no end with her,
I fall deeper every day,
But falling implies an end to this way,
This way that I feel about her
My blood races with thrill that I met her.

> I am above her, around her
> I love her.

When the song ended, Molly was speechless. She felt like she had been dipped in honey, licked off, and left to dry under a warm June sun. Every last bit of anger and doubt evaporated, and she felt a grin the size of a hot air balloon billow upon her face. In this moment, the one she was in, she loved him.

"Wow." Looking at Liam.

"Do you like it?" Blushing slightly. "I've been working on it for a while. I wanted it to be perfect."

"It is." Caressing his cheek. "No one has ever written any-thing for me before—that is if you don't count the Valentine poem Kenny Childress wrote for me in fourth grade."

"Did it go something like 'roses are red, violets are blue'?"

"How did you guess?" Smiling at Liam. "You are soooooo smart."

"I know, I know. Genius."

"I really love it. Thank you."

"You're very welcome." Squeezing her hand. "Hungry?"

"Starving."

Molly forgave him, time passed, and things were okay. But while she made peace with her boyfriend, Elena was a whole other story. One more check on Molly's "hate her forever" list. She just never seemed to give up! She was always in the background scheming, judging, hissing—anything to steal Liam's gaze away from Molly. No matter where they were, somehow Elena would figure out a means to interject herself into the situation like an umlaut or exclamation point. But the real problem lay in the fact that Liam never really saw Elena's true nature, as he was so accepting and trusting of others almost to a fault. Liam was oblivious to what lurked behind her perfect orthodontic smile and lithe size-two frame, while Molly couldn't even keep count of the number of times Elena showed up at just the right time to triumph over her. Like when Elena arrived uninvited at a dinner when Elizabeth was in town for a night and monopolized the entire conversation. Or when she used her bevy of salesgirl spies to stalk Molly and then strolled into Liam's CD release party in the exact same top Molly happened to be wearing. Of course her perky bra-free boobs looked runway perfect. Elena was sort of Veronica to Molly's Betty, but Betty stayed friendly while Molly wished for a tornado and a flying house.

Elena's first real strike came about two months after Molly and Liam had begun dating. There was this big Hollywood music fête in the Hills above Sunset. An all-day barbeque and musical jam, with babes, booze, and big shots. Liam invited Molly to be his date, and she was thrilled. It was their first real foray into Liam's public world together and Molly wanted it to be perfect. She wanted to represent. For a week, she planned her outfit. Trying on the contents of her wardrobe five times over to find the right mix of casual, sexy, fashion forward, yet blasé. She blew almost her entire month's salary on the right shoes, the right bag. Lucky for her discount at Jane Doe or she would have been even more broke. Molly wanted her armor to be wrapped and whipstitched snuggly around her form. Liam picked her up and his eyes lit up the minute she opened the door.

"Wow." Spinning her around. "You look beautiful."

"Thanks." Smoothing her hands down the front of her pink silk Indian printed tunic she was wearing over jeans. "It's not too much?"

"Nope. You are perfect." Kissing her long and hard. "Your chariot awaits."

The conversation flowed out the windows of Liam's car like a melody. Everything was sunny and light, they were inside each other's rose-colored glasses. When they arrived, Molly grabbed Liam's hand tightly and blinked, sending herself shooting away from their easy banter of only seconds before and right back into her fit of nerves. For some reason, even though she had been to a million parties, and met a million people, Molly felt extremely vulnerable. Maybe she wasn't yet comfortable in her seemingly perfect relationship. He squeezed three times and Molly was brought back.

"My dad used to do that," Molly remembered.

"What?"

"The three-beat hand squeeze. It was our secret code for I love you."

"Mine too." Kissing her cheek.

Molly blushed, swooned, and let herself feel the tiny champagne bubbles fizzing up and down her body. They walked into the party and it was already in full swing. Music and laughter filled the rooms and tumbled through the sliding glass doors onto the lawn. Exquisitely rock-'n'-rolled children with their hippie fashions did cartwheels while their parents held beers or played bongos. Molly was taking it all in when Liam handed her a drink and a small white pill.

"What's this?" she asked, holding it in her palm.

"Some E I just got from Elliot. I thought it would be cool to do it together."

"Now? Here?"

"Sure, everyone is already rolling." Gesturing to a group huddled around Elliot holding water bottles.

"I don't know." Looking at him. "I'm not the biggest fan. The last time I did this I was in the bathroom, curled up with Jay in a bathtub for about two hours."

"It'll be fine. This time you're with me."

"Are you going to do this regardless?"

"Well, actually, I already took some."

"Really?" Getting a little weirded out.

"I'm sorry, I thought you'd want to too."

"It's fine." Trying to smile. "You just have to promise that you aren't going to ditch me. That's a mighty big yard and I have a tendency to wander off."

"I swear, I will be your buddy for the whole day." Sticking out his hand. "We can shake on it."

"Fine." Shaking and then swallowing the pill before she could rethink her decision.

"Besides," taking her hand again, "you are the only one I want to pet me later."

Molly smiled at him and let him think the whole thing was just the best darn idea in the whole damn world, but she knew she was in for a nasty ride. Molly and E just did not get along, and she knew she would either freak out or puke. Bad decision, but it was give it a go or be the only one to not give it a go and be trapped with strangers for hours while Liam tripped. Wasn't she too old for peer pressure? That fucking smile of his would be the end of her.

About an hour later, when Molly's tongue started feeling thick and her body was on vibrate, Elena strolled into the party, coiffed and radiant. The girl had the fuck-me look and glamorous glide down pat. It took Elena all of about two seconds to insert herself into Liam and Molly's conversation. She sat herself down on the grass and started right in.

"Wow, Molly, you look seriously fucked up. Your pupils are enormous."

"Thanks." Swallowing. "You look great too."

"What did you guys take? Got any more?"

"Go ask Elliot." Liam gestured to the house.

"Cool." Getting up. "You should really drink some water because your jaw is super clenched, Molly. It looks kind of intense."

Molly raised her hands to her face, and traced her lips and teeth. They did feel funny. She looked at her hands and it was almost like they were butterfly wings slightly beating. Her heart and stomach swelled.

"I think I am going to be sick." Jumping up and running into the pool house behind them.

She pushed open the door to the thankfully free back bathroom and promptly threw up into the toilet. Liam followed after her and shut the door. Molly eased herself onto the floor and pushed her hair back. Her entire body felt wretched and she started to cry.

"Baby." Sitting next to her on the floor. "What happened? Drink some water." Handing her his bottle.

"I knew this was going to happen." Trying to focus.

"We were doing fine." Rubbing her neck. "Everything was mellow."

"I know. Maybe I'll be better soon." Trying to calm herself down. "I just feel really racy."

"Okay, let's just hang in here for a while. Turn around and I will rub your back."

Liam evenly stroked Molly's back trying to reset her internal clock. Just when Molly felt like maybe she was coming to some sort of equilibrium, someone pounded on the door.

"Liam!" Elena called through the door. "Are you in there?"

"Yeah, what do you want?" Still rubbing Molly's back.

"You are wanted out here. This journalist from *Rolling Stone* is here and wants to meet you."

"I'll be out soon."

"You have to come now. She's leaving."

"Elena." Getting up and opening the door. "I can't come right now."

Elena looked over to Molly, catching sight of Molly's tear-stained face.

"I knew you were too fucked up."

"Can you please get out of here?" Molly asked, trying to wipe off her face.

"Look, Molly, Liam needs to come out and meet this woman—now."

"Fine, I heard you the first time. Go." Looking up at Liam. "I'm going to stay in here a while. I'll be fine." Trying her best to be convincing.

"No, I'll stay."

"Please don't. I'll feel even more shitty if you do."

"Good." Elena grabbed Liam's hand and pulled him out the door.

Molly was alone, on the floor of a strange bathroom, wishing she were anywhere else. Time passed, who knows how long—

minutes, hours—and the cold tiles beneath her began to feel like a Chinese torture chamber. Maybe she was better? She stood up and felt herself wobble. Apparently, the drugs still persisted in her system despite the purge. She splashed some water on her face and it felt wonderful: cool and calm. Molly redid her lip gloss and grabbed the water bottle off the floor, refilling it from the sink faucet. She unlocked the door and wandered out of the pool house. It had gotten darker, dusk had settled on the grass, and the party was still blaring. More people migrated about, and Molly scanned the yard for Liam. She walked toward the house, shivering in the oncoming night air. Then she saw them, or really Elena, coiled up around Liam on a white leather couch in the living room. Elena was starry eyed and had her hands all over him, stroking his leg. Liam was talking animatedly to the few others sitting across from him while he rubbed Elena's feet. Molly's vision blurred and she felt hot. She felt like the Invisible Man. Not only had Liam forgotten about her but he was also a layer of clothing away from a scene in some Cinemax porno flick. Molly didn't even go inside—she couldn't. Instead, she walked to the car, huddled in the backseat, and cried herself to sleep.

"Molly, Molly," Liam purred in her ear, gently shaking her. "Wake up, sleepyhead."

Molly opened her eyes and tried to focus. She sat herself up and looked at the clock. It was almost eleven.

"I have been looking everywhere for you."

"Sure." Pulling her hair into a bun. "And it took you four hours to find me." Climbing out of the car and shaking herself out. Her neck felt like a pretzel, and not the soft, chewy kind. "Can I have the keys? I want to go home."

"Are you upset?" Still smiling. "The party's still going on. Come inside."

"Did you take more?"

"I think so, but I'm not sure how many."

"Great." Looking down at her feet and kicking a pebble by her toe. "Look, I want to go home. I know Elena or another one of your lackeys will be more than happy to give you a ride. I'll get Jay to follow me tomorrow and I will drop the car off."

"You're upset." Putting his arms around her. "What did I do?"

Molly almost burst out laughing, his puppy dog face was so pathetic. He really had no clue. Her sweet, dumb, fucked up boyfriend.

"Nothing, nothing." Realizing that she would have to let this go. "Go have fun. This is just not where I want to be."

"Why? Everyone is having a great time. Amazing stories."

"I just feel burnt and I definitely can't deal with one more interaction with Elena."

"She's not so bad. She was looking for you."

"You're joking, right? What, from the permanent spot she claimed by your side? She looked like a pig in shit the minute she had you to herself."

"When?"

"When she was giving you a full-body massage while you caressed her feet. I thought you didn't want anyone else petting you?"

"I don't, I didn't caress her feet. I didn't touch her." Thinking as hard as he could to grab a memory he couldn't recall.

"You did, and I'm happy you don't even remember, but I just really want to leave. This has been a big nightmare for me, and my comfy bed and a TV movie is calling my name. Plus, I'm freezing in this outfit."

"Let's leave then." Pulling off his Adidas jacket and putting it around Molly.

"No, it's fine, you want to stay, so stay."

"Nope, what I want, and what I wanted the whole day, is to be with you. All this," gesturing back to the house, "is really quite insignificant."

"Really?"

"Really. Here." Handing her the keys. "But you may have to entertain me with more than a movie."

"Deal." Jumping in the car.

Molly and Liam got back into their bubble. During the entire ride back to Molly's, Liam kept trying to get her to scratch his head. Like a two-year-old, the minute she would stop he would whimper, nudge her hand, and lick her until she would start up again. In no time, she was laughing and they were back to them. Everything was always better when they were alone together. If only life could stop interjecting itself.

The sloshing of liquid awoke Molly from her half-dreamy state. Alex stood above her with a bottle of Jack Daniel's, shaking it in front of her face. He smelled oily. A briny mixture of sweat, meat, and salt. Molly sat up, rubbed her eyes, and wrinkled her nose. The clock read 12:13.

"I will never get used to that smell."

"What?" Sniffing himself. "I don't smell anything."

"You reek." Holding her nose. "I hope you shower before you subject your poor wife to your, uh, unique odor."

"She likes it." Walking into the kitchen.

"Yeah, right!" Following after him. "I'm asking tomorrow."

Alex went over to the cabinet and retrieved two shot glass.

"Perfect." Twirling the small cup in his hand. "Orlando circa the early nineties."

"Is that the trip where Mom had Teresa fax us the entire Haggadah because Mom insisted we have Passover?" Taking a seat.

"Yeah, she made some weird charoset from airplane crackers."

"It's not even like we are so religious."

"It's strange, but now that Renee and I are expecting, I feel like being a better Jew." Pulling out a chair and sitting down at the table.

"What does that mean? Are you doing Shabbat?"

"No, but I do think if we have a boy, I want to have a bris."
Pouring the amber liquid.

"That would be cool." Taking her glass. "But I don't think I
can watch a knife travel near any male's nether regions."

"Me neither. I instantly think of the name Bobbitt, but I still
think it would be a good idea."

"Just make sure you get someone with a steady hand. Cheers."

"Cheers." Clinking her glass.

They shot down the booze and Alex quickly filled another
round. That went down like the first and Alex poured another.

"Easy." Molly eyed Alex. "We've got all night."

"What?" Drinking the next shot.

"You just have this uncanny ability to get your sister way too
fucked up."

"I have honed that skill all my life. It is a very important one
to have."

"Like New Year's in Aspen?" Tossing back another shot.

"I can't believe you actually fit in that foldout couch."

"I can't believe I let you fold me into it!"

"It was brilliant!"

Alex got up and poured himself a glass of orange juice to use
as a chaser.

"Want one?"

"No, but some water would be good." Looking at her brother
closely. "Got any weed to go with the whiskey?"

"I thought you gave all that shit up."

"I did, I have. I just . . ." Molly's eyes welled up a bit. "I just
think it would be a good idea."

"Sorry, Renee and I quit for now, getting ready for the baby."

"Okay, probably better that way." Molly poured herself
another round.

"So, are we going to talk about what is going on?" Alex asked
his sister as he placed the water in front of her.

"He OD'd."

"What?" Staring at her.

"Apparently, he snuck out of our party, went over to Zander's to supposedly write down some song, and the great influence that he is, Zander happened to have a pharmacy at arm's reach. Liam has been so good lately, so clean, but when it was sitting in front of him he couldn't resist." Looking at Alex through quickly drunken eyes. "He promised me he would never touch the stuff again after what had happened, and well, he did, did too much, and almost died. Zander called me in a panic from his cell on the way to the hospital. I guess Liam was shaking and sweating. He had a seizure in the emergency room. By the time I showed up, he was stable and I stayed a while watching him. But then the whole thing just got to be way too much and I bailed."

"That's fucking intense, Molly. It's almost surreal. I've never seen anything like that before." Shaking his head. "But what do you mean 'after what had happened'?"

"It's another long story I don't feel like telling, but let's just say he made me a lot of promises that I stupidly believed and then he decided to break them all in one fell swoop."

"What are you going to do?"

"Well, fleeing pretty much was the only thing that came to mind. Fight or flight and I chose flight. It's over." Feeling the liquor loosen her. "I can't do it."

Something broke in Molly and a dam of grief rushed forth.

"I'm so fucking tired of crying!" Molly sobbed. "It's like I'm caught in the midst of every bad Lifetime tearjerker."

"I don't really know what to say to make you feel better."

"I know." Taking a deep breath. "Let's just keep drinking."

Alex leaned over and gave Molly's hand a gentle squeeze. He felt completely helpless. There was nothing for him to do to soothe his sister's tears, to make her feel better even in some small way. When they were little, he prided himself on his grizzly bear power to protect. Anyone other than himself who messed with his sister was toast. There was many a bully who met the end of his fist or wit. When a sister is delicate, artsy, and a late bloomer, the tags children put on her can be cruel. Alex hunted and stalked his prey, eviscerating them within one or two seconds of attack. Molly never really knew why kids started being nice to her, but she certainly didn't care. Anything that hampered their shrill voices taunting Molly with "What note are you singing, Molly, b-flat?" would suffice. Now, in this moment, where all Alex wanted to do was shove his entire hand down Liam's throat, rip out his heart, and serve it up with pan-seared salmon for tomorrow's special, all he could do was pour another round and wait.

five

Helen woke up early the next morning and found her two children crashed out in the living room. An empty bottle of whiskey lay on its side on the glass coffee table. Shoes and socks and sweaters were scattered about the room. Alex lay in a heap on the floor, a blanket covering him so that just the tips of his toes and the top of his head were visible. He looked like tomorrow's laundry load. Molly had one leg thrown over the high end of the couch, the other dangling below. Her hair covered most of her face, and

the pillows a twisted cyclone of brown and red straw. They smelled overly sweet, a too ripe melon left in the fridge a little longer than necessary. Helen leaned down and pulled Molly's blanket over her, tucking her in. Molly barely stirred, her soft snore kept rhythm. She left Alex alone, not wanting to disturb his hibernation. Thank goodness it was Sunday because she really didn't want him wielding anything sharp today. To think these were supposed to be her grown up children.

Helen leaned back against the wall and lowered herself to the floor. She pulled her knees into her chest and smiled. When the kids were little she would do this for hours in their rooms. The patterns of their breath made Helen feel truly a part of something. All that quiet and stillness only interrupted by a small sniffle or snore was meditative. These unique, ridiculous creatures were hers, hers to protect, to guide, to be guided by. Helen remembered that when she was little, she would carefully tuck all her dolls into their respective beds, kiss them on their foreheads, and wait until she was sure they were asleep before she could tear herself from their side. Being a mother was going to be her big purpose, her life's biggest feat. Like Henry ultimately finding his calling in the kitchen, Helen found hers sitting in Molly's or Alex's room watching them sleep. That's why it was so difficult when they both left home. The very things that made Helen most satisfied were gone, and her world was tossed out of balance. Coupled with Henry's insane work schedule, which didn't allow them much time together, Helen lost her focus. Maybe it wasn't very women's lib to be completed by one's children and husband, but it was in these nurturing shoes that Helen felt the most at ease. Everything made sense in those intimate moments she shared with her family. She felt just a little more centered, just a little more whole, when they were around. It was because Molly had come home. All their puzzle pieces were in the same place for the first time in a long time. Helen had missed her daughter.

Helen always knew Molly had to fly. She knew those little five-year-old legs that would never cease moving would one day carry her daughter out and away. That was something Helen had to brace herself for. What does a mother do when her best friend is her daughter? The person who makes you laugh the hardest you ever have, the person who can make you weep in the garage with a simple sneer, the person who looks at the world in ways you could never conceive of. Molly never ceased to amaze her. Alex was always more earthbound, more like Henry. He was logical and focused and metered. She never worried about him, never worried where he would fall. His roots spread long before he could walk. As a baby, Henry and Helen would constantly compare him to a tree trunk. You could put him down and all of a sudden he was connected to some invisible magnet six feet underground. Helen knew he would not stray too far. On the other hand, Molly would never, could never, sit still. A hummingbird with beating wings, a school of fish. She saw colors in the stars and shapes in the clouds. The world was her theater, her stage, and at seventeen, she was gone. Helen could swear she smelled burned rubber when Molly steered her car out of the driveway. Molly couldn't wait to get back to LA, get to art school, get away. Helen knew Molly craved the "new," craved independence and space, but Helen couldn't wait until she came back, and here she was. However, Helen wasn't as overjoyed as she had hoped because for the first time she saw a stillness in Molly. She had stopped beating. Helen caught her breath and a small tear ran down her face. She wiped her eyes and eased herself up from the ground.

At about one o'clock, Molly rubbed her eyes and coughed. Her head seemed like wet felt. She rolled off the couch and slowly crept to the kitchen. Helen was sitting at the table doing the *New York Times* crossword puzzle. Molly walked to the fridge and reached for a Coke. She brushed her hair from her eyes and sat down next to her mom.

"Hi, sleepyhead." Kissing Molly on the cheek. "Want a latté?"

"Yes, but in a minute. I think I need to go die in the shower first." Getting back up.

"Eggs? Toast?"

"Check, check." Walking out of the room.

Molly gingerly climbed the stairs and shoved open the door to her room. Bed, bathroom, bed, bathroom. A small chant. The dilemma of the century. The sudden urge to pee answered, and then Molly turned on the hot water. After a good scrubbing, Molly fell into a clean pair of cords and a red tank top. She combed and braided her long hair, twisting it in a clear rubber band. Clear. Clear could be the color for the day. Clear was clean, pure. Clear was also nothing, a noncolor, a cop-out. She grabbed her favorite velour hoodie and went back downstairs. The smell of coffee and bacon beckoned. In the kitchen, Alex was hunched over a steaming mug, his hair doing the punk rock toddler.

"Did we finish that bottle?" Sitting across from him.

"Yeah," Alex mumbled.

"Did I puke or anything?" Picking up the latté her mother placed before her.

"Nope. But I think I did. I have this vague memory of staring at the blue bathroom tile."

"And you two are supposed to be adults?" Helen asked as she flipped the bacon.

"Adult? I'm far from it." Sipping her coffee. "Let's lay it out. Crisis + the need to flee – any desire to deal with it alone = a trek back to the nest. I'm ten all over again, except now I have a few unwanted wrinkles and a hangover."

"I think I see a gray hair too." Alex stared at her.

"Fuck off, Daddy."

"Oh, shit!" Alex's face paled. "Renee must be freaking out."

"Don't worry, I talked to her earlier. I told her that you, Molly, and Jack had a lovely evening together."

Easy familial chitchat went on for the rest of the meal, after which Molly went back up to her room. She had been gone two days, only two. Somehow it felt longer. That happened when she came home. Time here moved at a different pace. Most days looked the same so they passed more quickly. Molly never really had a schedule at home, every day was like laundry: a big messy pile of events that unfolded and sorted itself out as the day progressed. She and Liam always had something to do, someplace to be, someplace to be seen. With his second album about to drop, there were parties, gigs, different people wanting different things from him, from her. They were the eye of the ever growing maelstrom of publicness. Maybe that's why he slipped? Maybe that's why he fell? Maybe that's why . . . never mind. Coming home was going to be a good thing for Molly. Give her some semblance of normal, routine living. In LA, Molly usually thrived on seat-of-the-pants living, but she always felt a little bit blurry. Liam and she used to joke about how Molly was this mysterious superhero because every photo she was in only had a piece of her or a smudge that vaguely resembled her shadow. A hand or half a cheekbone. Molly was there, but always moving, always thinking ahead to the next thing, the next moment. She forgot how to be still. She felt still now, but still was like feeling a little dead.

For their one-year anniversary, Liam had made Molly a collage of all these photos. He'd spent hours at Kinko's blowing things up, shrinking things down, turning everything inside out in order to perfect his little Picasso-esque masterpiece.

"Here you go, my dear." Handing her a poster tube.

"What is this?" Opening one end.

"A gift."

"For?"

"You."

"Duh . . . what's the occasion?" Sliding the poster from its wrapping.

"One year together," Liam stated.

"Really?"

"You don't remember? You are making me feel like such a girl."

"I do, I just thought it was next week." Leaning and kissing his cheek.

"When are you counting from?" Asking.

"Our first real date." Unscrolling.

"See, that is where you are wrong." Holding one side of the paper.

"Why?" Molly, wondering.

"Because, the count started the minute we met."

"But, Liam, I didn't like you then." Trying to keep a straight face.

"Okay, miss walk-into-walls and make-out-at-the-beach girl."

"I mean, I was still deciding." Molly, laughing. "Wow."

Molly was looking at a picture of her and Liam holding hands, leaning against a wall, and laughing, but it was made up of a million little images of her and him. Small little pictures equaling a bigger whole.

"This is so cool." Looking closer. "I remember that shot from Mexico. You got so sunburned."

"Someone forgot to wake me up."

"Sorry, again." Kissing his nose. "This really is amazing."

"Well, with your photographic problems, I had to get a little creative."

"I love it. You should tell my mom how you did this because she is constantly looking for ways to get me into the family albums. I think she's used to only seeing my elbow or the side of my head. She would absolutely love this."

"I will make her one of you for the holidays."

"She would like that." Kissing him again. "Thank you, but you seriously suck."

"What? Why?" Staring at her.

"You have raised the gift-giving bar far, far over my head. I only have a week to top you."

"But today is our anniversary. You're late."

"I'm telling you, next week is our anniversary."

"Nope. Sorry, sister."

"Can't we have two then?"

"We can have as many as you want, but let's just remember who really remembered."

"Fine, fine. You win." Eyeing him. "I think this will look great in the bedroom."

"I'll get some tape." Jumping up.

They raced, and, in a flurry of arms and legs, they fell into each other and into bed.

Molly sat down on the bed and picked up a framed photo next to her. It was of her family in front of Helen's when it first opened. Renee, Henry, Liam, Helen, Alex, and Molly, with her head turned the wrong way. They had been together for about ten months when that was snapped. He had just gotten back from his first tour, their first major separation, and they were reintroducing themselves to each other. Feeling out if they had become disconnected. They took a road trip, hitting all the canyons and trying to remember how each liked to be touched. He had been gone for most of the summer, and except for a few stolen weekends, it had been a period of phone calls and emails. It had been hard. Probably harder for Molly. She felt nervous with him being gone. It had taken such a short time for them to become so attached that she often felt someone else could easily come along and sneak in just as quickly. Learning to trust in love and intimacy was hard enough for a regular guy and a regular girl, and here Molly was madly in love with a musician. All of those cliché paranoias of groupies and girls waiting around after shows were all of a sudden feeling very real and very possible. But that was her issue though, not his. It was her own fault that she dove headfirst into that obsession, her own inability to be confident that he was still hers, that she still had his heart even though he was far from her.

Maybe part of this out-of-sight-out-of-mind insecurity stemmed from growing up and constantly looking for Henry's acceptance, his attention. Things hadn't always been so jovial and cozy in the Stern house. Not that her father had been unloving or cold, he just hadn't been around. Seeing him now was like getting to know a whole other man. He was lighter, freer, more centered, and more available. The restaurant had changed him, made him more of who he was always maybe supposed to be, and Molly was grateful, but it didn't change the past. When she was younger she tried and tried to catch his eye, with her art or her schoolwork, whatever she could do to shine a light above her head, and she knew her dad had been proud. However, all the missed recitals and shows, the paintings only glanced at and put away, or the short conversations from art school that always ended after a few minutes with a "Need money?" added up and made Molly wary. All of it left this residue of doubt in her that even if she jumped through hoops and did a triple flip in the air, no one would be there watching. Henry would probably be devastated if he knew his daughter's need, and Molly would keep it somewhere inside when around her father, yet it just became compounded with Liam, the other man in her life. After all, everyone is a product of their family and emotional transference has to be a common human flaw.

Molly never really counted on falling for a public guy. A guy with people: band mates and agents and managers and publicists. Every other man she had dated had been an almost-this, almost-that kind of fellow. Struggling artists or filmmakers, writers or actors, like John the aspiring documentarian. She loved the thrill of their creativity, loved that they could understand her passion for art and culture, but she never really had to face what it meant to be with someone talented who was actually getting noticed for

said talent. Being with wannabe this-or-thaters was safer, easier.
When there was just a studio with canvases or a desk filled with
notebooks, their world was smaller, more manageable. It was her
and them and a bucket of dreams. Molly was comfortable with
that world even though sometimes it felt claustrophobic and
depressing. Molly had a string of affairs that came on strong and
dwindled when the dreams began to dry up. Then came Liam.

He was actually living it, the all-encompassing it that children
fantasize about when they are four and banging on kitchen pots
or singing with a hairbrush in the mirror. He had a deal in place,
a first full-length album in the works, and enough buzz to maybe
get him noticed because he had a loyal following of celebrity
friends. Initially, it intimidated Molly. Sure, she still fell fast and
hard, but she herself felt a little unpolished, unrealized when
standing beside him. She had always enjoyed being the one more
centered, more driven. Even though her dreams of painting and
doing some kind of art full-time were far from happening, she
did enough to feel superior to the other guys she had been with.
She organized a small show of her work at a bar in Hollywood
and it sold out, she did a mural at some school—baby steps to a
bigger goal. Liam's success and being with him made Molly see
that she was languishing, unable to truly commit to herself. She
was half-assing her life. When she was first with him, it crystal-
lized how lazy Molly had become—participating just enough to
keep herself afloat but never living as large as she wanted. She was
being a coward, too fearful of failing or falling to really get up
and go for it. The girl whom her parents had watched rush out
into the world, eager to eat it for lunch, had changed. Or, really,
she had gotten good at giving good face, showing everyone just
enough to let them believe in her fearlessness without putting herself out there at all and, thus, no one really noticed how Molly had
shrunk and instead of her still climbing and swinging, she could
barely muster a leg up. She had become stagnant, growing mossy
roots in a moldy pond. Molly knew she was not built to sit still in

pools of water so cloudy and filled with algae that she couldn't see her feet, but until Liam, the water felt nice, the water felt safe. Liam's belief in himself, and subsequently his belief in her, lit a fire under her ass and she began to really live her life. She wanted to be proud of herself, and she wanted him to be proud of her.

Jay came to keep her company that first weekend Liam was away, and when she walked into a whirling tornado of paint, canvas, fabric, and glitter, Jay couldn't help but laugh.

"Holy shit!" she exclaimed. "It looks like Pearl Arts & Crafts blew up in here."

"Really?" Molly absentmindedly looked around.

"And, you, my dear, look like a raving lunatic." Grabbing Molly's shoulders and dragging her into the bathroom.

"Whoa." Molly stared in the mirror above the sink. "How do you think my hair got like that?" Trying to pat down the paint-flecked fro.

"When was the last time you showered?" Taking a step away from Molly.

"What's today?"

"Saturday."

"Uh oh." Hanging her head. "Monday."

"All righty then. You are going to stay in here and I'm going to try to go unearth the couch." Jay turned around.

"I guess I was feeling inspired." Molly laughed.

"Which is fantastic," Jay agreed. "But not at the expense of basic hygiene."

Molly peeled off her clothes and let the water rinse away the paint and sparkles. It had been so long since she had gotten lost in her work and it felt fabulous. She felt clean, alive, and full of promise again. With her finding herself and getting extremely motivated, she felt like she finally had something to truly offer Liam. Something to prove she was worth his careful attention. But, unfortunately, he wasn't around to see it, and these bouts of

creativity were still peppered with off-weeks of self-doubt and
artistic paralysis. Molly would work like a dervish, spinning
around her apartment, high on paint fumes and glue, patching
together canvas after canvas, yet on a dime she could paint over
all the work she had done and stare at the blank slates. Molly,
while she was finally on the right path and digging back into her
art, still couldn't keep focused and figure out how exactly she
wanted to express herself, and with her sounding board so far
away, the cycle remained.

Molly looked at the photo of Liam and her family again. She
remembered feeling like she was split into two people on their
post-tour road trip. One was completely and utterly head over
heels in love with Liam, unquestioning and eager to jump back
and believe in him, in them. She was nauseated all the time with
a zillion butterflies doing the hokeypokey in her stomach. The
other Molly was scared, more scared than she had ever been in
her whole life. She watched his every move, every nuance, to see
if she could discern if he had betrayed her in any way. She
bobbed between wanting to heed his words and wondering if she
could really trust him, trust a musician coming off a road strewn
with more babes than a chain of Hooters. She was becoming
schizo, but she was trying to maintain her façade.

The first three days of the trip had been amazing, full of
sleepless, sexy nights and perfect car chattiness during the day.
They were both nervous but transferring that energy into a balls-
out good time. The wave of giddiness culminated in an evening
of eye-to-eye "I love you" lovemaking. The hotel room was
sparse, basic beige walls with a teal carpet and brown fake wood
furniture. The bedspread was mauve with a spray of flowers and
the neon NO VACANCY light flashed through the partially blinded
window. Molly remembered every detail, how many chips were
on the ceiling, how the headboard was slightly higher on the left
side. Everything was in high-relief, exaggerated. Molly felt like

she was on acid—the room was breathing, and every touch felt like Jacuzzi bubbles times ten. When they woke up, they both were quiet, too quiet. Their eyes barely connected, and as they showered and dressed, they moved in two solo dances around the room. Every time Molly tried to say something her mouth wouldn't work, her tongue, tied, her mind, blank. She was beginning to worry.

As Liam loaded up her Rover, Molly went in the room to grab the last of their things. She accidentally knocked over his guitar case in trying to close it and all these Polaroids spilled onto the floor. She kneeled down and collected them into a pile, smiling to herself at the silly pictures of her boyfriend and his band. Then one caught her eye—she sat down on the bed and looked closer at the image. It was a side view of Liam down a hallway with a girl whose face was obscured by long hair but whose hands were both looped through the belt buckles on his jeans. He was gazing down at her, and they were almost touching, embracing. He was smiling at her. Molly's mouth went dry, and all of a sudden she felt hot. She looked again at the picture and it became animated. She could see them down the hall, walking, coming together, laughing, kissing. This strange girl was getting her grin. Molly barely felt herself get up and place all the photos but this one back in the case. She tucked the incriminating shot into her pocket and it made her ass burn. She walked to the car, silently handed him his guitar, and got into the front seat. She tasted blood from biting her lip so hard to prevent the tears from streaming.

Molly bought a paper from a machine in front of Denny's before they sat down. She wanted something to occupy her at the table. Something other than fiddling with her hair or tugging at the waistband of her cargo pants. Something to keep her mind and eyes busy. Liam grabbed a couple of menus, and they sat down. Both of them quickly buried their heads in the plastic shields.

"What can I get you two?" a large blond woman with an orange apron asked.

"I'll have a spinach egg-white omelet, sourdough toast, and a coffee," Molly quietly answered while handing her the menu.

"I'll have the same, plus a side of bacon, crispy, and an orange juice."

"It'll be right up."

"Thanks," Liam responded.

Molly flipped open the paper, and began to read. Her lips hurt.

"Umm." Liam cleared his throat. "Anything interesting going on?"

"Not sure yet." Not looking up. "Do you want a section?"

"Sure. Business."

"Here." Handing him the paper. His fingers grazed hers and she felt a shock.

They both buried their heads for a spell and read. Coffees arrived and without thinking, Liam fixed hers for her.

"Thanks." Taking a sip.

"No problem."

Again, they both returned to their distractions. A few more minutes passed.

"Did I do something wrong?" Liam asked her.

"What do you mean?" Not catching his eye.

"Molly, put down the paper and look at me."

Molly folded in more ways than one, and she started crying.

"Molly, what's going on?" Looking at her.

"Nothing." Wiping her eyes with a napkin.

"Right, and you're just spontaneously crying. Are you getting your period?"

"Yeah, sure, something like that." Still not really looking at him.

"Please, just tell me what's up."

"I can't believe you."

"What? Did I do something?"

"Can't you just be honest with me?"

"Look, I really don't have a clue what this is about. I thought that after last night everything was fine, well, more than fine, actually. What could I have done in the short time since we woke up?"

"It wasn't what you did this morning, it's what you did before. I saw the picture."

"The picture?"

"The picture of you two. I know what happened." Taking a sip of water, hoping it would help her gain composure.

"Of me and who? Tom? Elliot?"

"Stop pretending. She was all over you and you could not stop grinning. You looked as if you were about to swallow her." Pulling the photo from her pocket and tossing it at him. "I knew I couldn't trust you."

"Whoa." Grabbing the photo. "Where did you find this?"

"Some compartment inside your guitar case. It fell out when I went to shut it properly." Tucking her hair out of her eye. "And the fact that now you are asking questions about it confirms you didn't want me to see it!"

"No, I'm asking because I was going to show you all these pictures when I first got home but I forgot where I stashed them."

"Yeah, right. Show me your little indiscretions, so I can't get mad because you are being honest. Was that the tactic you were going to take?" Raising her voice.

"Calm down, you're being totally irrational."

"Whatever, I should have trusted my gut. He's a musician, he's on the road, he's lonely, well, looks like not that night." Getting riled up even more.

"If you would just chill out for one minute and stop referring to me in third-person, you are going to feel very stupid for being so mad at me."

"So, now I'm stupid!? Screw you." Starting to get up from the table.

"Molly." Grabbing her arm and pulling her back down. "That picture is of Anita and me."

"What?" Pulling her hand away and onto her lap. "Anita who?"

"My sister-in-law Anita. She and Teddy came to one of the shows."

"Anita?"

"Yeah. I swear. You can call her to confirm if you don't believe me. Check out the ring and the star tattoo on her wrist."

Molly looked again at the image, and sure enough, it did look kind of like her. There was also no mistaking the vintage wedding ring Molly loved or the ink art. Molly turned bright red and put her hands to her face.

"I'm such an asshole." Crying again. "I'm sorry. I just, fuck."

"Molly, how could you even think I was with someone else?"

"I don't know. I sort of snapped when I saw it." Trying to find the right words. "Especially after how intimate last night was. All of a sudden here was this picture of a girl and you, and all these questions and doubts and . . ."

"Doubts? Questions? About what?"

"About this and you and everything."

They were momentarily interrupted by their breakfast.

"Thanks," Molly meekly said as the waitress set her plate down.

"No problem. Need anything else?"

"No, we are good. Thanks." Liam answered, putting a napkin on his lap. "Molly, you need to figure out a way not to worry about all that shit. I'm going to be gone a lot, it's part of the gig, and if every time I leave, you freak out that I am with someone else, we are not going to make it. This is going to get tired fast."

"I know that, I do. I want to trust you and believe in us, but sometimes I think that I am not enough for you. That you are going to leave and meet some sparkly girl with perfect tits and tattoos who steals your heart."

Liam got quiet and stared at Molly. He cleared his throat.

"After nearly a year together, practically living together, how can you even think that?" Getting a little annoyed. "Sometimes I feel like no matter how often I tell you I love you, it's not enough. It's like you don't even listen. Do you think I just toss those words around to be polite?"

"No, I know you love me." Quietly. "I really do. I just have this nagging feeling like this is all some big practical joke, and pretty soon someone is going to pinch me and I am going to wake up somewhere married to some boring accountant with garlic breath!"

"Why do you have such little confidence in this? In us?" Shaking his head. "It really bums me out that you don't see how special you are. Did I do that? Was it something I did that made you feel like this relationship is so unreal?"

"No. I don't really understand it either. I used to be this supremely confident girl and I know how annoying I must be." Taking a sip of coffee. "I hate insecure people, I hate feeling meek and fragile. It's such an easy copout from living your life."

"It's not annoying." Looking at her. "Well, actually, it is just because it has no merit and it's really hard being around it. I feel like all of a sudden I am on eggshells."

"I'm sorry. Lately I just have been feeling, I don't know, blah, I guess. I've been trying to motivate, to do good work, but nothing seems to jump out. After a week of mad creativity, I putter out and everything looks derivative." Pushing her omelet around. "And you not being around has been harder than I thought it would be. Everything was different, dull."

"It was for me too, but babe, that isn't going to go away. The separations are going to happen. But when we aren't together it doesn't mean that I am thinking about you less, or loving you less. Just like I know that your dad thought about you all the time when maybe he wasn't there. You are everywhere to me, in everything."

"I know."

"Maybe all this insecurity is because things are starting to come together for you."

"What do you mean?"

"Well, I know that after I got my deal, for a while I was elated. Living large and feeling like I was fucking Leonardo cruising in the front of the *Titanic*. And then, when things were starting to really get going, I sort of lost it. It's like you spend so long wishing and hoping that it fills you with this incredible amount of emotions, and once you succeed, all that longing disappears and you feel kind of empty. And then, just when you feel the most unstable, your stuff hits the marketplace and you are totally naked and vulnerable."

"I guess that makes sense."

"Molly, you're an amazing lady who's doing amazing things that people are going to love. I think your work has more direction and originality in it than you think, at least what you have shown me. Maybe you just haven't found your medium, but you definitely will and you will start feeling all of that goodness soon."

"Thanks. I'm sorry I'm such a drama queen." Reaching for his hand. "I promise that I will try to snap out of this."

"Good." Squeezing three times.

"I can't believe I thought you got it on with Anita! I just for the last few months had nightmares about girls in tight shirts slithering about your hotel room."

"Well, there was that one . . ." Winking at her.

"Really?"

"You're just going to have to trust me." Laughing.

"Was she really hot at least?" Eating the rest of her now cold omelet.

"I think she may have been a bunny of some kind." Eating his bacon. "Her chest was like . . ." Holding his hands way in front of his chest.

"Okay, okay, enough." Molly laughed.

"Look, I love you pretty much more than anything ever, I am committed to you, and that is a promise I take seriously. I will keep my promises."

"I just think I love you too much sometimes, and that scares me."

"And I don't think there is ever too much of anything." Pulling her toward him. "I am not going to let you down."

He kissed her, and it was earnest and true like a school morality lesson. She swallowed and believed.

Molly placed the photo of her family and Liam on the bed. She leaned back against her pillows and took a deep breath. She gave herself to the relationship on that trip, and she let go of her insecurities the best she could. Yes, they had already been together for a while at that point, but every relationship has moments where things morph and are altered into something new. There are milestones at every turn. The month, the three month, the meet the parents, the first holiday together, the first trip, etc., etc. The list goes on and on. Some days you wake up, look at the person next to you, and think, "If I hear him snore one more time, I will become Lizzie Borden." Sometimes you watch him scratch his nose and think, "I will kiss every freckle tonight three times." On that trip, Molly chose to believe and trust in Liam, and really to trust and believe that she was good enough, good enough for him, good enough for herself. She knew if she walked around wrapped in a shawl of doubt, she would succeed in pushing him away. Something of a self-fulfilling prophecy. She decided to let herself really go and allow this man to catch her. Where were his arms now? She had jumped, headfirst, and he had picked at the loose thread and unraveled the refashioned safety net beneath her.

"Molly!" a voice bellowed from below.

Molly got up and walked to the door.

"Yeah?"

"Renee is on the phone for you," Helen called.

"Thanks."

Molly went back into her room and picked up the phone.

"Hey, Renee."

"How are you feeling?"

"Okay, still have a headache though. Remind me not to get into a shot contest with your husband."

"He's asleep on the couch right now, snoring."

"I think I can hear him through the line." Snickering.

"In the mood for a movie?"

"That sounds great."

"I'll pick you up in an hour."

"Great."

Molly hung up the phone and threw herself back on the bed. Unfortunately, she knocked the frame onto the floor and the glass shattered.

"Shit." Getting up.

Molly leaned down and gingerly picked up the glass shards. She tossed the broken pieces of the frame in the garbage can under her desk. The picture she folded and slipped under her pillow.

At the beginning of the next week, a package arrived for Molly from LA. It was sitting on the kitchen table when she returned from a morning yoga class. She recognized the loopy scrawl and picked the box up on the way to her room for a shower. Jay had drawn silly little butterflies and flowers all over the brown cardboard. Bursting petals and flush wings ringed the box in the vivid purple of a summer day. Purple. It meant passion. Sex toys, Harlequin novels, and eggplant. All very ripe and fertile cre-

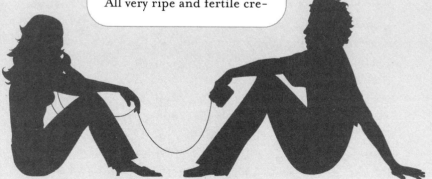

ations. Then again, purple also was the color of fresh bruises. Dark, deep, ringed with pain. Today, everything about Molly felt swollen. Her skin had a slight itch and swell, tender yet alive with feeling.

She placed the box on her bed and went to her desk to find a pair of scissors. She carefully slit the sides and opened it. Inside were her tools and boxes of beads as well as a velvet case of finished pieces. There was a large manila envelope sitting underneath everything. Molly unfolded the letter.

Mol—

Hope I didn't forget anything. If I did, just give a ring and will get whatever. Well, give a ring anyway, just to check in. Hope you are doing better. When are you coming home? I'm here if you need me and I'm really sorry you have to deal with all this. I love you.

—Jay

P.S. On a totally separate note, I saw this great little retail space on Third that the present renters are leaving at the end of next month. It may be perfect. Should I check it out?

Molly had forgotten all about her new big plan. She was so wrapped up in all the chaos that her sights had somewhat clouded over. She folded the letter and placed it on her bed. Then she opened the velvet box. There were five necklaces and three pairs of earrings. Some silver, some gold, with precious and semiprecious stones. The jewelry findings all were delicately carved with various floral motifs, and each piece looked like it had been born in a French garden circa 1600. Molly had designed and cast everything herself, and she also had dulled various parts of the metal to make it look antique. Molly wanted her pieces to be like small treasures from a different time. With bits of lace, ribbon, buttons, or other small charms, she fashioned one-of-a-kind objects of art. Each piece had something truly old incorporated in it, maybe a locket or a dollhouse-sized spoon. Some gems were mismatched, some edges were frayed instead of tightly faceted. Everything looked new but had the weight of history tied up in its cords.

The idea for the collection—or really the theme for all her work—came to her at the end of last summer when Liam and she had gotten back from their post-tour road trip and decided to move in together. The moving in thing had been Liam's idea and Molly hadn't remotely seen it coming. Even after Molly's minor flip-out at the diner—the rest of their time together had been amazing—she wasn't thinking about taking such a new leap. For her, spending all those weeks of concentrated time nurturing their relationship, indulging each other, and reconnecting was enough.

They pulled into Molly's apartment complex driveway and Molly hopped out of the car to begin unloading her stuff.

"Babe, this may take a while." Eyeing the trunk. "Everything has exploded and intermingled." She tried to see where to begin.

"Let's just leave it like that." Liam joined her by the trunk.

"What do you mean?" Trying to pull out her black Kate Spade travel bag. "We can't just leave all this stuff in the car."

"No, I mean, let's just leave it intermingled. Let's leave it all together."

"Are you planning on living out of my trunk?" She laughed at him.

"No, but we should plan on living out of our place."

Molly stopped pulling at bags and looked at her boyfriend. She stared at him carefully to see if she could figure out what the heck he was implying.

"Our place?" she repeated.

"Yes. I think we should find a place together. No more separate apartments, no more 'Your bed, my bed, where should we sleep tonight?' conversations."

"You want us to move in together? Really?"

"Really. I love you and the fact that we didn't take steak knives to each other or leave each other in the middle of the highway after spending so much time together in a confined space proves we are ready for this."

"Okay." Surprising herself with the lack of hesitation.

"Okay? That easy?"

"Yup. I think so." Kissing him.

"Thought I would have to do a little more dancing to convince you."

"Maybe if you had asked tomorrow or yesterday I would have hedged, but fuck it." Shrugging her shoulders. "Can't always be so cautious, sometimes maybe it's about jumping in."

"That's my girl!" Kissing her again. "Molly, this is going to be great."

"It will." Hugging him. "But only if we keep my bed, yours is really uncomfortable."

"It is not!"

"Baby, when did you buy that bed?"

"When I moved here, it's practically new."

"Almost ten years new! My bed or the highway." Laughing at him.

"Fine. You drive a hard bargain, missy." Kissing her back.

They stood by the open trunk making out like hormonal teenagers for what seemed like forever. It wasn't until a neighbor honked that they separated.

"We still have to unload the car." Molly giggled.

"Let's just do it later. I have a better idea of how we can spend our time." Hopping back into the car and pulling it into Molly's spot.

A few days later, they found their three-bedroom, two-bath apartment on Sycamore. When Molly unpacked all her boxes, some of which had not been opened in years, she found an old music box of hers from when she was five. Inside were old velvet ribbons, a tiny ballerina charm made out of copper, a pendant of ballet shoes, a picture of her and Helen, a dried rose from her first recital, and five loose ruby-red shiny crystal beads. It was an artifact from a special, more innocent time. Molly wanted some of that innocence with her and decided to try and incorporate the contents into a necklace. She knit the ribbons together to make them stronger, slipped on the pendant and charm, glued the rose petals onto the photo that she had mounted on a piece of leather, and tied the beads all about. Although it was crude, every time she felt the weight of the totem on the pool of her throat she felt more connected to the girl she had been and the woman she was becoming. It was a moment of clarity, for she could finally articulate what she wanted her art to say. This was the feeling she wanted to capture. Something beautiful and new but completely tinged with the memories and comfort of the past. She wanted to infuse her work with the joy and determination a little girl has when she takes the time to create a little memory box, fill it with hair from her first short haircut, a card from the tooth fairy, or maybe even a jack she got with her dad from that penny candy reward game in a Reno diner. Her work was driven by the need to not forget the past but to bring it forward and make it part of the present and future. She had never before considered that her means toward personal expression would take root in making jewelry, but somehow it just made sense. It was small, easy, related to fashion, and had a short distance between conception and completion.

The first few necklaces she made weren't perfect. She collected odds and ends from friends and worked hard to figure out how to unite the disparate materials. The more she made, the more refined and precious the finished products became. She took basic jewelry casting at a UCLA extension class, and, coupled with her art school background, was soon creating her own charms and findings to mix in with what she found. Jay utilized her first-year business school knowledge to help her incorporate, name, and brand her business. Molly chose Annabelle as the name for her line. It was old-fashioned, feminine, catchy, and happened to be her middle name. Henry helped her legalize everything and she was on her way. Everyone, even Liam, offered their expertise to get her up and running. He had helped her make her first "stranger" sale. He had been conveniently working on a few new demos with a producer who also happened to be working with a young songstress on her second album. Liam flirted and wooed, did a number on her, and soon Molly's creations were gracing the songbird's neck on the cover of *Rolling Stone*. He used all his connections to maintain Molly's momentum. He also helped organize her first big sale/show in the garden of his friend Elliot's restaurant. Molly remembered that afternoon well. Again, another series of swooping highs and mind-numbing lows.

Molly worked for a solid month beforehand getting things ready. She wanted everything to be perfect since this would be her first chance to get the kind of major exposure that could fully launch her career as a jewelry designer. Every piece slaved over, every display agonized over. Liam and she ran around town collecting stools, tables, fabric, mannequins, and various sizes of trunks to create the space. Molly wanted people to imagine that they were walking into a large-scale music box. They had an old tailor's mannequin dressed up in a pink tutu and pink toe shoes that they rigged to spin like a dancer, and mirrors everywhere to reflect the gems of her pieces like prisms. With the roses in bloom and champagne for everyone, it was going to be a fabulous event. Sure, it cost Molly an arm and leg to buy all this stuff, but it would hopefully pay off tenfold.

The afternoon started off exactly as planned. Molly and Liam's friends fluttered around oooing and ahhhing over Molly's work. The turnout was huge, with many little starlets whipping out their checkbooks and fastening the goods onto their bodies immediately after purchase. Liam had his publicist do a little magic, and a photographer showed, as well as a reporter from a small but well-known alternative fashion magazine. Pictures were snapped, information exchanged, and Molly was on cloud nine. In a lull, Liam came over to her and handed her a glass of champagne.

"A toast to my beautiful, talented girlfriend."

"Thanks." Taking a sip and kissing him. "Thank you for everything."

"My pleasure. I really am proud of you. I told you everything you've been working on in the last few months would come together. It was just about finding your niche. And if an up-and-coming rock star can't use all his connections, and all the people he pays to further his career, to facilitate his love's coming-out party, then who can?"

"Rock star, huh?"

"Well, the emphasis is on the up-and-coming." Kissing her cheek.

They laughed and flowed back into the party. Molly made a few more sales and her face became stuck in perma-grin. Nothing could topple this moment.

Then, just within earshot, Molly could hear a loud voice. One that rang high above the din. It was drunk and belligerent and kept rising as seconds passed. Molly turned her head to see Elena and Zander holding court at a small table. Two empty bottles and a third half full sat in the middle and all the flowers that had been the centerpiece were shorn of their petals and lying like corpses on the brocade cloth. Three others surrounded them, all with various subculture accoutrements of style. They were a scary group of those hipper-than-thou cool kids that immediately intimidated Molly even though she had dealt with them daily at art school. She gulped and edged closer to hear what they were saying. Zander's voice bellowed above all.

"It's all crap. This whole thing!"

"She would be nowhere without him." Elena spit. "What does

he see in her? All her little old-fashioned quaint ideas. It's like she is Little House on the fucking Prairie."

"She must be fucking great in bed," Zander stated, pouring some more drinks. "That has to be it because all this is just too precious."

"Like that's what I wanted to hear, Zander." Elena, giving him the evil eye. "But it must be true for miss plain-Jane to keep him interested."

Molly's face went crimson and hot tears formed. Elena always knew just what to say. Liam caught her eye from across the room and gave her a big smile. She weakly grinned and turned her head, bringing her hands to her face. His look changed and he weaved through the crowd to her.

"Baby, what's wrong?"

"Nothing." Wiping her face. "I'm fine."

"No, you're not."

Just then, Liam heard those same voices. Heard the things they were saying. He paled.

"Oh, come on. I'll be right back." Walking over to his friends.

Molly hurried after him.

"Liam, don't."

It was too late. Liam had rammed headfirst into the pack with a look of anger flashing in his eyes.

"Please leave," Liam stated simply enough.

"What?" Zander asked.

"Leave, all of you. Ta ta, good-bye." Grabbing their glasses off the table and tossing them into the trash nearby.

"Did I just hear you ask us to leave?" Elena questioned.

"Yup." Waiting.

"You have got to be kidding!" Elena blasted.

"Nope, I'm not."

"And that's it?" Elena, asking.

"Exactly."

"Give me a fucking break!" Exclaiming. "Zander, I think our friend has lost his mind."

"I agree." Standing up. "Is this over her?" Getting angry.

"Zander, dude, just get out of here." Losing patience.

"It is about her." Starting to yell. "Everything's about her."

Zander grabbed his jacket off the chair and spun around quickly. His coat caught the edge of one of the tables and before Liam could stop the chaos, half of Molly's display came crashing to the floor. Mirrors shattered, the mannequin fell off her stand, drinks spilled, and everything fell to pieces. Zander tried to grab what he could, but instead was left standing in the middle of the disaster.

"Dude, I'm so sor . . ." Stuttering. "I didn't . . ."

"Don't bother." Interrupting.

"I didn't mean."

"Look, just go."

Molly came running over and bent down over the mess. There was no holding back the tears now. She reached to collect her jewelry and her hand came in contact with a shard of glass. Molly felt a sharp pain and then a heated trickle. She looked and her hand was covered in blood. Liam grabbed her and ripped a tablecloth off to wrap around her hand.

"Jay! Jay!" Yelling.

Jay pushed through the crowd that had now gathered around watching the drama unfold. Elliot also came to Liam's side.

"Molly, are you okay?"

"I think so." Weakly. "I don't think it is that bad, really."

"Liam, what can I do?" Elliot, asking.

"Why don't you get some guys to clean this up? And maybe start clearing people out of here."

"No problem." Rushing. "Okay, everyone. Just a little mess but everything will be fine. Why don't you all take your champagne and head into the restaurant? The festivities will continue in there."

As Elliot corralled the crowd, Molly unwrapped the cloth around her hand and looked. She felt her knees buckle and Liam caught her.

"I lied." She smiled.

"Okay. I think we need to go to the hospital."

"I think so too."

"Jay, will you deal with all this? Pack up everything? Whatever?"

"Of course. Just go and call me when you get there."

Molly and Liam proceeded to spend the next five hours in the hospital. Twelve stitches later, they got home. Molly felt like a wet rag. Wrung out, limp, and smelling like antiseptic. Jay was sitting with Zander and Elena in the living room of their apartment.

"Look, I already feel like shit. I really don't need anymore." Molly eyed the evil ones. "Could you just leave?"

"Molly, I'm so sorry. It was an accident." Zander, hanging his head. "I'm really sorry. I was drunk."

"Fine." Unenthusiastically. "Liam, could you get me some water and give me one of those pills they gave me."

"Yeah." Settling her onto her couch.

"Everything is fine, all the jewelry is still perfect. I put it all away the best I could and the cash box is next to your bed." Jay, sitting next to Molly. "They helped clean up and sort of followed me back here."

"Whatever." Trying to get out of her jacket. "Help."

Jay got Molly out of her jacket and a large bloodstain ran the length of Molly's pink silk shirt and vintage lace skirt.

"Why don't we go get you changed?" Eyeing the blood.

"Okay." Getting up again with the hand of her friend.

"Molly, can I do anything?" Elena asked.

"I asked you to leave, that would be nice." Walking to her bedroom. "I heard all the things you were saying about me."

"I know. I didn't mean them. I was wasted."

"Yeah, you did, and that's fine. I don't like you much either." Shutting the door behind her.

Molly, with Jay's help, stripped off the stained clothes and fell into a nightgown. Her hand ached, as did her whole body.

"Do we know how to throw a party or what?" Molly attempted a smile.

"A total showstopper." Sitting next to her. "One that will not be forgotten in a while."

"How bad was it?"

"Pretty bad, but . . ." Leaning over and grabbing the cash box. "You made bucks, baby!"

"I did?"

"I think you had only eight pieces left, and they are doing one of those who's who party pieces in the magazine."

"Oh great, before or after the big finale?"

"Does it matter? I think it made it more of a scene. Kind of performance art. I also wooed the photographer a little to make sure that there were no pictures of you know who used. No sense in them getting the press."

"Thanks. He was kind of cute. Dug the shaved head and retro glasses."

"I know, me too. We have a date Wednesday."

"Go you. Even if that were the only good news you had for me, I would say it was a success!"

There was a knock on the door and Liam opened it slowly.

"Hi. Here's your water and medicine."

"Thanks."

"I'm going to take off." Jay, getting up. "Call me if you need me. I'll be around in the morning to help reorganize."

"Thanks for everything."

Jay slipped out of the room and Molly could hear the door lock behind her.

"They left." Lying down next to her. "They both are really sorry and sheepish."

"I don't really want to talk about them anymore. Actually, I kind of don't really want to talk about them ever again."

"I'm sorry."

"It's not your fault your friends are assholes and hate me." Curling into him the best she could.

"They don't. They're just jealous."

"It doesn't matter."

"It does to me."

"Maybe it's time you made a choice."

"I think I already made it." Curling around her and holding her tight.

Molly traced her finger along the scar on her hand. Another wrong choice Liam made the other night. The decision to spend time with old friends, old friends who brought out the worst in him. Were all the things he said to her made of cotton candy? Yummy, fluffy, and devoid of any nutritional value? Nothing seemed to stick with him—why should she? Molly set everything on her desk and stripped off her cotton black pants, red tank top, and black jog bra. She jumped into a hot shower, dried, dressed, and headed to the kitchen to grab a coffee before she took off for the restaurant. She picked up the phone, checked messages, made some calls, and finally, dialed Jay's cell.

"Hey, it's me."

"Molly, I was just thinking about you. I'm on my way to get waxed."

"Okay, that's a little weird." Starting to laugh as she poured herself a mug. "You're thinking about me as you head to the waxer. Yuck."

"That didn't come out right." Laughing with Molly. "I just ran into Stolen Memories and picked you up some great old lacy ribbon. Annie had it held behind the counter because she knew you would love it. I'm putting it in the mail later."

"Thanks. Sounds great. I got the box by the way."

"And?" Jay asked over the cell static.

"And what?"

"Should I go find out details? Take pictures? Do whatever?"

Having gained some confidence in her business, Molly had recently been entertaining the idea of opening up a work space/shop to make and sell her wares. Jay, having just graduated from UCLA business school, was keen on stepping in and capitalizing on Molly's talent. She already had taken over all of Molly's sales, orders, et cetera, acting as Molly's representative. Jay was eager to turn this mom-and-, well, mom operation into a bigger business. If Molly was unwilling to totally commit before Liam's meltdown, now she was unable to even toy with the notion. Jay's plan for her to be the next Me & Ro was going to have to wait. Molly couldn't handle anymore big changes. She was full.

"I don't know, Jay. I can't really get my head around that now."

"Things still hard?"

"Yeah, getting better though. I only cry once a day instead of breaking down every five minutes. It's been good being with my family. Also, I'm sorry for being so bitchy to you when I left. I know you were just trying to help."

"No need. I'm glad you're feeling a bit better. I . . . never mind." Breaking herself off.

"What?"

"Nothing."

"Jay."

"I talked to Teddy yesterday. I called Elizabeth, and Teddy was there too."

Molly took a deep breath and sat down. She pulled her jean-clad legs close to her and tucked them under her chin.

"He said Liam was out of the hospital and in a treatment center a few hours out of town. I think it's a monthlong program and then follow-up with a group here."

"How's he doing?"

"I think okay, but Teddy didn't have details. I guess in the first week of the stay there is no contact with the outside."

"That makes sense."

"This is good, right?"

"Sure."

"So maybe . . ." Jay pushed.

"Jay, maybe what?" Setting her feet back down on the ground.

"Maybe this changes things." Trying to be helpful.

"It hopefully will change him, but I don't know if it changes us." Taking another deep breath. "I don't really want to talk about this anymore."

"Okay. Listen, I just pulled up. Think about the shop, okay?"

"Jay." Getting a little frustrated.

"I know, I know. I love you, Molly." Starting to hang up.

"Wait." Catching her friend.

"What?"

"I bought you a massage at Burke Williams for all your help this week. It's all in the computer there, so you can just call whenever."

"Molly, that's very sweet, but totally unnecessary."

"You've had to clean up a few messes lately. It's the least I can do."

"Well, thank you. I'm not one to refuse a free rubdown."

"Enjoy. Talk to you soon." Hanging up the phone.

Molly downed the last of her coffee and stood up. She set the mug by the sink and looked into the backyard. She felt a twinge. Jay bringing up Liam was hard. Molly should be there for him. She shouldn't have left. How could she have left him like this? She pictured him in a room by himself, lying in a tiny dorm-sized bed, staring at the ceiling and counting cracks. She pictured him crying and alone and suffering. She saw the curve of his back and his eyes ringed in red. She imagined him aching. Molly felt a swirl in her stomach and her coffee returned all over the sink. Molly wretched again. Her face went hot. And she stood there hunched over for what seemed like an eternity. The nausea slowly ebbed and she splashed water on her face. She also rinsed her mouth out. After drinking a cup of water, Molly swallowed hard. She wiped off her face and steadied herself. Molly walked slowly over to her mother's desk that sat in the corner of the kitchen. She took a deep breath, sat down, opened the first drawer, and pulled out the Yellow Pages. She flipped it open, found Susan's number at the store, and dialed.

"Hi, is Susan there? It's Molly Stern."

"Hi Molly, it's me. How are you? Your mom said you were in town."

"Pretty good. It's been nice being home." Passing pleasantries. "How is everything going this summer?"

"Great, actually. I already sold all but two necklaces from the order."

"You're kidding?" Molly asked, surprised. "I just sent those to you, like, three weeks ago."

"I know. I made a little display with old dollhouse furniture and music boxes for them. I think people really respond to their sense of nostalgia. Women will pay anything to grab a piece of their past."

"I love that." Smiling over the phone.

"Did you bring anymore with you?"

"I have a handful, and I just got my tools and supplies to make some more."

"Why don't you bring in what you have so I can see?"

"Sure, and if there are certain stones or colors you think people are gravitating to, I can make the new ones in that direction."

"Sounds terrific."

"I'll be by in about fifteen minutes."

"See you soon. I also just got in these amazing reworked antique lace blouses. I think you will love them."

"Great, 'bye, Susan."

Molly bounded upstairs with a grin on her face. She forgot all about her puking attack and conversation with Jaycee. Her mind was trained on the elation of selling. Most of the time, when stores bought Molly's wares, she felt this enormous sense of guilt. In the pit of her stomach, she had this gnawing doubt. People were investing in her to make their own business profitable. That made Molly nervous. When she would see certain pieces languish like droopy, stale dime-store candy in glass display cases, she would feel terrible that people had paid her and had yet to be paid themselves for their risk. Molly hated risks, hated being the blue-chip stock others wagered on. She knew she needed more confidence in her worth, she knew she had to try to believe. She would try harder.

Molly pulled alongside of Sorella and hopped out. In one of the windows, her necklace was on display. It was a piece with turquoise, a tiny set of silverware, and pale pink ribbons. She had found the charm at the Rose Bowl with Liam a few months ago. They had been looking for a new small couch for the living room. The red couch that now had Noah's Ark burns on the cushion.

"Hi, Susan." Molly pushed open the door.

"Molly." Susan answered as she pulled Molly into a hug. "You look a little tired."

"I know, it's been a long week."

"Everything okay?"

"Fine, thanks." Giving her best smile.

Susan was a small woman around forty with a slight frame and a short auburn pixie haircut. She had on a black off-the-shoulder tunic with a slanted hemline, a pair of worn-in jeans cuffed past the ankles, little white lace socks, red high heels, and a big leather belt slung over her hips. Her fantastic sense of style permeated the store, which was filled with every designer you already knew and others you knew would be in upcoming issues of *Vogue*. If Sorella was in LA, it would be making Fred Segal–type bucks, serving every fashionable lady. But, here in Idaho, only the lucky ones got to check out her stash. Susan loved Idaho, and had the store simply because she loved fashion. Molly admired her and tried to do most of her shopping at the store.

"So, where are those tops you mentioned?"

"I pulled them for you. They are in the dressing room. There are no sizes because they are one-of-a-kind and recycled. I just put them all in there so you can pick."

"Great. Here is what I have now. You can look while I try." Handing her the velvet case.

Molly headed into the curtained closet and looked at the shirts. They were right on: Victorian, lace, asymmetrical. Molly's staple look lately had been jeans on bottom, cool blouse on top—and these were perfect. Like with her jewelry, Molly mixed the old with the new. Most of the time, she knew she looked like a cartoon: lots of color, texture, and eras, but somehow it all worked together and Molly had no intention of changing. She plowed through the shirts and found three. One was black with a deep V-neck and lace inserts along the sides, one was patterned with pink flowers and off-the-shoulder with a ruffle, and the other was white with a lace turtleneck and cap sleeves.

"Molly, these are great," Susan stated as Molly went to the counter.

"So are these." Handing her the shirts. "I'll take them."

"And I will take all of these necklaces. I can't do the earrings." Handing back the velvet pouch. "I have no way of displaying them properly."

"No problem." Putting it in her hobo brown suede bag.

"Should we trade?" Susan asked.

"Let's do it separately. Different money."

Molly paid, then wrote Susan up a receipt. She handed her a copy and placed the check in her purse.

"Can you make me something in coral and maybe let's do a really delicate one in ruby?"

"Sure."

"Everyone is gravitating to the reds this summer."

"I'll bring them by next week." Taking her package. "Thanks again, Susan."

"No problem." Coming around and giving Molly another hug. "I'll see you later."

Molly threw her package in the car and decided to leave it parked. The restaurant was only a few blocks away. The walk would do Molly good. She still felt a slight tingle in her skin and her stomach felt a little queasy. Maybe she was catching a bug. She took the blocks double-time hoping some exercise would flush it out and burst into the restaurant with a slight sweat on her brow. Her mom was hunched over a table with her laptop in front of her.

"Hi, Mom." Giving her a kiss on the cheek. "What are you doing?"

"Doing the menu for the private party we're throwing at the end of next week. Dad made a few new dishes he wanted to add, and he found this poem you wrote a few years ago that he wanted to put on the cover."

"What poem?" Leaning over her mother.

"I'll recite it for you." Clearing her throat. "Here goes."

THE SADISTIC CHEF

Spitting in the soup gets me excited
I always sneak small trails of drool into my pot
Avoiding, of course, big, phlegmy, mucousy, loogeys
Those can't be whisked away so easily and hidden
**   in the broth.**

When I'm bored I'll quietly pick and gnaw on my cuticles
Flick the torn pieces of skin into the salad
Toss it with tomatoes, lettuce, croutons
And a tangy balsamic vinaigrette.

The other day I scratched my head over some mushroom
**   risotto**
Just before it sailed out the doors balanced atop a
**   humble hand**

My dandruff danced with Lady Parmesan
Graceful snowflakes waltzing upon their last stage as
    they melt
into their curtain call.

You never know where I am,
Cleverly disguised in your made to order meal,
I am never caught in the act of desecrating your dinner.
I mark the perimeter like a dog.

"You're joking, right?"

"Nope. Dad thinks it's funny and different. The hosts are really expecting a unique evening and I think this is a perfect intro." Not looking up from her work.

"Whatever you say, but in my humble opinion, a restaurant promoting a sadistic chef is a little off."

"And your point is?" Helen turned her head and winked at her daughter.

"Nothing, nothing at all." Heading back into the kitchen.

Molly smiled as she walked. She liked that her father found that old poem she had written for him when he opened the restaurant. She liked that he had saved it, read it, and used it. It was a sign that he had noticed and maybe had all along, but now it seemed more tangible and Molly enjoyed the touch.

Early seventies rock played softly on the old radio, and everyone seemed settled in the retro, hippie melody. Her dad was by the stove with Alex, pondering a big black pot.

"What's it missing?" Henry asked, turning to his son.

"I'm not sure." Taking a sip. "It needs a kick of some sort. The sweet potatoes are a little too sugary. People won't get through the whole bowl."

"I know." Taking another sip.

"Let me try." Molly walked between them and dunked a spoon into the soup. "Did you do the base with pancetta?"

"Nope, I want it to be vegetarian."

"Well, what if you threw in some roasted garlic and sprinkled the top with some salty spicy nuts—like a pecan." Taking another taste. "That might balance it out."

"Leave it to the prodigal daughter to fix things." Kissing his daughter on the forehead. "Does Liam appreciate the talented chef he has?"

Molly's face fell and Alex threw Henry a "What the fuck are you talking about, Dad?" look. She carefully set the spoon down and backed away from the stove.

"Oh, Molly." Henry, realizing what he had said. "I'm so sorry. It just slipped out. I wasn't thinking." Going over to her.

"I know, Dad. It's okay. I'm fine. Better. Never mind. Is Renee around? I thought I might help her a bit."

"Yeah, she's back there and I know she would love the extra hand. Ashley has the flu," Alex answered.

"Well, then I do have perfect timing." Walking toward the back. "And Dad, Liam actually did most of the cooking. I guess I just feel comfortable with men who like to feed me."

In the back kitchen Renee was hoisted up on a stool, lining little tart pans with dough. Her back was to Molly and her once slight frame returned for a moment. Her blond ponytail curled down her narrow shoulders. She almost didn't look six months pregnant.

"So, I have two fairly nimble hands, which I am offering up to you. How may I be of service?"

Renee swiveled around and smiled. All her roundness returned, and she set her hand on her belly out of habit. She brushed back a lock of hair and pointed to the walk-in fridge.

"Inside, you will find a flat of cherries that need pitting, as well as one of peaches. The cherries then need to be made into a compote, and the peaches need to be mixed with some flour and spices and topped with cobbler dough."

"Yes, taskmaster. You waste no time!" Opening the fridge.

"Sorry, but I'm so behind today. I feel like I am moving underwater."

"We will be on top of things in no time."

Molly and Renee returned to work. They moved about each other in a tacit ballet, a fluid dance of rolling pins, pans, and fruit. Molly always felt at ease handling food. There was something very comforting about slicing and dicing. The repeated, methodical motions were almost trancelike. As her hands kept busy, Molly's mind was still. With so many tasks at hand, there was no time to fritter away worrying about anything. Hours past, desserts were made, and Renee's "to do" list shrank. At around four, Vanessa came back. Vanessa was a tall, gangly teenager, with freckles and red hair who plated appetizers and desserts every night.

"Hey, Renee." Opening the fridge and pulling out whip cream and bunches of mint. "Anything new?"

"Nope, same menu as yesterday. I think you need to make more chocolate sauce for the banana cream pies, and if you have time, I would love you to make more ganache for the chocolate cakes." Taking off her apron.

"No problem." Beginning her tasks. "I'm Vanessa by the way." Smiling at Molly.

"Molly." Untying her own apron.

"The daughter?"

"That's me." Hanging it on a hook.

"Nice to meet you."

"Likewise. Have a good night."

Renee and Molly walked through the kitchen and into the front. Helen was setting the last of the tables and the wait staff was milling around, getting everything ready.

"I thought you had left," Helen stated as she caught sight of Molly.

"Nope, the little tyrant over there put me to work." Gesturing to Renee.

"You volunteered." Renee, grinning at Molly. "I'll see you tomorrow, Helen."

"I'll see you later, Mom. Renee and I are going for coffee and then I think I am going to head home and do some work."

"Work?"

"That box was filled with all my tools from home. Susan bought everything I had made and wants more."

"That's great. I'll see you later."

"Anyway, I love you." Grabbing her purse from behind the counter.

" 'Bye, girls."

Molly and Renee walked to Renee's navy Volvo station wagon.

"I used to be cool." Renee, looking at her car. "Now I'm driving a station wagon."

"Uh, oh." Getting in the front seat. "Pretty soon you will be donning a yellow sweat suit with a very large fluffy cat on the front and be used to getting puked on."

"I will never wear a cat sweat suit." Starting the car.

"Sure, Mommy, whatever you say. I seem to remember when you were fifteen you were the only girl to match her shoelaces to her outfit." Tapping her lightly on the shoulder. "I'm sorry to say, but you were never cool."

"Fuck you, sister." Renee laughed, knowing just how true the statement was.

While Molly had always believed that she scored that day in middle school when Renee sat down and joined her for lunch, and never really had questioned why Renee could so easily embrace the new girl at school, Renee knew that it was truly the other way around. For Renee that fateful day meant she had met one of those special girls who knew how to make her, someone with braces, glasses, and twenty extra pounds of baby fat, glow. So while it may have looked from the outside like two oddballs finding a home with each other, Renee had found her first real friend. When they became friends, Renee felt smart and funny and beautiful for the first time. Slowly she blossomed and eventually what she saw in Molly's eyes felt real.

Molly especially helped Renee escape from under the judging eye of her diet-obsessed mother. Every ounce of Renee's frame was catalogued and weighed, measured and pinched. Whether it was pushing Atkins or Weight Watchers or fat camp in the summers, her mother constantly critiqued her daughter and undermined Renee's self-esteem. And all the negative energy only made Renee obsess over food even more. Early on, Molly somehow got a sense of Renee and her mother's battles, and always tried to deflect and compensate for the ego blows she knew Renee suffered at home. She wouldn't let Renee degrade herself and encouraged, with the help of the rest of the Stern family, a different attitude about food. With regular sleep-overs and hanging out after school, Renee finally had a safe, nonthreatening space to explore cooking, and her love for baking was freed.

Junior year in high school, Molly threw her a perfect birthday party. Henry was on hand to cook up a Renee feast. Everything Renee loved was prepared specially.

"Henry, this is too much!" Renee beamed. "It's like my very own Vegas buffet."

"That's the point, my dear." Handing her a plate. "Not a thing is missing from Molly's 'Renee's favorite foods' list."

"This is the best party I have ever been to," Corey, one of Renee's and Molly's school friends, praised through a mouthful of food. "You Sterns really know how to do it."

"Corey, there's plenty. No need to eat as you go." Molly laughed.

"True." Stuffing another mini quiche in his mouth.

"No manners." Renee giggled. "But he's right. All of you are awesome."

The rest of the gang, Lisa, and Abby all moved through the maze of munchies and piled their plates high with macaroni and cheese, sushi, bacon-wrapped dates, chicken sate, and more. They hurried into the living room and tucked away everything from the banquet. After an equally insane dessert bar, Lisa, Abby, Corey, and Molly huddled around Renee while she opened her presents. A candle, some CDs, a hand-knit scarf. Then came the gift from Molly. Renee opened the slim envelope and inside was a card for a subscription to *Food and Wine* magazine.

"I love it! It's my favorite magazine!" Renee gushed. "I always sneak a peek when I come over here."

"I know." Molly grinned. "My dad will be happy now that he doesn't have to hunt high and low for his."

"Thanks, Molly." Giving her a hug.

"You're welcome. But there's a condition to this gift."

"What?"

"We," gesturing to the gang, "get to be your guinea pigs. Lots of mouths here eager for good food."

"Food? Did someone say food?" Abby groaned.

"What?" Corey jumped up and grabbed a cookie from the coffee table. "I know you want it." Hovering over Abby.

"Stop, Corey!" Abby yelled, trying to cover her mouth.

"Open up, here comes the birdy!" Corey went on.

"Corey!" Laughing harder. Soon the room dissolved into laughter.

Renee smiled at the memory and looked at Molly. Here she was, years later, still her best friend, but now also her sister. She was one lucky girl, for the family who adopted her as a shy, unconfident teenager and encouraged her to find her passion and herself, was now truly her family.

"Okay, no cat, but maybe the sweat suit will have a horse on it. At least that is very Chloe 2000," Molly went on.

"Hysterical. You and your keen fashion memory." Pinching Molly's arm lightly. "Just wait until you get pregnant and fat. Only then can you comment on elastic waist bands."

"Ow!" Slapping her hand away. "That's going to bruise. And, by the way, babies and me are not going to get together for a long while. I am perfectly satisfied being a moderately thin aunt who spoils and then returns child to parents."

"To be honest, that sounds pretty good to me too." Rubbing her belly. "By the way, Abby and the rest of the gang have been asking about if and when you are going to make a move to see them."

Molly thought about her high school pals. There was Renee, of course; Abby, newly back in town with a husband and a new medical practice; Lisa, a stay-at-home mom with a very cute toddler whose pictures Molly proudly displayed on her fridge in LA; and Corey, a lawyer at his father's firm, which used to be her father's firm. In high school, they were all inseparable. A small, tight group in a small, tight town. They all stayed in contact peripherally over the years, a few phone calls here and there and greetings over the holidays. When Molly took off to LA for college, she sort of set off alone. They used to call her the "lone rider." They even gave her a mask affixed with feathers when she left. Molly had worn it for her first Halloween in LA. Everyone thought that she would come back after school, open a painting school or something, but she never did come back, minus a few weeks here and there. They all found comfort in the quiet; it just made Molly long to be louder.

"Everyone must think I'm a supreme bitch." Fiddling with the radio of Renee's wagon.

"Actually, 'bitchy' is the word Lisa used, not 'bitch.' "

"I just haven't felt like dealing."

"Molly, we're your friends, you don't have to deal with us." Pulling up to the coffeehouse. "You should call."

"I will. We'll get drinks." Looking at Renee's stomach. "Well, we will drink and you can sip some water."

"I just keep getting more and more boring." Getting out of the car slowly.

"You and Alex make a nice pair," Molly cooed.

"Come on, Molly. You're buying."

Molly and Renee went in and ordered: a latté for Molly and a hot chocolate for Renee. They found a small wood table in the back and settled in.

"I must smell really bad." Molly, taking a whiff under her arms.

"I think I must be immune. Alex and I sometimes have smell-offs when we come home from work at the same time."

"Smell-offs? I don't want to know."

"No, you don't." Redoing her ponytail. "I think it's one of those couple things better left secret."

"Couple things." Repeating after Renee.

"Okay, Molly, what the hell happened? I've been getting all these little pieces."

"It's been really hard to talk about. Certain things I can't tell my parents because I feel too ashamed. And then, what if I go back? We get back together, which isn't going to happen, but if it does, then they will never be able to look at him or me the same way."

"Look, I'm family but we are friends too. Well, really we are friends first. I can just be your girlfriend right now and not your sister."

"I know. Renee, why is it when you decide to end something, your brain keeps replaying all these moments when you were so in love? I keep flashing back to all these memories and while some really awful ones pop in, I usually am overwhelmed with this need to go to him and love him and feel all of that all over again."

"Because you are human, and Liam has been a huge part of your life for a very long time. And he fits into your whole teenage romance-novel archetype."

"What type?" Feigning ignorance.

"The one born from the hundred-plus *Sweet Dreams* books you read all through middle school and high school detailing your perfect rebel with the perfect tender heart fantasy."

"I don't shape my relationships from some silly girl books." Defending herself.

"Really?"

"Well, maybe." Giggling a bit. "But I did not, I repeat, did not, read them in high school."

"You so did."

"Did not!" Laughing. "I guess I did find my cliché rocker boy."

"Yup. Rough around the edges until he met you and swept you off your feet by playing a few jingles on his guitar." Renee, elaborating.

"It's humiliating how tacky that sounds when you say it out loud." Molly laughing harder.

"Kind of." Laughing with her.

"I remember this one time early on in our relationship when I had the stomach flu. I was nasty and beyond gross, and kept telling him to stay far, far away. Instead of listening he showed up, brought me every fashion magazine, a case of ginger ale, washed me in the tub, and cleaned up the mess in the bathroom without even flinching."

"Everything?"

"Everything. I was still in the too-afraid-to-poo-at-his-place phase and he just rolled right through it."

"What made you leave then? Seems like this is fantasy fulfillment at its finest."

"Let's just say that he is a constant maker of bad decisions." Grabbing two sugars and pouring them into her drink. "His promises don't last because he can't resist. It's like he is drawn to the light socket even when his fingertips have already been burned."

"So it is an issue of trust."

"I guess. I'm afraid that no matter how hard and fierce I love him, he will always do the wrong thing even though he promises me he won't."

"I think that it all depends on what these wrong things are. No one is perfect. I think to love is to ignore the perfections and embrace all the flaws. If you can love them that way, then that's true and real. To sustain love is to love all the shitty things about someone." Taking a sip. "Well, maybe not love but accept."

"I know what you have accepted and sometimes I think you are a saint." Smiling at Renee. "How my brother managed to snag you is a mystery we Sterns pondered daily."

"I know, I know. I'm perfect." Rolling her eyes. "He's not so bad either."

"Have you heard that snort, hacking, spitting thing he does?"

"I have ordered him to do it only in the privacy of the bathroom. What is that by the way?"

"No idea, but it is the grossest thing I have ever heard." Chuckling. "Mom and I used to stop the car and make him get out whenever we heard it starting."

"It's pretty bad." Laughing harder. "Okay, enough. Obviously, Liam's issues are a little more unsettling than unusual body noises or we wouldn't be having this conversation."

"Yeah." Taking a deep breath. "He made me a deal a little while ago and in one evening he proceeded to do pretty much everything he agreed not to. At least he did it all in one fell swoop. No half-assing his fuckup. I have to admire that."

"I note some sarcasm."

"Of course." Sipping the last of her coffee.

"Look, what it comes down to is, is this incident the deal-breaker?"

"I don't know. Part of me thinks it should be and part of me knows he's dealing with a sickness and that he's trying to get help and that should count for something."

"Well, take the time you need to figure that out. If you are strong enough to trust him again and try, then do it with everything you have, and if you're not, it doesn't make you less of who you are or less compassionate. This is your life as well." Getting up all of a sudden. "I hate to run right in the middle of this, but I have to go home. I have this nagging urge to pee, and my back and feet feel like they are going to fall off. I feel like I am swelling exponentially. Do you want me to give you a ride to your car?"

"No thanks. It's just around the block. I think I'm going to sit here a while."

"Thanks again for your help today." Kissing Molly on the cheek. "I'm sorry to bail right in the middle of things."

"Don't be, thanks for listening."

Renee walked out of the café, and Molly stared at the leftover foam in her coffee. It felt weird talking about all this. She felt like she was on an episode of *Oprah*. Was she becoming some clichéd story of when a good girl loves the wrong man? Molly hated being a cliché. Hated having anything about her be normal or usual or predictable. How had things come to this? A simple meet and fall turns into a pathetic melodrama of bad influences, being under the influence, and wondering whether or not to let all that influence the future. This was not how their *Behind the Music* was supposed to be. They were going to be the Bon Jovis or Paul and Linda. They were supposed to make it through the pitfalls of fame together. Does the whole future they planned come down to one night? Well, in reality it wasn't one night, it was a myriad of small things that culminated in a one-night scenario. Could she move on and move past and love him, or could she move on and move past and learn to live without him?

seven

Sunday morning, Molly woke up to the smell of pancakes. Her whole body soft-ened and she yawned herself downstairs in her snowman pajamas. Her mother was sit-ting at the table reading the *New York Times* and her father was manning the griddle. Molly poured herself a glass of orange juice and sat down. She stealth-ily weaseled the magazine sec-tion from beneath the pile.

"What do you think you are doing?" Helen asking with-out missing a beat.

"What do you mean?" Set-tling into her seat.

"It's not going to happen."

"What's not going to happen?" Leaning back in her chair to grab a pen off the counter.

"Don't you dare."

"Dare do what?" Slowly inching away from her mother.

"There's no way you are getting first crack."

"Really?" Jumping up and running into the living room.

"Molly!" Helen jumped up as well and chased Molly.

Mother and daughter proceeded to play tag all around the house. Shrieks of laughter echoed and both ran back into the kitchen.

"Hand it over, Molly."

"Never." Molly giggled

"Molly, give me my crossword puzzle."

"Yours? Dad, who bought the paper this morning?" Hovering around the other side of the table.

"I did." Lifting pancakes onto a plate.

"I see, so Mother, this really isn't your puzzle, it's Dad's."

"And?"

"And, Dad can I have it?" Waving it back and forth just out of Helen's reach.

"Sure."

"Sure!" Helen shot him a death grin. "Henry, you just blew it."

"I did?" Sitting down between them.

"Yup, buckaroo. Totally blew it." Giving up and sitting down.

"What does that mean?" Henry asked.

"You will find out later." Winking at him.

"Gross." Sitting down. "Too much information. Here, Mom, I was just kidding." Tossing Helen the paper.

"Thank you." Taking the magazine and stuffing it under her bottom. "Just to be safe."

"What are you going to do today, Molly?" Henry asked as he dished.

"Some work and a yoga class with Renee later on. Mom, you want to come?"

"What time?"

"Four-thirty."

"Sounds good, then maybe all of us can grab an early dinner."

"I'll call Renee later and ask." Taking a large bite.

"How come no one ever asks me if I want to go to yoga?"

"Do you?" Molly asked.

"No, but I would like to be asked."

"Okay, Dad." Rolling her eyes and taking another bite.

All of a sudden, Molly felt nausea rise up. She threw down her fork and rushed to the bathroom. Barely making it on time, Molly threw up. This was becoming a really bad habit. Any questions about bulimia were definitely answered with a resounding "no." Her parents both had concerned faces when she returned to the table.

"Honey, are you okay?"

"Yeah. Must be a little bug. I'll be fine." Taking a sip of water.

"Maybe you should go lie down?"

"That's a good idea."

Molly went upstairs and fell into her bed. Soon she was asleep.

The bar was crowded. When she walked in, the wall of heat melted over her and instantly dampened her brow. She traced a finger along her neck and licked the sweat. It tasted sweet and sad like a ballad. Everything was dark and red. Pulsing, dancing, beating like a heart. It was a tangle of leather and lips. Molly started swaying, moving through the collection of faces. In the distance, Molly could see a band on a small stage. She wanted to get closer. Soon she was in front. It was Liam, singing. He didn't see her. She felt beads of his sweat landing on her. They burned. Tiny blisters popped up where they landed. He looked down and smiled. He finished singing and left the stage. Molly waited. Wait-

ing. Wait, she turned around and the place was empty. A bottle rolled and rested by her heel. She leaned down to pick it up.

"He left."

Elena.

"He knew I was waiting."

"He's gone. I'm sorry."

"No you're not."

"I love him too."

"I know."

"He loves you."

"But he's gone."

"Not forever. He's trying to get home."

"I don't live there anymore."

"He's trying to get home."

Elena turned around and walked away. Molly was alone again. She started running, sprinting for the door. She threw it open and tumbled into the daylight. The streets were empty. She kept running.

Molly woke up bathed in sweat. The light was fading and the clock read 5:10. So much for yoga. Molly sat up and felt her head spin. Maybe she really was catching a bug. She lay back down and stared at the ceiling. She swallowed hard and searched the bed for her CD remote control. She pressed PLAY and the Cowboy Junkies' "Misguided Angel" filled the room. Molly quietly mouthed every word to the tortured dirge. There was a small knock at the door. Helen poked her head in. She came in and sat down at the edge of Molly's bed.

"I saved it for you." Handing her the magazine section.

"Thanks."

"Want to do it together?"

"Sure."

"What are you listening to?" Helen asked.

"Some tragic song about being in love with the wrong man."

"Sounds good." Sarcastically.

Helen flicked on the light and snuggled in next to Molly. For an hour, the two of them quietly worked and eventually finished all but a few clues. Helen had a knack for all those long theme-related answers and Molly was stellar at utilizing her expensive verbal SAT tutoring sessions. Molly curled into her mother and took a deep breath. Helen's cashmere sweater caressed Molly's cheek. Molly felt safe for the first time since she left the hospital. As Martha Stewart would say, "It's a good thing."

"Feeling better?" Helen asked.

"Yeah, my stomach still feels a little fluttery, but I'm fine."

"It's been nice having you home."

"I know."

"How long are you thinking about staying?"

"Don't know."

"You can't avoid the situation forever. It's not like you to run away."

"I just want to figure things out before I go back."

"That's a good idea, but don't get stuck here or anywhere, Molly. That's something I always admired in you, your drive. You're idling, baby."

"Mom, what do you think?"

Molly rolled on her side and looked up at her mother. She could tell Helen was pondering the question because her brow was slightly furrowed. Molly knew Helen was running down the list of all the stupid things Liam had pulled over the years. Helen was probably focusing on the time that she and Henry had come to visit LA for the sole purpose of meeting him and wound up never even catching a glimpse. It was post–bowling birthday, pre-tour. Molly and Liam had settled into that comfortable couple phase where there were fewer and fewer questions and more time spent just having a good time. Molly should have known that this is precisely the time one does not introduce parents into the equation. Why rock the boat? The whole weekend wound up being a huge disaster. If Helen and Henry knew the real reason they failed to meet him, they would have advised Molly to dump him immediately.

Helen and Henry had flown in on the way to their tropical weeklong escape to Hawaii. They planned one whole day and night in LA before their flight to Maui. Simple enough. Molly picked them up at the airport, settled them into their hotel, and placed a call to Liam from the lobby to make a lunch plan.

"Hi, babe."

"Molly, are they with you yet?"

"Yeah, we just checked in and now are plotting the lunch stop. Where should we go?"

"I can't make it after all."

"Okay." A little disappointed.

"This meeting came up and I have to go into the studio sooner than I thought. I'm so sorry."

"It's all right. I guess we will just meet up at dinner then?"

"I'll be there. Little Door at eight-thirty."

"See you then."

"Love you." Hanging up.

Molly stuffed her phone back into her vintage Gucci blue doctor bag she bought on eBay, and grabbed her valet ticket from the maw. A small twinge was beginning to form at the base of her spine. In retrospect, it was a physical premonition. Helen strolled over to her daughter and linked her arm through hers. Henry followed suit on the other side.

"Guys." Unwinding herself. "I am twenty-seven years old. The double-hook job is a little nineteen-eighty-six." Snapping at them.

"Sorry." Blurting in unison.

Molly looked up and saw a bit of crest fall.

"No, I'm sorry. That was really rude." Reattaching herself. "I didn't mean to snap. Looks like Liam won't be meeting us for lunch after all. Something came up."

"That's too bad." Understanding his daughter. "He is coming tonight?"

"Definitely. And so is Jay."

"Oh, good. It's been too long since we saw her last."

"So what would you two like to eat?"

"I have a craving for the Ivy's chop salad," Helen mused.

"The Ivy it is."

Molly and her parents had spent the day much how they usually did when they went on city vacations together. They ate and then shopped. After hitting pretty much every shop near and far, Molly dropped them at the hotel for a rest and a shower. She headed home for a rest of her own. She unlocked the door, threw her packages on the counter, and grabbed a water from the fridge. After a mini stretch routine using the kitchen counter as a ballet bar, the twinge still would not cease to exist. She picked up the phone.

"Jay, will you pick me up tonight?"

"Of course, but what about your parents?"

"They're going to take a cab. They said they would catch a cab back or we can drop them. Is that cool?"

"Yup. What about Liam?"

"He is meeting us too, or at least he is supposed to meet us."

"What does that mean?"

"Nothing, never mind. Get me at eight-fifteen."

"Coolio."

Molly grabbed her shopping bags and went into her bedroom. She set them on the bed and went to run a bath. After starting the water, she returned and unpacked her new things. She spread them all on her bed and smiled a little. Free fashion was always a cause for glee. The new black boots would be perfect with the black lace chiffon vintage dress she bought last month at the Fairfax swap meet. Maybe she would toss on her stretchy Seven jeans underneath to dress it all down a bit. Molly put everything away and got in her tub. After a long soak, she primped and preened, and before she knew it the doorbell was ringing.

"Hi." Kissing Molly on the cheek. "I'm a little early because I wanted to borrow a shirt." Breezing in and pulling off the sweater she was wearing.

"What do you want?" Following her friend into her bedroom.

"Something girly. I'm feeling very ribbons and bows tonight."

"How unlike you."

"I think I am premenstrual." Opening Molly's closet.

"Tight? Loose? Color preference?"

"Loose, flowy, and white."

"Try these." Handing her two blouses.

Jay tried on the first, a peasant top with red embroidery. It was short sleeved and soft.

"Done."

"Well, that was easy enough." Molly, hanging the other one up. "Usually you take forever."

"I always wanted to borrow this so it was a perfect match." Spinning on her heels. "Okay, a little lip gloss and we are off. Nice outfit by the way. Are those the Marc boots you wanted?"

"Yeah."

"I need my parents to come to town."

"Might I remind you that they live here?"

"Oh yeah, you know what I mean." Grinning. "Let's go."

Molly grabbed her purse and noticed that her twinge had eased slightly. Her best friend's attitude always seemed to set her straight. Jay was a mean mental chiropractor.

Henry and Helen were sitting when they got there. The chair next to Helen glared at Molly.

"Hey, Helen. Henry," Jay gushed, giving them both big hugs. "I'm so glad to see you." Sitting next to Henry.

"You look great," Helen complimented. "I like you with shorter hair."

"I'm still getting used to it." Tugging at her bangs. "I had a recent battle with a pair of nail scissors that did not end well."

"They've already almost grown out." Molly, sitting next to her mom. "Remember when I did that?"

"Do I? You almost took off an ear! Your hair was lopsided for months."

"I thought it looked cool."

"I don't think so," Henry interjected. "I seem to remember a few tears were shed when you realized you couldn't tape your hair back in place."

"I did not."

"I think it was duct tape no less. We have pictures."

"Well, they do say it has a thousand uses." Molly laughed.

"Shall we have an apéritif?" Henry asked the group of ladies.

"But of course!" They all agreed.

The waiter arrived at just the right moment.

"A round of Kir Royales, please," Henry ordered.

"I'll bring those right away, along with some menus."

Twenty minutes later, their glasses were empty, and the menus sat closed on top of the table. Pleasant conversation tinkled all around Molly, but she was nowhere to be found. Lost in the seams of the upholstered cushion covering the empty seat. Maybe if she gazed long enough, he would materialize from amid the stripes in the fabric. Another five went by and Henry glanced at his daughter, then back at his wife. Helen nodded quietly.

"Molly, let's order and he can catch up when he arrives." Squeezing Molly's hand across the table.

"Of course." Snapping back to attention. "I'm just going to go outside and call him and see what happened. Mom, I'll have the scallops to start and the lamb."

Molly bobbed and weaved through the tables and pushed open the door of the restaurant. She almost ran smack into Liam.

"Hey, careful there, kid." Holding onto Molly's arm.

"Sorry." Pulling him into a hug.

Molly could smell the alcohol all over him. He was sticky, drenched with the perfume of vodka and pot.

"What the fuck!" Pushing him away from her and glaring.

Liam fell back and had trouble steadying himself. He grabbed her arm again for balance and Molly quickly shook him off.

"You're completely wasted! You're such an asshole!" Raising her voice. "Did you drive yourself here?"

"Nope. Elena and Zander dropped me off."

"Oh, fuck you! Of all nights." Shaking her head.

"Everything's fine, really." Slurring his words. "Stop yelling." Putting his hand to his head. "I had, like, one drink." Looking at her with buzzing eyes.

"More like five and God knows what! You can't even focus."

"I can. Watch." Putting his head back and doing the finger to nose drunk test. He missed.

"My parents are in there waiting to meet you."

"I know, let's go." Grabbing for her again. "That's why I'm here. Henry and Ellen."

"Helen. Look, just go home."

"No, I want to meet them."

"Just leave—you are not seeing my parents like this." Molly dialed a cab company. "I need a cab, please. The Little Door on Third between Crescent Heights and La Cienega. The name is Liam. Thanks."

"Molly, I don't want to leave."

"Well, how about you do what I want for once and get the fuck out of here!"

"Molly?" Jay popped her head out of the restaurant. "I just was checking . . ."

"Jay!" Liam interrupted and threw his arms around her. "Hi!"

"Hi, Liam." Patting him on the back as she tried to extricate. "You're kidding."

"Nope, I called him a cab. There is no way in hell he is going in there."

"Good plan." Still trying to extricate. "He's a mess."

"I can't believe this."

The cab pulled up and Jay deposited Liam into the backseat. He rolled in without further protesting. Molly leaned in.

"Do you have money?"

"Yeah." Pulling rumpled bills from his pockets as he turned them out.

Molly closed the door and told the driver where to go, then she turned around and took a deep breath. The cab pulled away.

"Never a dull moment with that one," Jay cracked, trying to lighten the moment. "Here." Handing Molly a tissue from her purse.

"The little fucker." Wiping off the tears. "The one thing I ask of him that's important to me."

"Look, shake it off for now. Let's go have a nice dinner with your parents."

"Okay." Straightening up. "I'll try."

Molly and Jay returned to the table just as their appetizers landed.

"Ah, I knew the old leave-the-table trick would work." Jay, joking as she sat down. "It never fails."

"What happened to you two?" Helen asked.

"Well, Liam got caught at the studio, and Jay wanted company while she smoked a cigarette."

"Still smoking, huh?" Henry asked.

"Yup, but I'm down to a few a day."

"Good for you, Jaycee. I'm sorry about Liam. I guess we will meet him another time."

"Next time." Changing the subject. "This looks great. I'm starving."

Knowing their daughter well, Helen and Henry dropped the subject and regaled the girls with the trials and tribulations of getting the restaurant up and running. It was coming down to a matter of months before they would open Helen's. They split a few bottles of wine, had both dessert and cheese, and all left satiated. Molly and Jay dropped Helen and Henry off at their hotel, hugged and kissed them good-bye, and headed back to Molly's. Jay idled by the curb.

"Wanna hang out a bit?" Jay, asking.

"No, I just want to go to bed. I feel buzzed and a little deflated." Kissing Jay on the cheek. "Thanks for everything."

"No problem. It'll all be fine in the morning."

"Whatever. I'm beat." Getting out of the car and throwing Jay a wave.

Molly flopped her bag, keys, and self down on the couch and let out a big sob. What a disaster. So much for carefully made plans. Apparently, Liam did not respond to carefully made plans. Molly fell asleep wondering if she would have the patience to make any more.

The next morning Molly awoke on the couch in her bra and panties. Her clothes lay crumpled on the floor. The sound of the doorbell eased her off the makeshift bed. She tumbled off the couch, rubbed her eyes, looked through the peephole, and opened the door. Liam stood there freshly showered and shaven.

"You have a key." Turning her back to him and walking into the kitchen.

"I thought knocking was a better choice." Following after her. "I brought you a latté and the paper."

"Thanks. Just set them down." Pouring herself some juice. "Want some?"

"Please."

"Advil?"

"I already downed a few."

Molly poured another drink and handed it to him. She slowly drank hers and could not bring herself to look him in the eyes. She didn't know what would come out of her mouth.

"I'm going to jump in the shower." Walking past him.

"I'll wait."

"Whatever."

Molly stripped and stood naked in the shower, water enclosing her. She heard the bathroom door open and watched Liam come in and take off his clothes. He pulled open the shower curtain and stepped inside. Molly shifted around so he could get into the spray. Liam picked up the shampoo and gently began to wash Molly's hair. It was a routine Molly had gotten used to. He caressed her head, then her shoulders, washed her back with the soap. Molly turned around and let the water wash over her. Liam leaned down to kiss her. Molly turned her head.

"It's not that easy. I'm not that easy." Finally looking up at him.

"I'm so sorry." Wrapping his arms around her. "I really had every intention of being there—well, being there with all my faculties."

"That's the problem. You seem to have this disconnect between your intentions and your actions. I just don't understand what would possess you to get super fucked up when you know I was counting on you to be there, be there for me?"

"I was in the studio with the guys, Zander stopped by, one thing led to another, and time just got away from me."

"It sucked." Biting her lip. "Things have to change. You have got to figure out your priorities."

"I know. I think part of me got so fucked up on purpose. I was nervous about meeting your parents. I freaked."

"That sort of makes sense, but if you didn't want to do it, you should have just said something in the first place instead of creating all this drama. It's not like I was pressuring you to meet them. You said you wanted to, you even suggested it!"

"I know I did, and I do. I don't know what is wrong with me sometimes." Putting his hands on her face. "And I know things have to change. I have to change. I promise to try harder and handle things better."

"I feel like I have heard all this before. I can't deal with empty promises from you. I hurt when you break them. I really do." Starting to cry.

"Shush." Trying to console her. "It's going to be different. I'm going to clean up my act."

Liam and Molly looked at each other for a long time, standing still and letting the water embrace them. Liam leaned down again to kiss Molly and this time she let him. Once again, two became one.

Molly rolled over again and touched her face. She could almost still feel the water and his kiss. Helen shifted next to her and looked at her daughter. Molly was a million miles away. Helen knew she had to tread lightly. Whatever she said, she knew in that moment Molly was still in love and would go back for another try. It was the way Molly was gazing at the ceiling with a soft smile tugging at the edges of her mouth. After Alex had told her and Henry the gist of what happened, Helen cried quietly in her bathroom for an hour. She was terrified for her daughter. But despite how afraid Helen was that Molly was involved with a man whose highs would be great, true, and strong and whose lows would be many, devastating, and life changing, this was her girl's path. All Helen could do was walk the tightrope between giving careful advice and accepting her daughter's decisions. It would be slippery and incredibly difficult.

"Molly, deep down he's a good man—smart, charming, successful. I like him. He's funny and easygoing. He has money and a career doing what he loves and I know he loves you. But I'm not all that sure he loves himself."

"So Alex filled you in?"

"We got the two-minute recap."

"And?"

"I think that he is a little afraid to just be. That's why he drinks and whatever else he does. That's why he gets swept into other people's moments and forgets where he really should be. Maybe he's not sure that if he says no to something, anything, that there will be other moments. He doesn't want to miss anything."

"So instead he says yes to too much cocaine and almost dies?!"

"Is that what happened?" Letting Molly tell her own story.

"We had a party. A celebration for him finishing the last song on the new album. Maybe I shouldn't have done it—you know, placed him in a situation like that when he's been doing so well lately, but I did. Anyway, Zander shows up and does his little number on Liam, and before I know it, the two of them have taken off on some musical adventure. The next thing I get is a call from Zander on the way to the hospital."

"It must have been difficult to see him like that." Stroking her daughter's hair.

"He looked so bad, Mom. He was so pale." Crying softly. "I thought he was already dead."

"This is a lot, Molly, for anyone to take. This man is really lost."

"I don't know how to save him."

"You can't, Molly. That's not your job."

"What am I supposed to do, Mom? Part of me feels like I have abandoned him and the other part feels like fuck all of this, I am done. He has broken far too many promises. He knew after the car incident, he didn't have any wiggle room left."

"Car incident?" Looking at her daughter with wide eyes. "What car incident?"

"The last straw before this last straw and I don't want to talk about it."

"Molly, what happened?"

"Mom, I don't want to talk about it." Raising her voice a pitch.

"Okay, fine." Swallowing through her clenched throat.

"I just, I don't know. I don't want you and Dad to think all these horrible things about him. I know that sounds so stupid seeing how Alex told you stuff and I'm telling you stuff already too, but part of me thinks that if you heard every single thing that

I have had to deal with you would look at me differently, you'd be ashamed of me." Wiping her nose with her sleeve.

"Molly." Holding her tightly, wrapping her in a hug. "No matter what, Dad and I will never be ashamed of you. We love you."

"I know. I just . . . I love him so much, Mom."

"I know you do, and love makes us do crazy, sometimes unhealthy things. You just have to decide for yourself at what point the unhealthy outweighs the normal crazy. Does he give more than he takes?"

"Most of the time. He's the most supportive person of me who isn't related by blood. He sees all of me and accepts me as I am. No man has ever just done that, just said, 'Hey Molly, be crazy and flighty, be emotional and tough, freak out on me for no reason and tell me how you feel, just be you, and I will love it all and I won't run away.' "

"You do know that there will be someone else who will do all those things if this doesn't work out."

"Not the way he does it."

"Molly, you can't just be in love with his potential, you have to be in love with the man that he is."

"I guess." Glancing at her mom.

"No matter what I say, tell you to stay, tell you to let go, or whatever, you have to make all these choices yourself. No woman ever has her ears open when people talk to her about the man she loves."

"Even you?"

"Yup. For a long time I internalized everything and let myself think it was fine, despite what my friends were saying to me."

"Your friends?"

"Yes, we talk about our love lives just as much as you do. Just because we are older doesn't mean we don't dish." Grinning at her daughter.

"Once a girl, always a girl."

"Exactly. Look, I love your father very much and although we had a rocky time for a while and I didn't know how things would work out, I had to work it out for myself, just like you do. I was lucky that he decided to reconnect and place all of us on the top of his list of priorities. To switch jobs so late in life and start a new path, I admire him for taking this chance. I know it's hard for him now to look back and see how distant he was for so many years. But Dad's issues and motivations were different. Dad wasn't an addict, he was a husband and father already committed to the people around him. He had no choice but to change because he was already living the life."

"So you're saying that what Liam and I have is not a commitment?" Staring at her mother. "That I am not enough to motivate him to change?"

"No, don't take it the wrong way. What I am saying is that Liam has a bigger problem that he needs help with. It isn't something he can just deal with, just flick a switch and be fine. He may need to lose more to be able to fix it."

"Mom, you are handling this very calmly." Eyeing her. "We are not talking about clean little problems."

"I'm not clueless." Nudging her daughter. "I know what's up. I watch MTV."

Molly burst out laughing. She had this flash of Helen late at night, watching videos and mouthing the words to Slim Shady.

"What's so funny?" Starting to laugh herself. "I really like that band Incubus." Starting to hum one of their songs. "Cute singer."

"You're going to be one hip granny." Giving her mom a big hug. "And, he is hot. I met him a few months ago at some record party with Liam."

"No?!"

"Yes."

"I'm officially jealous of my daughter." Giving her another squeeze. "Hungry?"

"I think so, thanks for listening, and sharing."

"It's my duty. One that I take great pride in." Getting up from the bed. "I have complete faith in your ability to know your limits and protect yourself. You'll figure all this out. We didn't raise a wilting flower."

Molly got up and straightened out her clothes. She was still in her pajamas.

"Wilting no, but slightly wrinkled, yes. I'll meet you downstairs." Gesturing to her clothing. "I think a new pair of pajamas is a must."

"What do you feel like? Soup? Pasta?"

"Spaghetti will be good."

"Meet you in the kitchen." Giving Molly one more kiss on the cheek.

Helen took the stairs methodically. She paused halfway down and caught her breath. While she was reacting as calmly as she could to all the things her daughter was saying and all that she knew Molly was still hiding, inside she was raging. Helen knew she had done the right thing, handled the whole situation in a manner that would not alienate her daughter, yet she hated herself for being so easy and calm. What if all the things Molly was still hiding were worse, worse than doing too many drugs or having too many drinks? What if Liam hit her or put her in danger? What would Helen do if something happened to her baby that a bandage and a cookie couldn't fix? Helen looked back toward Molly's bedroom and mentally crossed her fingers, said three hundred Jewish Hail Marys, and tossed her hand out to ward off the evil eye.

Once downstairs, Helen busied herself in the kitchen. There was a note from Henry on the table that he had gone to the movies with Alex. Molly strolled in. She had washed her face and braided her hair Pocahontas style.

"I always love it when you wear your hair like that. It reminds me of when you were little."

"Whatcha makin'?" Plopping at the table.

"Alla checca."

"Perfecta."

Molly and Helen sat around the big steaming bowls of pasta and spent the rest of the evening talking about Alex and Renee and the upcoming birth of the newest member of the Stern family.

The next morning, Molly felt a lot better. Her stomach felt a bit more settled and she felt a little lighter having shared some with her mother. It was freeing to actually talk about things. Thank God her mother listened without really judging. That made Molly feel safer, stronger. She picked up the phone and dialed her brother's.

"Hey, Alex, it's me."

"What happened to you last night? I thought we were going to do a little family powwow?"

"Some stomach thing. How was the movie?"

"Predictable. Lots of kung fu and a bad dialogue."

"Glad to have missed it. Let's do dinner tonight instead."

"Sounds good. Renee and I have an appointment this afternoon with the doctor, and we are getting more pictures. I can't wait to see how much he's grown."

"He?!"

"Whoops! I didn't say anything."

"He!!! I thought you didn't want to know!"

"Renee didn't. I did, so I made the doctor spill it. Renee doesn't know I know, so you better keep your big mouth shut."

"He!!! A little nephew. I am so excited!" Screaming into the phone.

"It's pretty fucking cool."

"Yes it is, Daddy. I'm really happy for you."

"Thanks. So, anyway, we will have more pictures tonight."

"Cool. Will you tell Renee I will be there in ten to get her for class."

"She's all ready."

"See you later. A boy, a beautiful baby boy!"

Now he was a real person with a sex and all. A little boy. There was nothing better. Well, except for a little girl.

Molly cruised by, gathered up her sister-in-law, and headed for the yoga studio. After a slew of down dogs, up dogs, and for Molly, a few dead dogs, the two girls headed back to Renee's. Molly followed her inside and did a few more stretches on the floor. Renee handed her a bottle of water and eased herself into a chair.

"I remember when my body looked like yours." Examining her belly. "Will I ever be thin again?"

"Of course. I bet you will look even better after. Look at all those celebrity moms. They look hotter after, and you are going to have those great tits for a while as well."

"For the first time ever I'm going to have a bustline."

"Alex must be loving that."

"I know. Lucky for me, though, he's a butt man. It's the only way we've lasted this long."

"Liam's a butt man too." Leaning and bending forward. "He always says that guys who are into boobs have a Mommy complex and really aren't into women. Butt men, on the other hand, really appreciate the finer points."

"Well, my ass is way more than a point." Putting her feet up on the table.

"What time is your appointment?" Leaning down again.

"Three-thirty."

All of a sudden another wave of nausea hit Molly, and she sprinted up and bolted for the bathroom. When she came out, Renee looked concerned.

"What's going on? You okay?"

"Something is off with my stomach. It's really strange. Out of the blue I have to puke."

"Maybe you should go to the doctor?"

"I'll be fine." Standing up. "Okay, on that pleasant note, I'm off. I'll see you later."

When she got home there was a message from Abby. Molly knew she couldn't ignore her old friends forever, so she grabbed the piece of paper and the phone. On the fifth ring the machine picked up.

Hi, this is Abby and Scott. We are not home. Leave your name and number and we will get back to you as soon as we can. Thanks.

Hey guys, it's Molly. Sorry it has taken so long to connect. I would love to catch up and see you. Thursday night, maybe at Jake's? Hope you are both well. 'Bye.

Done deal. Easy enough. Molly looked outside and the sunflowers were still blooming. Molly grabbed a scissors and went into the backyard. She carefully clipped a handful and added a few wild roses to the bunch. They were bright yellow ringed with a fiery red on the tip of each petal. They looked like sunset on an island in the South Pacific. Molly took the flowers into the kitchen, trimmed them, and placed them into a vase. She set them in the middle of the table, just where the light caught the edges and cast a warm glow on to the room. Molly bounded upstairs and grabbed her box of materials and tools. Hunched over and intent, Molly worked the rest of the day stringing, winding, and tying beads and baubles. Time fell away, and the golden shade of the room enveloped Molly.

eight

When another small package arrived from Jay, Molly had to smile. She knew what was inside. Her friend had the knack for perpetual optimism and driving insistence. Jay was turbo-charged, an Energizer bunny minus the cheesy commercials and drum kit attached to her paws. The fact that the two of them were slowly forging a real partnership did not surprise Molly. Jay could always see three or four steps down the road, while Molly was about the moment at hand. It made sense that Molly grew

up drawing and designing Shrinky Dinks and Jay was a local chess champion. Their brains did not function on the same level. Perfect complements. Within the manila envelope was a stack of pictures, a sheet detailing the terms of the lease, a rough budget of what they would need to get the store up and running, and sketches of ideas for the space. Molly had to admit, it was a dynamite space, affordable and in a location that had both restaurants and other shops around it. As Molly was stuffing everything back in, Henry walked into the living room.

"Helen!" Henry, calling upstairs. "I'm leaving. I'll see you later."

" 'Bye!" Calling down. "Have a good day."

"I love you."

"I love you too."

Henry was dressed in his chef's coat and clogs. It was still so weird not seeing her dad freshly shaven and in a suit. He looked so different now, longer hair, a beard. He actually looked happy, his mind calm and not wrapped up in what he had to do three months from now. Molly actually felt she would choose to be friends with this new version of her father. She wished he had been around before. Did he know how much he had changed? How his kids looked at him? How Helen did?

Since she had been home, Molly had caught glimpses of her mother watching her father. There was this schoolgirl quality that washed over her mother's cheeks. Helen's eyes would twinkle, beam like a cheerleader watching her quarterback sweetie throw the winning pass. Even how freely they would exchange "I love you" was exciting. It was as if Helen was rediscovering herself and her husband, and what she was finding was better than it had been before. And Molly knew that her father's asking her mom to come and work at the restaurant made her mother feel needed again.

What Molly didn't know was that when she initially left the nest, now more than a decade ago, things were colder, Helen's life, chillier. Molly knew times had been tough, but she never knew the details. These were the things Helen would allude to with her daughter but never fully share even in their most intimate conversations like the one they had had last night. Helen walked a fine line with her daughter because she didn't want to scare her or make her see her father as an ordinary man with ordinary issues. She still wanted Molly to have some of her fantasies about her dad, even though Helen knew Molly was an astute observer and saw what was left unsaid.

It was when the house was empty, when Henry was at work all the time and there was no one around to nurture or to laugh with or to yell at to make their bed, that Helen lost her center. She spent hours alone, weeping uncontrollably. She would wander around the house looking for something to do and hours later would find herself half dazed and pruned in the tub or shivering outside on the porch in nothing but a thin T-shirt. She went to a doctor, who prescribed some pills. Helen would hide the bottles in her tampon boxes to keep them from Henry. She didn't want him to know just how fragile she was. She was embarrassed by her dependency on him, on her kids. When had the peace-loving activist girl inside her transmuted into a woman who could barely get dressed in the morning?

She lived with this secret until Henry, one afternoon a few months into her "treatment," really looked at his wife across the table, really looked at her. Helen was too even, too calm. Helen was a ghost of herself. She saw him watching, looking, wondering, and she began to cry. Everything flowed from her then, and she talked and wept and yelled until she felt empty and clean. Henry reached over, took her hand, and swallowed all she had released. He saw her stripped and raw and embraced her, then he began to change. It wasn't until that moment that he really understood how disconnected they all had become—or really how he had become from his family. He unwittingly had become his father, just giving enough of himself to allow him to stay in control of his emotions. It was in this moment that he decided to be different, act different, love harder. Helen noticed the subtleties after a while and stopped taking the pills. She stopped crying, wandering, or forgetting where she was. She started sculpting again, as she had done in college, and working at the library in town part-time. She did her hair and bought new lingerie, and felt butterflies everytime she looked at her husband. Even now, when years have passed, she still gets the giggles about him and thinks it's a blessing. Helen knows this is what Molly sees, and this is what Molly wants to emulate in her relationship with Liam. The ability to change and evolve. Molly sees how people can grow and become better versions of themselves, truer to themselves. This is a lesson to hold on to, but maybe Liam can't change what he has become like Henry could. Maybe that's why it needs to end and Molly needs to move on with her life.

"What do you have there?" Henry, coming over and giving Molly a kiss on the cheek.

"Jay sent me some information about this space she found." Pulling the pictures out and showing her dad. "What do you think?"

Henry glanced at the photos and sat down on the couch next to Molly.

"I think this place looks great. You guys could make it into a very interesting little shop. The rent seems reasonable."

"The people who own the building really want these tenants out so they are trying to give good incentive."

"You guys wouldn't need that much start-up money. Is Jay going to invest?"

"Yeah, fifty-fifty, her parents are into it."

"Is this what you want to do?" Looking at his daughter.

"I don't know. I seem to be having trouble making decisions lately."

"I noticed." Scanning the pictures again. "Your mom says

that your jewelry is selling really well and getting on all the right necks. That should tell you something. The snaps and clippings you send her are absolutely beautiful."

"You've seen those?" Sort of surprised.

"Sure, Mom prints them out for me."

"Still can't turn on the computer?"

"Nope."

"I think you were one of the only lawyers to not touch the thing."

"I bet you're right, but I just can't get the swing of it." Looking over the pics again. "This seems like a good move."

"It does, but this is not what is making me confused."

"I know that, but maybe a shop and a new project would make all the other stuff fall into place. Your life can't be about just one thing."

"It's a pretty big thing, Dad."

"Look, Molly, when you were younger, your mom and I never had any trouble figuring out what you needed. You were so self-sufficient and independent."

"Only on the outside." Molly whispering.

"What?" Henry's eyes widened a bit.

"Well, I wanted you to be proud of me. I wanted to be perfect." Admitting more than she wanted or realized. "I didn't want you to have to bother with me too much."

"Molly, did you think that if you had trouble with something we would love you less? That's insane. Bother us? You are our daughter, you're supposed to need us."

"That you would love me less." Looking down.

"Oh, man." Running his hands through his beard. "Is that why you never wanted help, why you had to do everything by yourself?"

"Yeah, maybe."

"Baby, it would be impossible for you to do anything to make me love you less. You could screw up royally, whatever that expression really means, and I would stick by you."

"Thanks, Dad." Hugging him. "I feel a little lost right now."
Opening up more.

"You have been standing still here too long. I know it has only been a few weeks, but you have to jump back into your life and get going. As much as we love having you here, this is not your home anymore. And as much as I miss you and hate that your life exists miles away from my protective gaze, you belong back in LA."

"Are you telling me to leave? Thanks." Getting upset.

"No, I am telling you to start living again. Your mom told me about Liam. I don't really know what to say about him except that it all sounds like something you need to start distancing yourself from. Molly, what are you doing?"

"I thought I just heard you say that I could totally fuck up and you would not judge?"

"I'm not judging, I am voicing concern." Staring at his daughter.

Molly could only hold her father's stare for a short second before she let her head fall. Her eyes welled up. Just the fact that they were having this heart-to-heart made Molly uncomfortable. It wasn't that she didn't trust her father or want to be frank with him, she just never had exposed herself so fully to him before. This was all new territory. Before, she hadn't wanted him to think she was weak, to think she wasn't tough enough to handle whatever she was thrown. And still now, she didn't want him to think that she wasn't perfect and perfectly in control.

"Oh, Molly." Pulling her into a hug. "You have to stop all this."

"I know." Wiping her nose. "It's just that . . ." Unable to finish.

"You love him."

Molly nodded her head and caved into her father.

"I don't know what to say to you." Shaking his head.

"Say something. Yell and tell me what to do." Pleading with her father. "Tell me to leave him, tell me what an asshole he is! Tell me I deserve better!"

"I could say all of that and mean every word, but I can't."
Holding her again. "I really want to, but would that really work?
I would just be yelling at you."

Molly didn't respond. They hadn't had a real heart-to-heart
with each other since right before she left for Los Angeles. Her
dad had come in her room late one evening as she was packing
and handed her this huge box to fit into her trunk. Inside was
every tool known to man, a mace canister, LoJack, an earthquake
kit, and one thousand dollars cash. It was the way Henry illus-
trated how worried he was, and the only way Molly would let
him be a dad and protect her. Their shorthand was through
wrenches, hammers, freeze-dried water, and emergency eco-
nomics, not conversation. Now they were talking and Molly felt
tongue-tied.

"I really don't want to yell at you. Molly, you have all the
information you need to make up your own mind. I love you no
matter what. This guy, though, has some serious problems and if
you want to help him and work it out, that's fine, but that's a big
burden to take on. If you don't do it, that's fine too. It doesn't
make you less loving. It scares me that you love someone so
unstable, but I am not going to scream at you and shame you into
doing what I think is best."

"Do you mean all that, Dad? You're so calm."

"Yes, and I know. Who have I become?" Cracking a smile.
"It's freaking me out."

"Me too."

"Should I scream at you a bit for good measure?"

"No thanks. I will take a rain check on that."

"Seriously, I guess the only thing I am absolutely sure of is
how headstrong and capable you are. You'll do what you need to
do."

"How can you be so certain about that?"

"Because I am certain of you."

Henry sighed and stretched out. He looked at his daughter

and felt a bit trapped. Much like Helen, he was trying to tiptoe around all the things he wanted to say. If he followed his heart he would tie her to her bedpost, dig a moat, fill it with alligators, ring it with fire, and never let down the drawbridge to anything with a penis.

"Molly, you have to live your dream and not be sidetracked by this."

"So, look out for number one?"

"Something like that," Henry responded. "You should do this." Handing her back the photos. "I'll write you a check for whatever it costs." Getting up and walking to the door.

"Thanks, Dad, but if I do this with Jay, I'm going to do it myself."

"But I want to help."

"I know, but I have come this far by myself and I kind of want to see if I can follow through."

"How about a loan then? I don't want you to spend everything on this and not have anything left in the bank. Pretend I am the bank—I'll charge interest and everything."

"I'll think about it." Looking up at her father. "I love you, Dad."

"Me too. I'll see you later. And, Molly, you are so much more than sitting in this house hiding from the world."

Molly went upstairs to her room and placed the package on her desk. A missive holding the key to a potential future. Molly grabbed a hair elastic and turned to head back downstairs when she knocked her cell phone off the tabletop. She picked it up off the floor and realized she had not checked her messages all week. Molly picked up the phone and dialed in her voice mail. There were a few messages from random friends, and the last was from Liam's mother detailing his progress and where he was. Molly swallowed hard. Molly's hands were shaking as she placed the call. She hadn't talked to Elizabeth since the call from the hospital, and even though she knew she would be gracious and kind, it was difficult to dial. On the third ring a woman's voice answered.

"Hi, Elizabeth. It's me." Clearing her throat. "Molly."

"Sweetie, how are you doing? I was hoping you would call."

"I'm all right. It's been good spending time at home with my family."

"That baby must be coming soon. You all must be so excited."

"A few more months. We just found out it is going to be a boy."

"Wow, that is terrific. Your parents must be thrilled."

"Yeah, it's all pretty strange though—getting my head around my brother being a dad. I can't really imagine having kids now."

"When the time is right, you won't even think about it."

"Maybe."

There was a long silence after the pleasantries. Molly didn't know what else to say.

"So, I have to be honest, but I don't really know . . ."

"It's okay, Molly. All of us are a bit out of it lately." Trying to be supportive. "I keep wishing things were different. That I had done things differently."

"Me too." Choking up a little.

"Listen, Liam will be away for a few more weeks and then I guess the rest is up to him. I haven't been able to really talk to him, but when we rode up there together, he felt very clear and ready. I think he's going to pull through this."

"I'm sorry I had to leave." Choking even more. "I just had to. When I saw him in the hospital that night, I freaked."

"I know. I did too. It's not the place you ever want to see anyone you love. Complete bad dream."

"I know." Swallowing again. "I'm really scared, Elizabeth."

"So am I, honey. It's all pretty overwhelming. All I know is that I love him and all I can do is be there for him and hope he figures it out."

"I love him too, but it's just not that simple for me. There's been a lot to deal with. And now I know my parents are freaking out too. They are trying to be mature and calm and careful, but I can see it in their eyes that all this overwhelms them and scares them."

"I can understand that. Should I talk to them?"

"I don't know. Maybe later. I really just want to figure this out on my own."

"Molly, I want you to know that I know all about the car and all the other—how shall we say—incidents. He told me everything when I helped him pack for the center. He went on and on about how he is amazed that you have had this much patience."

"Me too."

"Sometimes I think he does all this crap to you, to me, to himself, on purpose," Elizabeth mused.

"What do you mean?"

"Well, you know that Liam's father split when he was five, and I think that in a lot of ways he has stayed that five-year-old boy inside. Stayed that small child who watched someone he loved more than pizza and comic books and sunny days just leave him. No matter how much I loved him and tried to prove to him that I was never going to leave, there has to be something in him that thinks when he loves something too much, it will up and leave one day."

"So he does everything possible to screw up and push away as a preventative measure?"

"Something like that. If he has an excuse like being too drunk or drugged up and you leave, then he has something to blame for it. It could then make sense unlike when his father left."

"But that makes no sense, Elizabeth. I don't want to hurt him, leave him. I love him."

"I know. Maybe he will figure all this out once he gets his head clear."

"Sometimes I think it is too late for us, but then I can't imagine anything without him. It's not like I'm so perfect myself, and maybe I am being too hard on him. I think there is also a part of me that subconsciously wants him to be fucked up."

"That, I don't understand."

"Like, maybe there's something in me that stays and allows all of this horrible behavior because it makes me look so together in comparison. Maybe I want him to mess up and come with his tail between his legs so I can stand on my pulpit and scold him and be right. Maybe it's my fault."

"Molly, it's no one's fault. And, yeah, maybe we all like to have poor little Liam, who is so blessed but can't seem to stay on the straight and narrow, be our fool, make us look better, but I think it's because we are used to it and we are scared to reevaluate our relationships. We're scared at what's to come."

"Maybe he won't love me if he's better," Molly said softly. "Maybe he'll see everything I hide beneath his addictions."

"Molly, I think he will only love you better."

"I just don't know what to do. I feel like I am in that Who song."

" 'Should I stay or should I go'? I think that was one of the first songs Liam learned to play," Elizabeth noted. "Everytime I hear it now, I cringe remembering how many times I had to listen to him."

"It does get a little grating."

"I do remember at the time being glad it wasn't 'Stairway to Heaven.' "

"Why is that the first song so many kids learn to play?"

"No idea." Laughing a bit. "Listen, Molly, whether or not you guys make it, I know my son loves you, I love you, and you have been a wonderful influence on him."

"Yeah, right! He almost dies under my loving eye and you think I am a good influence!"

"You are. You are loving and thoughtful. Every anecdote he shares of the two of you tells me how true-blue you are. He's getting help because of you. Wanting to save what you two have.

That's what is important. Imagine where he might be now if you hadn't eventually tried to change things?"

"Elizabeth, I have to go." Cutting her off. "But, I guess, fill me in?"

"I will. I really do think that he is going to be fine and pull through this. You know him, and once he sets his mind to something there is no stopping him. Take care of yourself, Molly."

"I will. 'Bye."

"Oh, wait, I forgot that I put something in the mail for you. You should get it soon. And, by the way, I loved those superhero dolls you had made for Liam. What a great idea."

"He showed you those? They are so silly."

"He brought them with him. Said something about them being his security blanket."

"Oh." Choking up slightly.

"Molly?"

"I'm fine, I'll look out for the package. 'Bye, Elizabeth. Thanks." Hanging up before she heard her good-bye."

Molly held the phone in her hand for a long time. The weight somehow was comforting. How can something made of plastic and wires relay every piece of news in the world? Each human emotion transferred to sound bites passed back and forth along a phone line. Imagine the days before Alexander Graham Bell. Urgent messages sent on the back of galloping horses. Was life then less insistent? Did it demand less because the speed of information was slower? Were horror stories or tales of good news duller since they had time to settle and cool before being shared? Were senses less acute without the constant bombardment of information? Sometimes Molly wanted to shut her eyes and stuff cotton in her ears just to keep the world a hand's distance away.

She felt uneasy. How could she have opened up so much to Elizabeth when she could only speak in fragments to her family? It seemed all mixed up. Should she have been so intimate, so fragile in talking to someone who could easily disappear if Liam did? Molly did feel lighter after allowing herself to free some of her thoughts, but she also felt more tender for letting them resurface so fiercely. It wasn't as if she had consciously picked Liam's mom to be her sounding board, it had just happened like a sudden leak in her resolve to process most of this on her own. Maybe she was using Elizabeth as a substitute for whom she really wanted to talk to, maybe it was time to let things out.

Molly also felt a deeper sadness when she hung up the phone with Elizabeth. One born in postcard memories of holidays, birthdays, and vacations spent becoming a new family. Elizabeth and Liam had all become part of her, part of her history. Their lives were inextricably woven together into a delicate pattern of love and loss. The dolls. He had brought the dolls with him. That touched Molly. She pictured them sitting on a tiny desk, in a tiny room, with Liam curled into an even tinier bed. Super Liam and Super Molly were watching over him as he slept and dreamed and craved.

Jay had found on the Internet a toy site that would fashion your own action figure. You could send the company pictures and details of what body, what hair color, and what outfit you wanted the doll dressed in. The company would then produce the toy and it would look exactly like the photos and specifications. Liam's birthday was a month or so away and Molly could not think of anything better for a comic-collecting, video-game loving, *Star Wars* accessorizing guy than a plastic doll emblazoned with his very own visage. Molly searched through various pictures one night long after Liam had fallen asleep. She collected a few of both of them from all angles and sent them in along with a copy of an "Archie" comic book. As much as Liam dug the more action-packed storyboards from the "X-Men" and

"Spawn," Molly knew that the first comic he had ever collected was "Archie," and Liam, unlike most, fell in love with idiosyncratic Jughead. He had Jughead sheets and even a lunch box. She was certain that he would love his face atop Jughead's gangly body, his head adorned with Jughead's pointy little cap. Molly would have herself transformed into Ethel and they would be a perfect pair.

Liam's birthday arrived and the two of them spent the whole day together. Breakfast in bed, having sex, laughing, shopping for dinner. That night Molly invited all of Liam's close friends—Elliot and his girlfriend, Maggie; Tom, Liam's drummer; and the other members of his band—to an intimate dinner party. Liam hadn't wanted a big shindig, thirty-one was not such an exciting age, so Molly thought this little party would be an ideal celebration. He helped her cook all afternoon, and they spent the time perpetually spinning in the bouncy chorus of their own infectious pop song. Love was in the air. The guests arrived, wine was drunk, food consumed, and all were satisfied. After Molly brought out the enormous chocolate-chocolate cake she baked from one of her father's recipes, Liam blew out the candles, plates were passed, cake was eagerly eaten, and Molly decided it was time for gifts.

"Okay, birthday boy, time for presents." Getting up from the couch. "It looks like you scored."

"Guys, you shouldn't have."

"Whatever, birthday's are no good without a little gift-giving." Elliot, answering. "Besides, you haven't opened them yet."

"So you're saying that your gift is going to suck?" Winking at his friend.

"You never know. Maggie picked it out." Squeezing his girlfriend's hand.

"Thanks a lot." She laughed.

"I'm sure I will love it, Maggie." Opening the small tie-shaped box. Inside were two tickets to the Hollywood Bowl for

Celia Cruz. "These are fantastic!" Getting up and kissing her on the cheek. "Thank you so much."

"Hey, what about me?" Elliot piped in.

"You said she picked them out."

"Yeah, but I wrapped them."

"Well then, thank you too." Giving his friend a pat on the back.

"Here, this is from all of us." Tom pushed toward Liam a very large, heavy, newspaper-wrapped box.

Liam ripped open the box and inside was a very old record player that had been reconditioned and now gleamed like a shiny penny.

"Wow. Where did you guys find this?"

"Some weird little music store on Sunset by the guitar center. The guy redid everything and it should run perfectly."

"I love it. Let's try it out."

Liam set the player down on the floor by their bookcase of records and picked from the stacks. Soon Bob Dylan filtered into the room.

"Sounds good." Liam smiled.

"He's going to be in front of that for the rest of the night." Molly laughed. "Baby, before you get sucked in, you have to open up my gift."

"There's more?"

"Yup, here." Handing him the balloon-printed bag.

Liam got up and sat back down on the couch next to Molly. He unwrapped the tissue paper.

"What are these?" Looking at the dolls.

"Look closely."

Liam held Jughead in his hand and rolled him around. He focused on the face and the hair.

"You have got to be kidding." Starting to smile. "Is this me?"

Molly nodded as Liam picked up the second figure and looked at the doll's face.

"No way!" Holding them up. "These are us!"

"Now you have your very own action figure."

"Molly, this is beyond cool." Kissing her. "Jughead?"

"Of course."

"You are so amazing for doing this and remembering."

"My pleasure."

Liam's eyes gleamed like a six-year-old high on too much sugar.

"Let me see," Elliot requested, and Liam handed him the dolls. "Molly, how did you get these made? I have never seen a personalized action figure before."

"There's this website that will make whatever you want. They do the mold from photos."

"They really look like you two."

"I know, it's a little creepy. I didn't think they would come out so well."

"What range of motion do you think they have?" Elliot asked as he bent the two together into a Spice Channel pose.

"Dude!" Liam grabbed the dolls away and unbent them. "Jughead and Ethel would never do it from behind."

"Are you sure about that?" Molly asked.

"Whoa, kids." Tom threw up his hands and stood up. "I think that's our cue."

"Mine too. Come on, Mag." Getting up and helping her up.

"Thank you so much for dinner. It was delicious," Maggie said.

"You are so welcome. Thank you for coming." Molly walked the entire group to the door.

"Thanks, guys." Tom kissed Molly's cheek and gave Liam a hug. "Happy birthday, buddy."

"Thanks. All of you." Hugging and kissing the rest.

Soon all the good-byes were made and their apartment was empty and swirling with "Tangled Up in Blue."

"So, about that position?" Eyeing her.

"What about it?" Eyeing him.

"Well?"

"You'll have to catch me first." Molly laughed and sprinted down the hall.

Liam ran after her but not before scooping the dolls off the table and tucking them under his arm like a football. The dolls never again left their bedroom and kept watch from the night-stand.

Molly sighed. Now they were watching Liam sleep alone. She wondered if they could tell she was missing. After a while, Molly got up and got dressed, stuffed the new pieces of jewelry she had made in her bag, and hurried to her car. She had promised Renee she would come help out again. The restaurant was having a huge private party tomorrow night and Renee had twice as much to do. Before Molly went to the restaurant, she parked the car outside of Sorella and popped in.

"Hey, is Susan around?" Asking the lovely dark-haired girl behind the counter.

"She's not in today."

"I have some more jewelry for her to take a peek at."

"You must be Molly. I'm Sarah." Extending her hand. "You make great stuff."

"Thanks. Why don't I just leave it all and Susan can pick whatever if any she likes."

"Sounds good."

Molly laid out her pouch and pulled the pieces.

"I love this one." Fingering the coral and citrine three-strand necklace.

"Me too. It reminds me of a sunset." Writing up a receipt. "I'll swing by tomorrow to pick up a check or the jewelry."

"Great. Thanks." Taking the paper and placing the pieces behind the counter.

Molly jumped back in her car and drove the few blocks to the restaurant. She was feeling a little lazy and knew the work ahead of her, so before she went in, she walked over to the bookstore across the street. She wanted to see if there were any books about all the shit she was going through. Some self-help book dealing with addictive and addicted musicians and the women who love them. She was curious to find out if any of Elizabeth's theories had some sort of psychological merit to back them up. She pushed through the heavy glass door of Chapter One and wandered into the appropriate section. She sat on the floor and began thumbing through books on the shelves: *Addicted to Love: Families Dealing with Addiction, Codependency: How It Hurts, When Loving Gets Too Hard*, et cetera, et cetera. Molly soon had a stack of books around her as she read through parts and chapters. She was so engrossed that she forgot all about the time and was startled by Renee's voice.

"So here you are. I have looked in just about every store." Sitting down on a chair next to Molly. "It's always nice when the help plays hooky."

"What time is it?" Looking up.

"Noon."

"Shit." Closing the book. "I'm so sorry, I've been in here for, like, an hour!"

"It's okay. I needed a little break anyway. Vanessa and Ashley are hard at work."

"I'm really sorry. I just thought I would check some stuff out."

"Think you are going to find answers in there?" Renee asked as she flipped through the titles.

"I don't know, maybe."

"I realized that we never finished our conversation the other day."

"It's okay."

"No, it's not. There's something I wanted to tell you, and I am not sure if I should, but I know you and I know your parents and I know that you are most likely going to go back to him, and everyone else is going to think you are nuts and stupid for doing it, but I don't and I understand because I did."

"You did what?"

"I stayed."

"Renee, what are you talking about?"

"Last year your brother cheated on me with some woman who came in for the holidays."

"What?" Molly's eyes widened.

"He was drunk at Whiskey's, I had stayed home, and he wound up at her place."

"I'm having a little trouble here. Are telling me that my brother cheated on you? That just doesn't compute."

"It didn't for me either."

"Why didn't you tell me?"

"I didn't tell anyone. It's your brother for heaven's sake! He told me right after it happened, he was crying and everything, and we worked through it."

"Renee, it couldn't have been so simple."

"It wasn't. For a long time I was angry and horrible to him and every day thought about leaving, but we kept talking about it and I decided that I loved him more than I hated him, and I tried to forgive him. Sometimes it is still there, I'm sure it will always linger, but him stupidly hooking up with some woman didn't end up being our deal-breaker. I thought it would be, but here we are, stronger and more honest with each other."

"Why are you telling me this, Renee?" Getting angry. "Why now after all this time? How am I supposed to deal with this? We are talking about my brother being a total shit! Am I supposed to just pretend I don't know?"

"You can do what you want in terms of your brother. I'm telling you this because I wanted you to see that every relationship has its demons, and people get past them, and that if you choose to continue this relationship with this man and accept these large flaws he has, I won't judge you. I understand that people are capable of much more than they ever imagine."

"So you shared this bit of family secrets for my benefit?"

"I guess. You're my best friend and, I don't know, I thought it would help. No one is perfect. We all make choices for ourselves no matter what anyone tries to tell you."

"My mom and I had a similar conversation the other day. And your telling me does help on some level, but Renee, you are also married to my brother, not some guy I get along with because I have to."

"I guess I didn't think it through." Hanging her head.

"No, Renee, you didn't, but my mom was also talking to me about my dad's flaws and I listened. I just, shit. All men suck!"

Both girls were quiet for a moment. Renee was torn between elation for finally being able to share with her closest friend and devastation for exposing Molly to a terrible truth about her brother.

"I was selfish to tell you. I really didn't think it through. I am so sorry."

"Stop, Renee. It wasn't. Don't apologize, this secret must have killed you. Like you said to me the other day, we are friends first, sisters second, and I really appreciate the idea behind this confession. I really do. I'll keep your secret and subtly be a bitch to my brother for a while, which he is already used to." Trying to smile. "I'm really sorry you had to go through all of that on your own. It must have been really hard."

"Yeah, it was." Wiping a small tear from her eye.

Molly stood up and gave Renee an awkward hug, then wiped off Renee's face with the tail of her shirt.

"Shall we go back to work, boss?"

"Yeah." Renee stood up slowly.

"It makes sense we are such close friends." Walking arm in arm to the door.

"Why?"

"Because we are both complete suckers for fucked up men."

"Our bonds are deep." Squeezing Molly's arm.

Molly walked with Renee back to the restaurant, her head

swimming with evil images of what she wanted to do to her brother: castration, starvation, humiliation. Why was everything playing out like a battle of the sexes? While by no means were all her ladies, herself included, without supreme faults, human flaws, and moments of bad judgment, it just was a fact that on this day, in this week, the ladies were smelling like roses in comparison.

nine

The front room of the restaurant was empty when Molly and Renee strolled in. Molly dropped her bag and keys behind the bar. Soft music floated out from the kitchen as they walked back.

"You found her!" Henry exclaimed.

"Not to hard in this town. She was lost in a book."

"Where's Mom?" Molly asked.

"I think she went on a hike or something."

"Looks like all the Stern women are playing hooky in the face of a fancy party," Molly commented.

"Perk of knowing the owner. She needed a little time today to wander. She'll be back in a bit." Winking at Molly. "Did you think any more about what we talked about?"

"Nope." Grabbing a carrot from the pile Alex was cutting. "It wasn't important or anything, was it?"

"Funny. Go get to work, I know that Renee needs your expertise." Flicking Molly with a towel.

The melodies of the front kitchen were in direct opposition to what Ashley and Vanessa had raging. Hole screamed from a little stereo. Courtney Love on volume ten.

"Hello, rage against the machine! What is going on?" Turning down the CD. "Feeling a little riot girl today? How can you guys work to this? The minute I leave here, it turns into a Hollywood club." Renee, teasing Vanessa and Ashley.

"It keeps us pumped up," Ashley answered.

"I will take your word for it."

Molly grabbed an apron and tied it on.

"Okay, Renee, so just tell me what to do and you can order me around for a few hours."

"Same as before, plus I need a double batch of biscotti. Make whatever kind you want." Tying on her apron. "Just nothing with hazelnuts, the new order hasn't come in."

"And the recipes?"

"On the back shelf."

"Got it."

"Good."

Molly again fell into the quiet kitchen dance, and the four women worked around one another gracefully. Molly was happy for anything that would calm her down. She wished she was an only child and not related to a cheating brother. Men could really screw things up. Even men who shared her last name. Everyone seemed to be capable of making completely bad decisions. Molly just didn't get it. To her, doing the right thing in certain scenarios, like where one puts his penis or what penis one lets into her vagina when you are in a committed relationship, seemed like taking a multiple-choice test with only one answer written on the page. Maybe Alex couldn't read. Molly would never look at her brother in quite the same way again. That made her sad—sad that he wasn't really as wonderful as Molly thought he was. Growing up and seeing your family members as just other people trying to get by really blows.

Time passed and the list of tasks grew smaller. Just when everything was either sliced, diced, baked, or caked, Molly knocked over a glass, tried to right it, shattered it instead, and felt a stab of warm heat. Not again. Molly looked down at her palm and, in an almost mirror position to her jewelry sale scar, a stream of bright red blood appeared. Molly quickly wrapped her hand in a dish towel and held it upright.

"I think we have a small problem." Trying to appear calm even though the pain started to spread.

"What?" Renee turned around and caught sight of the growing crimson stain. "Shit!"

Renee rushed to Molly and unwrapped the dish towel. The blood still flowed and the cut looked deep. A small piece of glass glinted from the ragged tear.

"That is going to need stitches." Rewrapping the cut. "Vanessa, you and Ashley can finish the rest."

Renee rushed Molly from the back and into the front kitchen. By now, Molly's hand had begun to throb and a simmering nausea crept up Molly's belly. She quickly leaned over and threw up into a trash can.

"What happened?" Henry cried. "Molly, are you okay?"

"She cut herself on some glass. It's pretty ugly."

"No big deal, I just happen to be a prime-A klutz. At least now I will have twin scars. Kind of like the Olsens."

"I'll get my keys." Undoing his apron. "Helen isn't back yet."

"I'll take her. We were almost done anyway and the girls can finish." Renee, asserting.

"Are you sure?" Henry looked at his daughters with concern.

"Dad, I'm fine." Molly leaned over and puked again. "Sorry."

Henry grabbed a plastic garbage bag from beneath the sink and handed it to Renee.

"Thanks. Wouldn't want to get puke all over Renee's car."

"Come on, let's go."

"Think I qualify for worker's comp, Dad?"

"Cute. My daughter the comedienne."

Henry helped situate Molly in the front seat, then kissed her on the cheek.

"I'll be home as soon as I can." Henry, continuing.

"Dad, you have the party." Molly, stating.

"I know, but . . ."

"Henry, I'll stay with her," Renee affirmed.

"Thanks, Renee."

"No problemo."

Renee drove fast and hard to the hospital. By the time they got there, Molly was even woozier and Renee had to help her out of the car. Molly's blood had seeped through the towel and had splatter-painted the front of both their aprons. Renee signed her in and soon Molly was again on a table with her hand propped, watching the doctor probe for glass.

"I think I'm going to be sick." Putting her free hand to her mouth.

"Here." The nurse handed her a pan. "Maybe you shouldn't watch."

"Maybe you're right." Wiping off her mouth.

"Molly, you have been getting sick a lot lately," Renee added from her seat in the corner.

"Is that so?" The doctor asked as he irrigated the wound.

"It's nothing. Just been feeling a little queasy every so often." Lying down on the raised bed. "How big was the glass?"

"I'll show you when I am done." Beginning the stitches. "I think you are going to need about six."

"Nice enough number."

"How often have you been throwing up?" The doctor asking.

"I don't know."

"It's been a few times in the last three weeks. Maybe five total," Renee answered.

"Man, you pay attention." Molly looked at Renee. "Must be MSP kicking in."

"MSP?"

"Motherhood special powers."

"Have you been taking any new medication? Or eating anything strange? It could be a side effect or an allergy."

"No, nothing new."

"When was your last period?"

"About a month or so ago." Molly, trying to count back.

"How 'or so'?"

"Maybe I'm a little late, but I have been traveling and let's just say stress is an understatement."

"Well, you are all set here. Nice piece of glass." Placing a bandage on her hand and showing Molly the shard. "Why don't I run a few tests and then you can be on your way."

"What? Like a pregnancy test?" Molly's face paled.

"That, and I will do some other cultures to see if it is bacteria of some sort. The nurse will draw some blood and if you can provide a urine sample, we will go from there."

"Fine, I do kind of have to pee." Sitting up and swinging her legs off the bed.

"Slow down a little, Molly," Renee asserted.

Molly stood up and took the cup from the nurse. She went to the bathroom and sat down. The twinge had returned and began attaching to every nerve in the base of her back. It slowly grew like a spiderweb, delicately lacing and coiling itself onto Molly's spine. There was no way in hell she was pregnant. Molly sat on the toilet and prayed for E. coli.

By the time blood was drawn, bloody aprons tossed in the

trunk, and Tylenol downed, Molly was in a state of panic. Renee
tried the entire ride home to elicit some sort of response, but
Molly just sat there, drugged and distressed.

"Relax. You probably have a stomach bug or something."

"Yeah," Molly responded halfheartedly. "Just a bug."

"The doctor said it easily could be a virus. No sense flipping
out until tomorrow."

"Okay, whatever."

Renee pulled into the driveway and helped Molly from the car.
They went inside, up the stairs, and Renee eased Molly out of her
dirty clothes. She fished in Molly's drawer for some pajamas.

"These okay?" Lifting out a pair of blue sweats and a faded
red T-shirt.

"Fine."

"Do you want to try to clean up a little?"

"I should." Looking at the spattered blood on her arms. "Can
you help me?"

"Of course. Sit tight and I will run some water in the bath."

Renee went into Molly's bathroom and ran a tub. Molly could
hear every sound amplified. The rush of water, the swirl of a
hand, the unfolding of a terry towel. Every quiet sound was a
cacophony blaring in Molly's ear. Even the whir of the air condi-
tioner made the hairs on her legs quiver with attention.

A few hours later Molly woke up and her hand felt like it had
grown into the Super Bowl blimp. It pulsed like a vibrator, only
it wasn't emitting stimulating beats. Molly slowly lifted herself up
and tread softly into the bathroom. Her hair was sticking out on
the left side and everytime she moved her arm she felt the
swelling pain. On the countertop was a bottle of Tylenol. Molly
popped two more, peed, and then carefully wrapped herself into
a black cashmere cardigan. Her mouth felt like sandpaper after
priming a summer deck. All she could think of was orange juice
and seeing if there was a chainsaw in the garage to amputate the
aching wound. When she got downstairs the living room was

overflowing with people. Renee was holding court from the couch with Abby, Lisa, and Corey. They were all in the midst of hilarity when Molly shuffled by and plopped herself on the couch next to Renee.

"Hi, guys." Trying to smooth her Medusa mane. "I guess our whole drink plan didn't work out too well. Sorry."

"No worries. We brought the drinks to you," Lisa answered as she got up and gave Molly a kiss on the cheek. "Margarita?" Tucking a wisp of her black bob behind her ear.

"Actually, just some juice. I just took some pain pills the doctor gave me and I wouldn't want to start drooling."

"Like senior prank night?" Corey got up to help Lisa and squeezed Molly's shoulder. "To this day I have never seen anyone puke up so much in so many colors."

"Thanks. Nice to see you too." Winking at Corey. "You were right there next to me, buddy. We both woke up facing the porcelain goddess."

"True, true." Laughing as he walked into the kitchen.

"How does it feel?" Renee asked, looking at Molly's wrapped hand.

"Like I wish I had a phantom limb."

"That bad?"

"Kind of. I'll survive." Readjusting. "Abby, where is Scott?"

"He had to work late."

"I haven't seen you guys in so long. I think since the wedding."

"Well, that's what happens when you move to LA, become fabulous, and start dating a rock star."

Renee tossed Abby a look, and Abby blushed with embarrassment. Her head of blond curls tumbled as she tried to recoup.

"I'm sorry."

"It's fine. I liked the fabulous part." Smiling at her friend. "Hey, Corey!" Yelling. "Think you could bring some food in here as well? I should probably eat something."

"I'll get it." Abby got up and pulled down her light blue work shirt. "I brought over some snacks, which now that I think about it was kind of stupid seeing whose house this is."

"It's a good thing. With the big party at the restaurant, there is zero food here. Plus, I never turn down snacks."

Abby got up to join the rest of the crew in the kitchen to assemble the poo-poo platter and Molly, feeling the effects of the medicine, tucked herself deeper into the couch.

"You didn't say anything about you know what to anyone?" Molly asked Renee.

"No, of course not. I told your parents that they stitched you up and everything was going to be fine."

"Ha!"

"Molly, just enjoy your friends tonight and we will go from there? Okay?"

"Okay." Leaning over and giving Renee a kiss. "Thanks. For this and before. I know you were trying to help and I am here for you too."

"Thanks. I feel a little shitty that I laid that on you about Alex."

"It does suck to know how absolutely awful my brother can be, but if you have learned to forgive him, which obviously you have seeing how your stomach continues to grow exponentially, then I can't create my own drama with him. I don't want to become one of those tsking friends who judge. It just is unfortunate that he lost some of his glow."

"I know, but it does slowly come back. New experiences, like our baby, kind of rebuff the surface and make everything shiny again. Maybe that will happen with you and Liam."

"Maybe, maybe I am not as forgiving, I don't know." Running her good hand over her hair. "By the way, how cute does Corey look? I love his hair longer." Changing the subject.

"I know. It almost makes me want to rekindle our torrid tenth-grade affair."

"What affair?"

"You remember. We made out for, like, a week in February before it all got too weird."

"No, I do not remember. Are you sure? Because I had a torrid affair with Corey junior year for about a week in March."

"That little prick!" Renee laughed. "I bet he made out with Lisa and Abby too."

"Perk of being friends with a group of girls."

"Did he do that weird tongue twirl?"

"Yes!" Shrieking with laughter. "Renee, what was that?"

"To this day I have no idea." Laughing harder.

Corey, Lisa, and Abby all returned to the living room carrying trays of beverages and food. They carefully placed everything on the glass coffee table and sat back down.

"What's so funny?" Lisa asked as she took a sip of her margarita.

"Did you ever make out with Corey?" Molly asked.

"What are you talking about?" Corey blushed ever so slightly. "Of course I did."

"Me too," Abby added. "Senior year fall."

"Senior prank night before the dueling pukers," Lisa noted.

"You slut!" Renee chided.

"I deny everything!" Blushing more.

"I can't believe you made out with all of us," Abby stated.

"What guy wouldn't have?"

"So you admit it!" Molly shouted

"Well . . ." Taking a large swig.

"Can I just ask one thing?" Lisa interjected. "What the hell was that weird tongue-twisting thing you did?"

Molly and Renee laughed even louder and harder, their giggles ricocheting around the room like rubber bullets. Soon all of the gang dissolved into the same hysterics and the evening progressed much the same way. At some point, Molly faded into the couch, and Renee and Corey had to help her upstairs. They settled her in her bed, turned out the lights, and left Molly to her dreams.

Molly woke up feeling hot pink and fleshy. Everything felt tender, like lips stung by a jalapeño. Her mouth was the Sahara and she crawled from the bed, tipped her head under the sink, and drank greedily. She ran some water for a bath and eased herself out of her clothing, being careful not to bump her hand. She slid into the tub and the hot water wrapped around her. Molly held her hand out of the water and looked at her nails. Some were still caked with blood. She took a washcloth and methodically cleaned her cuticles. The cut didn't hurt as much today—all that was left was a dull ache. Molly was used to dealing with those. Molly placed the washcloth on her head and rewound yesterday's activities. Talking with her father, Elizabeth, Renee, being at the restaurant, getting the stitches, seeing her friends, and then, the potential disaster awaiting her. It had been too big of a day and Molly felt turned around. She was definitely struggling to find which end was up. Her head was lolling about somewhere by her feet while her toes brushed the ceiling.

Molly thought about her parents and what this whole saga was doing to them. She could imagine them huddled together in their California King worrying about their only daughter. Wondering what they did to encourage her to get mixed up with a guy who lives on an edge not even they saw in their hippie pot-smoking days. Wondering if anything they say or do will push Molly one way or another, wondering if they should speak their minds or hold their tongues. Wishing that their daughter could have found some nice, normal man with a normal job and a less extensive list of problems. Wishing Molly had someone like Renee to come home to, someone who they knew would remain centered and supportive and forgiving in a way they would never fathom. Knowing that there was no way in hell Molly was going to listen to anything anyone says because she never has. Praying that Liam would love her better. Hoping things would get better.

Molly took a deep breath and went underwater feeling the need to be submerged and held down. She wanted to feel weightless, to feel nothing. She broke the surface and ran her healthy hand over her face to brush the water from her eyes. She stared at the ceiling and counted the tiles. There were twenty-five yellow ones. It was right then that Molly knew she didn't belong lounging in her childhood any longer. She was too old to be so young. And what if she was pregnant? What if some little thing was growing in her? Then what? What the hell was she going to do? Molly ran her hand over her flattish stomach and looked at her belly button trying to see what was inside. No way. It was just a bug, some sort of flu. She kept her hand there just in case.

Molly got out of the bath twenty minutes later, her whole body a giant prune. That was one way to tone down the fleshiness she had felt when she woke up. Suck all moisture from her skin. Nice illusion. Molly threw on some black yoga pants and a blue T-shirt. She sat down on the floor and folded her legs under her. She reached for the phone and dialed Jay's number.

"Did I wake you?"

"Sort of." Her voice rolling with sleep. "Hungover and in serious pain."

"What did you do last night?"

"Went out with Elliot and Maggie to some new club in Hollywood. Kind of fun, until Tom came in and started the whiskey train."

"You hate whiskey."

"Yes, but I love Tom."

Tom was a short, built guy with a shaved head and a tribal tattoo on his bicep. He and Jaycee had a yearlong flirtation going that went in circles.

"And?"

"And obviously nothing happened because I am talking to you, but somewhere last night I think I rolled my ankle."

"Oh, Jay. Do you think you fucked it up again?" Molly, worried.

"I don't know. I'm more into complaining about Tom."

"Jay."

"I'll go to the doctor tomorrow if it still hurts."

About six months earlier, Jay had microscopic surgery on her ankle. Something to do with decaying bones. They pulled some out, put in some tiny pins, and sent her home with crutches and a cast. Molly drove her home from the hospital, trying to avoid any jarring potholes. She half carried Jay into her apartment and settled her on the couch. Molly went to the kitchen to fetch some water.

"I still don't quite get why you planned this surgery when your parents were out of town," Molly called from the kitchen.

"I didn't. There was some emergency business thing they had to go to." Adjusting the pillows. "My mom was going to stay, but I told her I had you."

"Thanks." Handing Jay the glass and opening the bottle of pain pills. "I love playing nursemaid."

"I know. Plus, you know how my mom can cluck and I didn't want her to make a big deal out of this." Downing a few pills.

"Jay, it is a big deal. You can barely walk and you won't be able to drive for a few weeks." Molly groaned. "I can't believe I have to deal."

"You don't have to."

"Who else will? Such a pain. I'm going to have to change my whole schedule." Complaining.

"Look, I'm sorry to put you out!" Whining. "Just leave and I'll manage. Fuck!"

"Sure you will." Molly headed for the door.

"Where are you going?!" Jay cried. "You can't leave me alone! You wouldn't! Please!"

"You told me you would manage." Molly eyed her friend and knew she had taken her little joke too far. There was terror all over Jay's face.

"Relax, Jay." Kissing her friend on the head. "I'm just going to get my stuff." Starting to smile.

"What?"

"My stuff to stay here." Grinning. "You just have no humor today!"

"Must be the anesthesia."

"Had you going there for a minute."

"Kind of." Smiling. "You were being such a bitch."

"I would never leave you here all alone. Think of the guilt I would have to endure when they found you, prone on the floor with a head wound, and your nightgown bunched around your waist exposing your Hello Kitty panties."

"I don't own Hello Kitty panties."

"Liar!" Molly squealed. "I saw them in your panty drawer."

"Stop saying 'panty,' I hate that word. And when were you snooping in my drawers?!" Laughing harder.

"Panty, panty, panty!"

"Stop!" Jay yelled.

"Panty, I got your panties!" Molly, singing.

"Seriously, it hurts to jiggle."

"I'm sorry." Catching her breath. "I feel like I took some of your Vicodin. I'll be right back." Molly ran out of the house.

Molly stayed at Jay's for a few weeks, constantly shuffling clothes and beads between her and Liam's pad and Jay's while tending to her friend. Jay knew it was an inconvenience, but Molly never once complained and indulged in Jay's every whim. Pizza fests, ice cream for dinner, eighties bad movie marathons, and their very own version of *American Idol.* But Jay also knew that a repeat performance of Molly as perfect nurse was not going to happen if Jay drank too much whiskey and fell over in stilettos she wasn't supposed to be wearing. Molly would kill her if she reinjured her ankle.

"I promise I will go to the doctor. I'm sure it's fine."

"Okay, but you can't mess around with your foot," Molly scolded.

"I know, Mol. Can we change the subject?"

"Sure. How about this? I had a shit day yesterday."

"What happened?" Lighting a cigarette.

"I thought you quit."

"How did you even know?" Jay, wondering.

"Psychic."

"I have allowed myself one a day."

"Anyway, I sliced my hand open again and had to get stitches."

"Are you okay?" Her voice rising slightly with concern.

"Yeah, I'm just a big klutz."

"Yup. Cute doctor at least?"

"Yeah, right. That only happens on *Friends.*"

"I know." Sitting up and ashing. "Does it hurt?"

"A little. I'll survive." Molly, picking at the polish on her toes. "I got your package."

"And?"

"Fuck it. Let's do it."

"Really?" Jay chirped.

"Yeah. My dad thinks it looks great and convinced me to give it a go."

"YES!" Jay screamed. "I'm so psyched! This is going to be so cool!"

"Easy, I think you just blew out my ear." Laughing. "I'll be back next week and we can get started."

"You are coming home?"

"It's where I live."

"Good. I'll call the peeps right now, get the lease going, and tell my parents you are in. Molly, you won't regret this. It's going to be awesome."

"I know, partner."

"I like how that sounds." Getting even more excited. "I'll start on our business plan."

"What do you think for a name?"

"I think we should keep Annabelle. It's cute and already has an identity."

"Are you sure that you don't want something of you in it?" Molly asked.

"Definitely. When we open our second store for men we can use my middle name."

"Francesca?"

"Frankie."

"I like it. You're always three steps ahead."

"That's my job. Okay, I'm so excited and I have to pee."

"Go, we'll talk later. And take care of your foot."

"I will. Love you."

"Back at you." Hanging up.

Molly stood up and stretched. A smile formed across her face. It was the first in a while that seemed to have a mind of its own. Everything that had been burning before now just glowed and her color had mellowed to a dusty pearl. Today was a day of new beginnings. Today she would start afresh.

ten

Helen was sitting at the kitchen table reading the paper. Her glasses perched on the end of her slightly crooked nose.

"Hey, Mom."

"Honey, how is the hand?"

"Feels a little tight and sore, but not so bad."

"You were out cold when we got back last night." Getting up. "Breakfast?"

"Eggs would be cool."

Helen got up and began busying herself.

"Is everything ready for to-night?" Sitting down.

"Yeah, Dad was there so

late and he left early this morning. I just need to go in and finish setting the tables. The flowers should be getting in about now."

"It's going to be great."

"It better. It needs to be perfect. Besides it being a bunch of bigwigs from the Allen Conference, *Food & Wine* is covering it for the magazine."

"Cool."

"It's great for Dad and the restaurant. They are doing photos and the menu for the October issue. Should get us on the map as more of a foodie destination restaurant."

"It will. Can I come help? I'm a bit of a gimp, but I can still set silverware and smile."

"Of course. We'll go as soon as you eat. Dad told me Jay sent some pictures of a space. I love that she is so driven."

"Yeah, I called her and told her that I'm in. It seems a little insane and fast, but why not, right?"

"Exactly. I'm proud of you. It's going to be terrific." Coming over and kissing Molly's cheek. "It's time to start something new."

Helen placed some scrambled eggs in front of Molly and she gobbled them down at warp speed.

"Let me run up and put some real shoes on and then we can go." Rushing out of the room.

"Grab something nice for the party. And make sure you're wearing one of your necklaces," Helen called. "I forgot to tell you that the hospital called and they'll have all the tests back tomorrow. What tests?"

"The stomach thing." Yelling over her shoulder. "They think it may be a parasite or something." Lying.

Molly had one more day to live in blissful ignorance, believing that the thing growing inside her was parasitic, and she was not going to waste one minute of it.

When Helen and Molly arrived, the restaurant was buzzing like a hive. Waiters and cooks, aromas and noises, were swirling around creating a mixture of sound, sight, and smell. Photographers were setting up in one corner and a journalist sat writing down a copy of the menu Henry had planned. Helen walked right into the center of the whirl, introduced herself to the people from *Food & Wine*, and went directly behind the bar to fetch the vases for the tables. Helen was all business and could switch hats at the drop of one. Molly set her bag behind the reservation desk and disappeared into the kitchen.

It was even more insane inside. Alex and Henry worked at the stove, stirring their sauces while the other staff prepared their stations, covering vegetables with olive oil and garlic and tossing them into roasting pans. In the oven went one tray, out came another: beets, potatoes, tomatoes, asparagus, mushrooms. She walked farther back and Vanessa, Ashley, and Renee were busy making all the various garnishes for the desserts. Peanut brittle was being broken into bite-sized pieces, strawberries were being chopped and fanned, mint was being sectioned and set in ice water, and lemon bars were being arranged on platters. Renee had decided to do one plated dessert, a chocolate-banana cream pie with the brittle and fresh whip cream, and trays of smaller petits fours like the lemon bars along with truffles, small cherry tarts, mini peach cobblers, and pineapple upside-down cakes. She also had made a fresh mango sorbet for a palate cleanser in the middle of the meal.

"Hey, Renee." Molly, giving her a kiss on the cheek. "How's it going?"

"Fine, actually. Vanessa and Ash rocked last night and really got most everything done. We are all squared away." Brushing a hair from her eye. "Though this is definitely my last big event before the big event. How's the hand?"

"Okay, a little sore. I feel pretty useless."

"Don't worry. Yours were extra hands anyway."

"I'm going to go back out front."

Molly wandered back through the kitchen feeling a little like a fish out of water. She returned to the front of the restaurant and her mother had already set out all the vases, filled them with water, and was wrestling with the buckets of flowers that had just been dropped off. She pulled both buckets behind the bar and wiped her hands on her jeans.

"Molly, grab the scissors from that drawer over there and go get a garbage bag from the back."

Molly returned with the items and while her mother cut and directed, Molly placed the flowers in the containers. They were all yellow tulips. Helen was a purist. She liked tightly arranged bouquets with a single type of flower. Simple and elegant without the fuss of competing petals. While they were arranging, photos were taken, smiles interjected, and banter bandied about. The task was finished rather quickly and the two of them next set out to create the tables. All the tables had been lined up in the middle of the restaurant, creating a long one for the thirty guests. Helen placed white tablecloths down and then on top laid out patchwork quilts she had brought from home. Each quilt was different, but all of them had squares of pastel fabrics that contrasted with the intense yellow of the tulips. It was homey and modern at the same time. The napkins were all white and held firm with a collection of mismatched vintage napkin rings. The end result was fresh and accessible without being too quaint. Molly loved how her mother could pull things from different eras or genres and create a new whole. It was something Molly was lucky to inherit, and a source of Molly's inspiration when it came to her jewelry. After they placed a smattering of votives along the table, they were done and set about cleaning everything up so it looked perfect. They only had an hour before the guests would arrive.

With Tom the bartender's help, Molly and Helen went back to the freezer and grabbed the milk cartons Helen had placed inside a few days before. Within each was a bottle of vodka that Helen had then frozen into a block of ice and within the ice were suspended slices of lemons, limes, and grapefruit. They ripped off the surrounding cartons and exposed the ice sculptures.

"Mom, these are really cool." Setting down a bottle on the tray Tom had prepared. "Where did you come up with this?" Looking at the beautiful ice-encrusted bottle.

"I actually saw it on Martha Stewart."

"She always thinks up the best stuff."

"Except those ice candles we tried to make. Remember?"

"Last New Year's. They never froze right and all the fruit and leaves we put in fell to the bottom."

"I found them still outside when all the snow melted this spring."

"Aren't these sort of the same?"

"Yeah, but I think the carton helped keep the fruit wedged. It will be a great way to serve the cocktails tonight."

Helen, Tom, and Molly finished up, more photos were taken, and Molly slipped into the bathroom to change. She carefully pulled a black wrap dress around her and somehow managed to fasten a large coral necklace with a cameo around her neck. She also wound a piece of black lace ribbon around her bandage to camouflage her injury. Very Madonna circa 1986. She slicked her hair back into a bun, dashed on some makeup, and spritzed herself with perfume. She slipped on her nicer black thongs and went to the car to leave the bag of dirty clothes there.

The sun was setting and it was getting down to crunch time. Helen was ready when Molly returned from outside. Her mother was wearing a crisp white button-down and a long camel-colored suede skirt. She had on one of Molly's necklaces as well, a carnelian multistrand with tiger-eye leaves. A good mother always advertises. Helen selected some Andre Bocelli, dimmed the lights, and poured two glasses of wine. She handed one to Molly.

"No, thanks. I took a few Advil for the hand and I don't want to be any fuzzier. Also the stomach thing."

"Perrier?" Handing the wine to Tom.

"Sure."

"It looks great, doesn't it?" Helen asked as she surveyed her restaurant.

"It's going to be a wonderful evening." Toasting her mother.

Twenty minutes later, the party was in full effect. People were laughing and mingling, enjoying the ambience. Molly helped pass around the appetizers, small savory tarts with onions and Parmesan as well as fried potato chips with avocado-tuna tartar, balancing the tray on her good hand and holding napkins wedged in her bad. Helen served the iced vodka martinis and the guests seemed to enjoy everything. Then it came time to start the meal. A snicker arose when the guests sat down to read their menus. Henry had been right about them getting the joke of Molly's poem, and a little round of applause as well as a slew of typical responses like "This is just a poem, right?" wink wink were directed at Molly.

The meal began with a small purple potato, halved, and scooped out only to be refilled with a mixture of green onions, hard-boiled egg, and sour cream, then topped with a large dollop of Sevruga caviar. It was served alone on the dish, the purple contrasting with the white porcelain. Simple and clean. The second course was one of Molly's favorite salads. The roasted yellow beets were layered like a Napoleon with goat cheese and a variety of baby greens. Scattered on the plate were more greens and candied walnuts. Then the whole thing was dressed with a lemon and olive oil vinaigrette. So far so good.

Molly and Helen continued with the wait staff to man the front of the restaurant. Pouring wine and water, clearing plates, changing the music when necessary. They knew things were going well when the plates were returning to the kitchen practically licked clean. The next course was Renee's sorbet. Just something a little sweet and cold to liven up the palate. More wine was poured and several guests stepped outside for cigarettes. When everyone had returned, Henry sent out the next dish. Home-made ravioli stuffed with sweet peas and ricotta salata, topped with the roasted tomatoes, small slices of fried garlic, and basil. Five guests asked for another serving if there was one. With each course, Henry asserted his skill at crafting fine flavors using fresh ingredients. He let the food speak for itself as opposed to drowning it in a sea of herbs and sauces. Everything was clean and tasted as it should. The guests had two choices for entrees: trout, of course, seeing how it was Idaho, roasted in the oven and served with vegetables and a turnip puree, all glazed with a balsamic reduction, and lamb, pan-seared crisp then finished in the oven, served with a mushroom bread pudding and summer vegetable ragout.

Molly went into the kitchen where the *Food & Wine* writer was huddled on a stool, sampling the dishes. From the look on her face, this piece was going to be glowing and definitely place Helen's on the map. Molly smiled and as if in an instant, everything felt lighter. She took a deep breath and knew all of her was now on the mend. Seeing success for her family and watching how they all worked together to produce this major high was ecstasy. With a little hard work, people's stomachs and hearts could be fed.

"Have you eaten yet, honey?" Henry asked his daughter as he wound down the service.

"Nope, and I'm starved! Everything looked so good, Dad."

"What can I make you? Alex, what do you want?"

The waiters walked past Molly holding Renee's desserts. Each looked like a little gift.

"The lamb, please. And if you have any more ravioli," Molly answered.

"I'll have the same, Dad," Alex added as he began closing down his station.

"Coming right up." Henry fixed his kids some dinner as the last plates were brought to the guests.

"Here." Serving them both a dish.

"Join us?"

"I think I will." Serving himself a plate as well.

Molly, Alex, and their dad sat on three little stools by the stove and greedily sucked back their meals. Molly looked up at her dad, then at her brother, and smiled. Another flash, another still moment captured, and Molly breathed another sigh of relief. About five minutes later, Helen came in.

"Henry, Alex, you guys outdid yourselves." Kissing Henry hard on the mouth and squeezing her son's shoulder. "They're asking for you both."

Molly stayed in the kitchen and could hear the applause. She could hear her father's humble voice, his easy laugh, and Alex's lower chuckle. Her mother's glow could almost be seen hovering around the kitchen door. This was a moment for them, and Molly was glad to have been a part of it. She had been gone for too long. Renee came and sat down on the stool beside her. She hadn't been down for but a second before Helen came in again.

"Renee, come on. They want to meet the maker of that banana cream pie."

Renee slowly stood and followed Helen. This time Molly poked her head out the door and watched. With a mental camera, she captured this moment too, and bore witness to the glory of her family.

When she got home, Molly finally picked up her journal and scribbled away. She gushed about her family and what it meant to her to be a part of something like that. She even gushed about her brother and knew that Renee had been right about new things coming up that replace the bad. She wrote about how complete she felt in their presence, how she had forgotten how much better she felt around them, how much she missed them when she was away, even though she knew that being away was where she belonged. As much as they loved her, Henry, Helen, and Alex were a three-pronged fork, and Molly was the spoon.

They had become a team, and Molly could only watch them from the sidelines and cheer loudly. Molly wasn't sad about it, surprisingly. There was no sense of not belonging, she just belonged somewhere else, and that was okay. Was that other place by Liam's side? There were too many questions, too many things that Molly couldn't yet figure out. Was she really ready to give up on Liam, on the life they had, on his mother, on the relationships she had invested in and spent time nurturing? Did she want to flip on the TV one day and see her life living on without her? She wrote until her good hand got tired, then closed the lavender notebook. She traced her fingers softly over the cover. Liam had bought it for her a few months ago. Journal writing was something they shared. It was something that bonded them early on in their relationship.

Molly remembered coming home one day when they had been living together for a while. The apartment was alit in candles and smelled like cookies. Liam was sitting on the couch surrounded by journals, all classic old-school black-and-white composition books. They were ordered, labeled, and neat.

"What's this?" Molly asked as she walked in and sat down next to him.

"Well, I wanted to share with you some stuff."

"Stuff?"

"Me, really." Pulling her closer. "I want to share myself with you, and these," gesturing to the books, "are all of me."

"Wow." Picking up a notebook. "I have an idea." Setting it down and getting up.

Molly went into their shared office and grabbed a large brown box from within the closet. She carried it into the living room and sat it and herself on the floor. She opened it and removed all of her journals. They were all different, a melange of color and texture, size and ornamentation. In comparison to his, all uniform and crisp like a Gucci store, Molly's were bursting with flea market chic like a David LaChappelle photograph. It was kind of amusing.

"You show me yours, and I'll show you mine," Molly stated. "But, first," sniffing, "are those chocolate chip?"

"Of course." Getting up and retrieving a tray filled with milk and cookies from the kitchen.

"I love you."

"I know." Winking at her.

"Okay, even though this is your thing, can I go first?"

"You never have any patience." He chuckled. "Did you go look for your Chanukah presents before they were wrapped?"

"Of course! Don't tell me you didn't search high and low before Elizabeth put your Christmas presents under the tree?"

"Never."

"You are such a liar."

"You're right." Laughing. "Mom had to get a padlock to keep me and Teddy out. We knew the minute it went on the closet that it was Christmastime."

"So, can I still go first?" Batting her eyes.

"Ah, a sucker for those baby browns. My secrets can remain hidden for a minute or two longer."

"Pick one, and open a page." Pointing to her collection. "That way we are not sitting here reading everything from fifth grade on."

"Sounds good." Liam slid onto the floor and pondered his selection, his hands running over the covers like a blind man reading Braille. "This one." Handing her an Italian handmade journal with brown-and-red swirling paper. "First entry, please."

"I think this is from senior year of high school. Abby gave it to me for Chanukah." Taking the book and opening it. "I remember thinking how cool a gift it was because it showed how much she knew me. It sort of cemented our friendship. Anyway, okay, here goes."

Well, it's a new year, so of course there's a new guy and another rejection. I decided to tell him directly how I felt and stuff because rumors got started. I am amazed how brave I have become. I really like being more forward and honest, nothing weighing me down. He was cool about it and not weird, but he likes us being friends, nothing romantic. Is there something so horribly wrong with me that all the guys I like don't like me? I want to fall in love so badly and be loved in return. I hate being alone. Well, that's not true, I just think there could be more that I am missing. The worse thing about nice guys is that even in rejection, they care about how you feel and are nice. It makes you like them more and more as they tell you no! Shit. I am frustrated. I hate him, no I hate that he doesn't like me, but you can't hate someone for that. It's life and how much did I really like him anyway, spur of the minute crush. Yeah right!! It hurts, I'll get over it. Soon, I'll be back in the saddle (this weekend, ha ha). Later.

"I am pathetic!" Molly groaned.

"No, you were so brave. I could barely talk to girls back then much less tell them I dug them. I think that is an amazing quality about you. You are fearless in your emotions."

"Thanks." Blushing. "It's weird, but that's the only place I am fearless. I think I wrote something about that. Where is it?" Looking through the journals. "Here, this was when I went abroad to paint in Paris after college."

I think I am a person that thrives on change and stimulus. I am not a physical thrill seeker but a mental and emotional one. I don't jump off planes but I hop on them and then go it alone. It's hard to sever ties with your life on purpose. It's kind of nuts and brave and intense. I am choosing to say good-bye, see ya later, take care. I am choosing

to go it alone. That's a fucked up choice and totally amaz-
ing at the same time.

"Has it been hard for you being with me all this time? It sort
of goes against your whole need to leave and change. No more
Molly in perpetual motion."

"All of this, you, me, living together, has been a huge emotional challenge in itself. A trip of some kind, I guess."

"For me too. I think that loving someone is the biggest, riski-
est, most intense adventure you can take." Running his hands
through his hair. "I didn't think I would ever be brave enough to
do it."

"What about all that stuff you told me the first night we met?"

"What did I say?"

"You went on about how all guys aren't weird about coupling
and you have to jump in and let yourself be vulnerable and feel
love to feel anything at all."

"Oh yeah, I remember. I probably was trying to get in your
pants."

"You suck!"

"I'm kidding." Kissing her cheek. "I think I knew that there
was something about you the minute I saw you. It made me say all
those things and want them to be true."

"My turn." Blushing more. "This one." Handing him the
book open to a page.

"Senior year as well."

I quit the baseball team. I want time to be with friends,
play music, do other things with my life. I'm burned out.
No more awards to win, things to prove. The joy of playing
is gone. The guys are going to kill me. Fuck it. Coach was
cool, sort of, not really. He's one of the reasons I quit so
who cares what he thinks? He's an asshole, plays favorites,
picked some junior to be captain after all the time I put

into the team. Maybe I am being an asshole myself, not a team player. Whatever. They lost today and I was happy. I am a dick. Besides working on my music, I am acting in a play. A musical. Never done it before because it was always baseball season. I hope I don't suck. Guys will give me shit for that as well. Can't win.

"I didn't know you played."

"Yep. Shortstop."

"I was an all-star pitcher myself."

"Really?"

"Yup. Did everyone give you a hard time?"

"Yeah, especially since I had to wear these tights for one of my costumes. What did one of my friends say? 'Guys do not let guys wear tights.'" Closing the book.

"I bet you look hot in tights."

"I'll show you later. So, more?"

"Sure."

"I like that book over there with the pink flowers."

"That was the one I finished right before I met you."

"Cool, I can see the you before the us." Opening a page in the middle.

I am in that blissed out state of sleeping too little and feeling too much. I slept at John's last night for the first time. We only made out, then fell asleep cuddling and it was great. I was nervous at first because when we talk it's really intense, no flirtiness, nor easiness, it's interesting and deep and kind of cold. Not emotional in a fuzzy sort of way. It made me think he wasn't into me in "that" way. But when he kissed me . . .

"Why am I reading this to you?" Shutting the book and looking up. "It feels weird."

"It is a little weird. John's the guy you broke up with when we got together?"

"Yeah. The guy who ceased to exist after we met."

"But it seems like you liked him a lot."

"I did, but after a while all that intellectual intensity minus the comfortable easy thing gets to be tiring. I just wanted to be sexy and spontaneous instead of always having to talk everything to death."

"So you're saying I'm not as smart as him?" Kind of hurt.

"No!" Grabbing his hand. "Of course not. You're just easier to be myself around. Like, we can talk about politics and art and then be goofy and watch *Blind Date.* With him, everything was so explained, so planned out. Our relationship was like a mental chess game and seldom were any moves unexpected or really that physical. I never felt like I could just be free. You let me be me, you feel like home."

"You too. When I am with you, I feel like you see me completely for who I am. From the minute I met you, Molly, you were this light that I could stare for hours at without blinking. Listen to this." Pulling out a book.

I met this girl last night. Molly. Freckles and the greatest smile. There is something about her, it's weird. The moment I looked in her eyes it was like I could see right through her. Not in a she is empty way, more like I could see all of her and then all of me reflected back. It freaked me out. Everything changed in that one minute. The smells, the air, me. It feels like I came home. That I have known her forever. Fuck! This is nuts. I have known her for a handful of hours and I'm tripping out. I close my eyes and her smile is there, just hanging out in my head. I hear her voice everywhere now, like we have been talking everyday for our whole lives. I am not making sense. Is there love at first sight?

"How did I get so lucky?" Molly asked. "Sometimes I wonder why you love me so much. I look at us and I think I'm in someone's big practical joke and soon it'll be exposed and you will in fact not exist. You're just a figment of my imagination."

"That's crazy." Looking at her. "It drives me nuts that you are so untrusting of this, of us! Do you not know how strong you are? How loving? How beautiful inside and out? You move away from your family whom you are so close with. You hustle and work, and you don't take everything your family wants to give you. You do it for yourself, by yourself, you start a business that is flourishing. You take care of me, feed me, make sure the bills are paid, see every one of my shows that you can, listen to my crappy first-draft songs, help me when I hit a wall. You listen to me, to Jaycee, to all of your friends. You do all this and you still think you aren't perfect and need to be more. Just being you is perfection."

"Wow." Molly was almost rendered speechless by his praise.

"Wow, is right. Where did all that come from?" Smiling at her, blushing. "Little intense?"

"Just a little."

Liam leaned over and kissed her long and hard.

"This is real," he said, looking in her eyes.

"I know." Looking at him.

"Do you?"

"Yeah, I do, and maybe that is what makes me think it's only a dream." Holding his face in her hands. "So it seems like we are stuck with each other."

"Forever."

The kiss they then shared was different from all others. Molly felt like she was melting into him, merging. Molly felt safe and solid and part of something that would grow and nurture her for the rest of her life. The kiss tattooed itself onto her and no other pair of lips would ever be a match.

Molly laid her head back on her bed and ran her fingers again over her journal. She knew that no other man would fit her like he did and that scared her. She let out a sigh. In a lifetime of forgettable men, Liam would always remain. Together or apart, she would never be free from him because in him she saw herself. They were each other's mirrors, soul mates. She knew right then that she was going back and she knew she was setting herself up for whatever came. Despite the voice within telling her to cut her losses, be tough, move on, there was a louder, more trained operatic aria telling her that she couldn't just leave without giving him an opportunity to set things straight. Yes, she had in the past made deal upon deal, promise upon promise, with herself and with him, but somehow knowing he was getting help, admitting the problems he had couldn't be solved all by himself, working on a solution, cleaned the slate—or at least washed off the old chalk. Maybe she was being naive or stupid, but those were her choices.

She also knew that she had to be strong enough to withstand the next chapter because she had to be with him. She just had to be. Whoever ran things out there, whether it was God or Fate or whatever, wouldn't have had them connect in such a profound way, only to make it so they could never be truly solid together. Also, "they" wouldn't make it virtually impossible for Molly to steer clear of Liam, if in going back she was setting herself up for total and complete destruction. She was a good girl from a good family who, even though she had bouts of self-doubt and drove the people close to her nuts with her lack of self-confidence, she deserved a shot at happily ever after. She prayed she could feel safe again inside his arms and trust him with her heart. If they could rebuild that, maybe they could survive. Maybe. Molly fell asleep easier that night than all the others that had come before.

eleven

The next morning when Molly woke up, she had this desperate need to connect with Liam. She needed to hear that he was okay and getting stronger. She had decided that she was going to support him, or at least try to. She still wasn't ready to talk to him directly, she hadn't planned the perfect conversation—or really the monologue she was going to deliver. Another call to Elizabeth would do the trick. Elizabeth would tell her enough to get her up to speed. Molly picked up the phone and

dialed Elizabeth's cell. It rang three times before being answered.

"Hello." A male voice answered.

"Um, hi. Is this Elizabeth McGuire's phone?" Not registering.

"It's me, Molly."

"Liam?" Molly choked.

"Hey, baby."

Molly was tongue-tied.

"Molly? You there?"

"Yeah." Clearing her throat. "I'm here. Where's your mom?"

"In the bathroom. She left her bag."

"I thought you couldn't have visitors."

"That was only the first week. No contact until you've detoxed and had some heavy doses of therapy."

"Oh."

"How are you, Mol? I miss you." His voice was light and normal.

"How are you? How are you feeling?" Molly bounced back.

"Better, stronger. It's been good to talk through some stuff and I feel clearer. But it's kind of crazy in here. You should see some of my compatriots in this getting clean thing. They have some wild stories." Trying to catch her up.

"Good." Still unable to come up with more than one-word responses.

"So, again, how are you? How's home? What's up? The last time we talked things weren't too pretty. They kind of sucked and I'm sorry."

"No, they weren't, but I'm fine."

"Fine? You're fine. Can't you elaborate a bit on fine? I've been waiting to talk to you again." His voice finally cracking. "It's been too long, baby."

"I don't know, I feel better, calmer, fuck. I don't know," Molly stuttered. "Listen, I have to go, my parents are calling me." Lying.

"Molly, don't hang up, please. I have so much to say to you. I love . . ."

"I gotta go. Glad you are feeling better. 'Bye." Hanging up quickly.

Molly slammed down the phone. Her hands were trembling. What she just did could be the video shown in the dictionary next to the verb "to choke." What was wrong with her that she couldn't have an adult conversation with a man she had just spent more than two years with? He sounded like himself, so normal, so strong, so real, so unexpected. She blew it, unable to give in, unable to articulate. Maybe her heart had decided to listen, but her head and ears had yet to catch up. She took a deep breath and headed downstairs. The whole family was gathered around the table. She tried her best to plaster a smile on her face and toss off the previous ten minutes.

Henry had decided to keep the restaurant closed and give everyone a day off. Pancakes and muffins were on the table along with eggs, bacon, bagels, and lox. Every possible breakfast food. The Sterns' Vegas-style buffet theme was alive and well in the kitchen. Everyone was quietly eating when Molly grabbed some juice and sat down next to her brother.

"A toast." Raising her glass. "To my family who seriously kicked ass last night."

"Cheers." Halfheartedly.

They all weakly clinked glasses and kept eating. Something felt off.

"What was the final verdict, Dad?" Pushing through the thick air.

"Everyone loved it. I booked another party in a few weeks, the restaurant is booked for the rest of the week, and instead of just a two-page piece, *Food & Wine* is extending it to a feature. We are going to have six or so pages plus recipes in the October issue."

"That's so cool!"

"It is, isn't it? Who would have thought a lawyer could become a gourmet chef?"

"The gamble paid off." Helen, stating.

"It sure did." Henry looked at his wife. "Mom tells me you decided to go for it with the store."

"Yeah, I told Jay yesterday."

"What store?" Alex asked.

"Jaycee and I are going to open a boutique in LA. Jewelry, obviously, and clothing. She found this great space."

"So you're leaving?" Renee asked.

"Yup, in a few days."

"I kind of thought that you would stick around a little longer."

"Me too," Alex added. "I mean, I'm excited about the store, but it just seems like everything was crazy in LA. You ready to go back?"

"I think so. I have to. It's where I live. I'll be fine."

"What about Liam?" Alex asked and everyone glared. "What? It's not like all of you weren't thinking it."

"I don't know." Lying because she already knew she was going to give him another chance, she just wasn't ready to tell. "All I know is that I can't hide out forever."

"Are you going back? Are you going to get back together?"

"Alex." Renee raised her voice. "Chill out with the third degree."

"Let's just enjoy our breakfast." Molly tried to change the subject.

"Look, we are all just looking out for you. You show up here out of the blue, all freaked out and upset because your boyfriend is a drug addict and almost dies, and then you tell us you are going home just like that." Alex, raising his voice. "You should also know that Mom talked to Elizabeth this morning and we know everything."

"What does that mean?"

Molly wished she had gotten up earlier and intercepted that call. It seemed she had missed by mere minutes. Elizabeth probably chatted with her parents right before she went to the bathroom and left her phone in Liam's grasp.

"Stop avoiding. The accident, does that ring a bell?" Yelling at her.

"Alex, come on," Renee pleaded.

"No, someone has to say something!" Yelling louder. "All of you are walking on eggshells, but I just can't. You all have been the whole time she has been home. She's not going to break! Molly, what the fuck are you doing?!"

"Stop screaming at me!" Molly cried. "What the fuck is your problem?"

"My problem is that my sister forgot to mention to any of us that she almost died in a fucking car accident!"

Molly's face paled and all the air got sucked from the room. She felt like she was in one of those infomercials demonstrating vacuum packaging, only she wasn't holding the gadget but being sucked into the bag choking on latex.

"It wasn't that bad." Bursting into tears.

"Molly." Helen came over and put her arms around her daughter. "Alex, please, you aren't helping."

"Mom, and coddling her is? Hello, Earth to Mother. He almost killed her. Don't just let this go. Molly, how can you forgive all that!? You are such an idiot!"

"It wasn't like that," Molly stuttered. "And you should not be lecturing me on forgiveness seeing how you yourself have been the recipient of someone else's."

"Molly, please don't," Renee pleaded.

"What are you talking about, Molly? This is not about me," Alex yelled.

"What this is about is loving people who fuck up and hurt others and fuck around on them and are forgiven because no one is perfect and maybe together is better even if it is flawed.

You, my dear brother, fit into that little equation rather perfectly."

Alex's face blanched and he looked at his wife.

"Yes, I know." Molly, continuing. "And you should not be so high-and-mighty judging someone else's relationship."

"What is all this about?" Helen asked. "Alex?"

"It's nothing, Mom, she's just trying to deflect."

"Fine, play it that way." Molly shook her head. "I don't care."

"Alex, let's go for a walk." Renee grabbed her husband by the shoulder.

"No." Refusing to budge and knocking her hand away.

"Now!" Glaring at him.

Reluctantly, Alex got up and left Molly with her parents in the kitchen. Henry came to the other side of Molly and sat down. Molly was trying to calm down.

"The accident wasn't really like that."

"Why don't you tell us what happened then," Henry told his daughter.

Molly wiped her face with her hand and steadied herself. It had been four months since the accident. Long enough to forget, but then again, not long enough to really pretend like it never happened. It had been a Wednesday night like any other. Molly had made them an early dinner because Liam had a special show later and she knew that if he didn't eat he would be hungry. They had steak and a salad with this new miso dressing Molly had found at Whole Foods. It was a good meal, and Liam left to go set up. He took her car—bigger trunk space—and Molly was getting a ride from Jay. He wasn't playing until eleven so she took a leisurely bath, had a glass of wine, and got dressed. Jeans, a Harley-Davidson belt Liam had bought her at the flea market, and a green, striped chiffon, off-the-shoulder top. Jay picked her up around ten and they went to Small's, a tiny, very hip, very cool new bar that Elliot opened near his restaurant. Liam was doing the unannounced gig as a favor to his friend, and it was a good way to test out some new songs for the second album.

It was already crowded when they got there. Word spread fast in LA. Elliot had saved them a table by the small stage. The place could maybe hold a hundred people max and it was full. Familiar faces abounded, including Zander and Elena. Both smiled meekly when they caught her eye and flew quickly to the opposite side of the bar. They all had reached a silent agreement to just ignore each other and back off. Liam barely saw them anymore so Molly felt like she had won. Childish, but it still made her smile inside. Jay grabbed them some drinks and the night wore on. Liam played, it was great, Elliot was happy, and soon it was time to go.

"You want me to give you a ride home?" Jay asked.

"Let me check and see how long Liam is going to be." She hopped off her seat and walked over to her boyfriend. "Baby, what's your ETA?"

"Soon, I think—stay. Let's go home together."

"Okay."

Molly walked back to Jay.

"I'm going to wait."

"Cool. Goodnight, my dear." Kissing Molly on the cheek and making her way out of the bar.

About a half hour later, Molly and Liam finished packing up the car and were ready to go. Molly was a little tipsy, so maybe she wasn't paying as close attention as she should have to Liam. He pulled the keys from his pocket and started the car up. He leaned over and kissed Molly hard on the mouth. He banged her teeth with his.

"Ow." Pulling her hand up to her mouth. "Easy, Tiger." Tasting a little blood.

"Oh, baby, I'm sorry." Clenching his teeth slightly. "Didn't mean to." The words sort of jumped out of his mouth like hot popped corn.

"Are you okay?" Looking at him, wiping her mouth.

"Yeah, fine. Why?"

"You're a little jumpy."

"Just pumped from tonight. It was cool playing some new stuff. I had a really good time."

"Me too. It was a good show and it was great for Elliot."

"The place is going to do real well." Overenthusiastically. "Did I cut you?"

"Yeah, just a little. I'm fine."

"I'm really sorry." Grabbing her hand and squeezing hard. "Can't wait to get you home."

"Liam." Prying off his fingers. "You may break me."

"Let's just go."

If Molly had been totally with it and not in her own little fuzzy bubble of a few drinks, she would have seen his eyes twitching, dancing, and his fingers tapping out the cha-cha on the steering wheel. Instead, she turned on the radio and sat back in her seat. About halfway home, in the middle of her favorite Ja Rule song, everything jerked left, then right, and it suddenly felt like the car was slipping. Molly looked up and thought she was cruising the length of a Slip 'n Slide or maybe lying flat in the middle of a spin art machine. She turned her head toward Liam and then there was the crash. The next thing she remembered was hearing her name.

"Molly! Molly!" Liam yelled.

"I'm okay." Opening her eyes and mentally cataloguing her body. Her back felt funny, like something had untied. Pain slowly spread out and wrapped around her like a sarong. Her wrist felt limp, something had snapped. "Oh, shit." She looked at Liam, who had a cut on the side of his forehead. Blood was running down his face. "Liam, you're bleeding!" Momentarily ignoring her back and hand.

"I'm okay. Are you okay?"

"I don't know." Undoing her seat belt slowly with her good

arm. "But, baby, you're bleeding." Grabbing her sweater off the floor and holding it to his face. "What happened?"

"I fucked up."

"What?"

"I'm fucked up. I fucked up," he kept repeating to himself. "I fucked up."

"Calm down. Take a deep breath."

Molly gingerly got out of the car and tried to stretch her back. No amount of yoga forward bends were going to fix this right now. The pain was starting to swallow her, and she had to catch her breath. Her wrist was definitely broken. She wiped the tears from her eyes, then looked around, fearing what she was going to see. Another car, more blood, major damage; instead, the front passenger side of the car was up on the curb with two large metal garbage cans crushed under the wheel and the front bumper smashed deeply into the base of a cement light. They had hit the curb, the cans, and finally plowed into the light. No one else was around: it was just them with a majorly dented car—her car, no less—on a small street near their home. Thank God they only had contacted inanimate objects; someone was on their side. Even though Molly felt like storm-preventing burlap bags were layered on top of her entire body, she knew they were lucky. Molly carefully walked around the car and opened Liam's door. Somehow, she was in caretaking mode, only able to focus on Liam. Visible blood took precedence over invisible broken bones. She took the sweater off his head to see if he was still bleeding. It had almost stopped, but it looked like it needed stitches. His brow was also beginning to swell a little and a bump had formed under the cut. Tomorrow, it would be a first-class shiner.

"I fucked up." Repeating.

"It's just an accident. Just some cans. It'll be fine, but Liam, we need to go to the hospital."

"No, we can't!"

"We have to. They should check your head. You could have a concussion. You might need stitches." Trying to calm him down. "And I think I'm really screwed up."

"No! Molly, you don't understand. I'm fucked up. I took a bunch of E." Casting his eyes down.

"Excuse me?" His words hitting her like firecrackers.

"I took some E at the bar, two hits. I thought I could get us home before I started rolling. I've driven on it before. I've been fine. But I thought I saw something and I turned the wheel too hard, and lost control."

"You fucking asshole!" Molly, igniting. "Why didn't you tell me? Jay could have driven us both home!"

"I'm telling you now."

"Oh, fuck. I can't even believe this." Walking away from him. "Okay, deep breath, Molly." Talking to herself as she ran her good hand over her back.

Her wrist was starting to throb. Memories of second grade and her pretending to be Olivia Newton-John in perfect *Xanadu* mode skating around the driveway and wiping out flashed. What the fuck! She brought her fingers to her face and held them there for a while hoping the cool pressure of her palm would transport her up and away from this disaster. When she brought them back down to her side and opened her eyes, she had not pulled the Dorothy she had wished for. She walked back.

"Can you get out, please?" Calmly.

"Yeah." Undoing his seat belt and getting out. "I feel fine. My head just hurts a bit."

"To be honest, I really don't give a fuck how you feel. Just get out and get in the other side, so I can get us out of here before people come out and start poking around." Completely sobering up.

Liam fully exited the car and walked to the other side of the curb while Molly got into the car and reversed slowly. She felt the cans loosen and she called out the window to Liam.

"Dislodge the trash cans and get in."

It took him a minute or so, since the cans were still somewhat caught under the bumper. Soon he got in, buckled, and Molly put the car into DRIVE. Luckily, it ran fine, and Molly eased them off the curb and drove them home very slowly. She parked and without saying another word, nor looking at the full damage done to her car, walked into their apartment. Liam quickly grabbed his guitar from the back and followed after her with his tail wedged firmly between his legs.

"Look, Molly, I'm sorry." Trying to get her attention. "I'll pay for whatever it costs."

"Save it. I can't even listen to the sound of your voice." She carefully walked into the bathroom, gritting her teeth in pain, and returned with some bandages, antiseptic, a bottle of Advil, and some ice. "Sit down."

Liam sat and Molly tended to his wound as best she could with one hand. She was a picture-perfect Florence Nightingale. The cut was still bleeding a little. Part of her wanted to make it deeper with her nail, but not being violent person she instead placed the bandage on tightly enough to slow the flow a bit. Too bad her wound wasn't so skin-deep. Molly knew it would be months before she felt better. Her injuries would linger long after a simple scratch had healed.

"Molly, please. Just hear me out."

"No. Liam, I really just can't even begin to deal with this. Pass me the phone."

"Who are you calling?" Handing it to her.

"Dial Jay."

He handed her the ringing phone.

"Hello." A sleepy voice purred.

"It's me. I need you to come over right now."

"What's wrong?" Still sleepy.

"We had an accident and we have to go to the hospital."

"What!?" Waking up.

"Just come over and I will explain later."

"I'll be there in ten." Hanging up.

"What are you going to say?"

"That we got in a car accident. They don't need to know the details and if they ask I'll tell them it was a cat or something."

"And what about me? What should I say?"

"Whatever you want."

Molly winced as she got up and went into her room to grab a clean sweater. She carefully put it on and waited for Jay. Her hand bumped into her side and she let out a cry. Fuck. Soon they were all in the car headed for the hospital. Jay kept her mouth shut—this was one she didn't want to get in the middle of just yet. She drove quickly and carefully so as not to hit any bumps.

"Jay, do you think he should tell them he's on E?" Molly asked. "Before they treat him?"

"What?" Shocked.

"Yep, he's fucked up and failed to tell me that. Somewhere between the bar and home, the car met with a cement streetlamp. And now I think my back is fucked and my wrist is pretty much broken."

"Are you a friggin' idiot!" Jay yelled at Liam, turning. "What the hell were you thinking?"

"Stop yelling at me!" Liam cried.

"You can be such a moron! You could have killed someone!"

"I know! Don't you think I know that! It was an accident."

"No shit, Sherlock!" Jay kept on. "A perfectly preventable one. Sometimes I wonder how you function."

"I get it, I know. I'm sorry!"

"Can you guys just shut up, please." Trying not to focus on the pain. "Just drive and get us there."

Jay again looked at Liam and scowled. She then looked at Molly and concern spread over her face. She drove a little faster. Jay pulled into the emergency entrance of Cedars and gingerly helped Molly out of the car.

"Liam, go get someone to help us."

Liam ran in and returned with an attendant who walked Molly into the hospital.

After about four hours, five stitches, a handful of lies, a few X-rays, two cups of coffee, and thankfully minimal questions, the group trudged outside and back into Jay's car. Molly's wrist was broken and was sporting a temporary cast. Tomorrow she would have to go to an orthopedist to get a more permanent one as well as to physical therapy for a routine to heal her sprained back.

During the ride home, she could barely move and focused only on her bed. Jay and Liam helped Molly up to their apartment, and after they settled her in bed, Jay got comfortable on the couch next to Liam.

"Looks like it's you and me, baby." Liam trying to joke.

"Don't bother." Flicking on the TV. "The only reason I'm here is to help her." Gesturing to the bedroom. "And she said the doctor told her that you needed to be kept awake for a few more hours in case you have a concussion. She, obviously, doesn't want you to fall into a coma and die, so here I am."

"Thanks."

"You're welcome." Turning to him. "Liam, you know how bad this is, don't you?"

"I do, and I'm so sorry. If I could take it back I would, Jay. I don't know what possessed me to drive."

"You better take care of her from here on out. You really could have killed her."

"I know." Quietly.

Jay and Liam spent the whole night on the couch, not speaking, not sleeping, just watching bad TV until dawn. Part of Jay wanted him to pass out, fall into a coma, and have more than a scrape on his head after almost killing her best friend, but she was never a violent person. Instead, she silently seethed.

The next morning, at Molly's insistence, Jay left to get some rest and Liam drove her to the doctor. Her doctor had prescribed

Vicodin and a long course of treatment requiring three days' bed rest then physical therapy mixed with massage that would last six weeks or longer, depending on how fast Molly healed. He also wrapped her wrist in a hot-pink cast that would have to stay on for about two months. It all seemed slightly unfair to Molly. She would be the one to cringe every time she moved for the next month and have to deal with a dull pain coursing through her body twenty-four-seven while he wouldn't even have a real scar. How was Molly going to do her work? No way was she going to be able to lean over and craft with a bad back and one good hand. This whole accident was going to X-Acto a slice of time out of her life that she would never be able to get back. She had been seriously fucked over.

They got home, crawled into bed, and slept. Later that day, Molly woke up and went to take a bath. Her back desperately needed the soak, seeing how the Vicodin had only slightly deadened the ache. She poured in a bottle of muscle-easing salts, lit a vanilla candle, and carefully settled in with her wrist propped on the side of the tub. Liam came into the bathroom and sat on the toilet next to her.

"Can I join you?"

"No." Not looking at him.

"Can I sit here?"

"Free country." Trying to get comfortable.

"Can you stop being so . . . ?"

"So what? Angry? Hurt? Scared? Pissed? No, I really can't." Raising her voice a little.

"Molly, I'm so sorry about last night. I blew it. I don't know what I was thinking."

"You were thinking about getting high and that's it. What you should have been thinking about is that I am driving my girlfriend, or how about even I am driving myself, home and I don't want to kill her or me or anyone else who happens upon my path."

"I know." He hung his head.

"Do you?" Looking at him finally. "I can't take this anymore." Feeling a tear run down her cheek. "We could have died, someone could have died. It's like we were the luckiest people on earth. This can't go on." Crying harder.

"What are you saying?"

"I don't know." Wiping her face off. "All this shit is getting in the way. I can't keep picking up after you. I'm the one who ends up getting more hurt. All the deals we have made, the promises as a couple to keep each other safe, have flown right out the window on the tail of whatever drug you're smoking. I'm scared of the next time. My body can't handle the next time."

"There's not going to be a next time."

"I've heard that before. How do you know? What if there is and what if you aren't so lucky? What if you get fucked up and die or I die! This is too much for me to handle."

"What do you want me to do?"

"Liam, you need to figure out how you want your life to go. There have been a million little things I have forgiven—my birthday, my parents, your friends, countless times you're late or flake or whatever. I just have nothing left. This all needs to change or . . ."

"Or what?" His face falling. "Molly, or what?"

"Or maybe I can't be here anymore." Staring at him, unflinchingly. "Maybe I can't be with you anymore."

Liam started crying, holding his head in his hand.

"Don't leave me. I love you so much," he whispered. "You are the single most important thing to me, ever."

"You say that and I want to believe you, but then what the fuck are you doing? Why on earth are you putting me at so much risk?"

"I don't know. I really don't."

"You need to deal with this. You've got to get help."

"I will, I'll stop everything. Cold turkey. I'll even go to some meetings. I'll do it for you."

"Not for me, for you."

"For us. Just give me one more chance. I swear nothing like this will ever happen again. I can beat this."

"I don't know." Laying her head back against the porcelain.

"Molly, I promise you I'm done, just stay with me. With you here I know I can do anything."

Molly pulled her knees into her chest and her whole body shivered. Another promise, another pledge. Would it last? She reached out and grabbed his hand. Touching him, holding him. Molly tried to think if they could once again be as solid as flesh and bone. They sat there for a long time like that, and four months passed without incident. Without a drink, a hit, without even the formation of a pack a day smoking habit. She forgave, Jay forgave, and their lives went on as usual. Molly was silly to think it would last, but she believed in it and him and tried to rebuild her trust. Trust that came crashing down when Liam was strung out on a gurney being shocked back to life.

"Molly, how could you keep this from us? Why didn't you tell us? I'm so upset." Helen voicing concern.

"I'm fine now. Yoga has helped and it is only tender every once in a while. And the wrist is completely healed. I didn't want you to freak out like you are now."

"Freak out? Of course we are going to freak out! My baby is hundreds of miles away hurt and I didn't even know!" Starting to cry. "How many more chances are you going to give him to hurt you? It's like you are putting yourself at the opposite end of a loaded gun. Your body is literally a landscape littered with his mistakes!"

"Your mother is right. What happens next time? You break your back? You break a leg or another arm? You get killed?" Henry yelled. "You need to walk away from this. He is dealing with things that are just so much more than what's normal."

"Dad, what is normal? Everyone has issues. No one is perfect. What if this were me? Would you walk away from me?" Defending him.

"You're our daughter. It's different. He's just a stupid boyfriend." Henry escalated in tone. "A boyfriend who put you in the hospital!"

"He's not just a boyfriend. You make it sound like I picked him up at the gym last week between sets of push-ups. It has been years. We are a couple, a family. We have a history."

"We are your family." Helen stating flatly. "And if this is your so-called history, you better come up with some revisionist theories."

"Mom, it's not all like this. Liam is my family. And there are just as many good times as there are bad."

"You're not married. You can leave."

"I know I can, but a ring and a piece of paper would not make me more committed than I am now. And what does it say about me if I totally bail on him after he finally really admits his problem and goes to get serious help?"

"It says that you are watching out for yourself and removing yourself from a dangerous situation. It says that you are cutting your losses." Henry confirming. "This is not your life."

"But it is my life. He is my life. Cut my losses! Stop talking about this so analytically! You didn't raise me to walk away from people who are in trouble. Besides, what about all that shit you told me the other day about respecting whatever I decided? And if I loved him then you weren't going to yell at me and make me feel like shit!"

"That was before this new information!" Shaking his head. "I just had to listen to news that my daughter was in the hospital and had broken bones and has been in physical therapy for months because of some preventable accident with a wasted boyfriend! This is a really fucking bad melodrama! It's almost funny if it weren't so pathetic."

"Thanks, Dad, my life is now bad TV. Sorry I can't be as *Leave It to Beaver* as the two of you are now!"

"Don't get fresh." Henry eyed her.

"Please, both of you. Molly, we are just trying to help. You're right about us teaching you to be a loving woman, but we also didn't teach you to lose yourself into an abusive situation. Boundaries need to be drawn." Helen, adding.

"I feel like I need to give him a chance to make this right, to get well, to create a life together."

"Molly, you're being so naive," Henry scolded. "Why can't you see this for what it is? Liam is a fuckup! How the hell is he going to support you if he can't even help himself!"

"Henry, easy."

"No! This is our daughter, Helen! I can't just sit back, I can't even listen to this anymore." Storming out of the room.

"Henry!" Calling after him.

"Just let him go." Molly, defeated.

"Honey, he's just afraid for you. We're both terrified."

"That's fine, Mom, and I'm sorry you are so scared and worried, but instead of him screaming at me, I needed him to listen. I need you to try and respect this." Looking her mom right in the eye despite her tears. "I'm scared, I feel totally alone, and I need you to help me."

"Molly, I don't know how to help, and that's what scares me."

"Look, after being here for the last few weeks, my head is finally clear again and I know now that I can't walk—or really run—away from him. It's weak to do it. That's not who I am. I have to give this one more try because I know the meaning of family from all of you. He is mine, and I have to try. I need you to say that's okay and that you will be there for me."

"Whether or not I think this is okay, I will always be there for you. I love you more than anything." Holding her daughter.

Helen and Molly stayed entwined for what seemed like hours. The phone interrupted their silent reverie.

"I'll get it." Molly ran to the other room to grab the phone. "Hello."

"Hi, is Molly there? This is Dr. Marcus."

"Who is it?" Helen called from the other room.

"Hi, it's for me, Mom." Clearing her throat. "Hi, Dr. Marcus."

"I have the tests back and there is no sign of any bacteria or parasite in your system."

"Well, that's great, right?"

"Right, but I have some other news. Congratulations! You're pregnant. You probably have been experiencing some early morning sickness, which should ease as the pregnancy continues."

"Excuse me?" Paling, even though she knew this was what he was going to say.

"You're pregnant. I would, when you get back to LA, go see your gynecologist who can help you get on a prenatal routine."

"Uh." Not knowing how to respond, feeling her tongue swell in her mouth.

"Molly?"

"Yeah, I'm here."

"Are you okay?"

"Not really."

"So, I take it this was not planned?"

"You could say that." Wrapping the cord around her good hand.

"Take some time for it to settle. You'll be fine."

"Okay, yeah." Whispering into the phone.

"By the way, I need you to come in in five days so I can remove the stitches, or you can get them removed back in LA."

"Sure." Spitting out the words as her throat closed. "Okay."

"Take a deep breath."

"Thanks."

"Congratulations, Molly."

"Yeah, yeah. Thanks." Choking out the words.

Molly hung up the phone and slid to the floor. It's all fun and games until someone gets pregnant. Molly swallowed hard. Although she had that creeping feeling that this was what was going on with her, it felt like a Mack truck ran over her the minute the words tumbled from the doctor's lips. The Mud Flap Girls were smacking her head. Hearing it out loud confirmed by another person made it stick. Molly was covered in glue. A baby. Her baby. Her and Liam's baby. How? When? They were careful. She had been sick recently, antibiotics fucked with her pill? She was the one percent? How? Why? When? A baby? Her baby? His baby? Molly swallowed again and took a deep breath. This definitely changes things. This changes everything. She set her hand on her stomach and rubbed. She didn't feel anything. A baby, her baby. Their baby. Molly stood up quickly and ran up the stairs to her room. She locked the door, threw herself onto her bed, and started to cry softly.

twelve

Henry went to bed that night with an ambidextrous four-hundred-pound gorilla on his chest braiding fishtails with his hair. He felt like an anchor—heavy, cold, and numb. Molly refused to come out or speak to any of them. He didn't blame her. He had acted like a real shit. Yelling at her when all she wanted was to be held tight and listened to. He had screwed up, but how could he play the easygoing dad when all he felt was rage? Rage at Liam, rage at her, rage at himself for not being able to

keep her safely tucked away from needy men looking to feast on the tender flesh of innocents. Henry had trouble keeping his emotions at bay; they were percolating under the surface. He was a terrible liar, no poker face whatsoever. He just wished for once he had reigned himself in instead of railing against Molly.

All he could think to do after his petulant exit was feed her. He made her a grilled cheddar cheese and a small salad and left it by her door on a ceramic tray. She had only eaten a few tiny bites when he went to retrieve it later. He couldn't even feed her the right way. He couldn't do anything right. What are fathers supposed to do when daughters grow up and move away? When they have their own issues, dilemmas, and crosses to bear? When no matter what the advice or help is, they remain stubbornly steadfast on their own path? Of course, it's truly what you want them to do. A father wants his daughter to be strong-minded, independent, and passionate, but he also wants to be able to somehow always keep her safe, keep her not quite strong enough, and keep her not quite independent. When Molly was born, Henry wept. He remembered sitting next to a napping Helen, holding his precious girl in his arms and weeping. Glad he had a girl, happy she was healthy, but devastated that one day she would leave him for another man and enter an embrace that was just not going to be as protected as it would be for a boy. She was so small and fragile, so easily hurt. Her skin was almost translucent. Henry was so fearful.

When Molly was a teenager, they seldom fought. Maybe it was the distance he maintained or the fact that both of them were not very good at confrontation, but once the gloves were on, the battles were vicious. Henry couched his fear for her in anger at her. He couldn't express to her how terrified he was, he could only yell at her when she was late or forgot to call. Gradually, as she got older and more mature, he let her live her life and he got on with his. He truly thought that he was done being frightened and overprotective, but he was mistaken. Every bone in his body was aching, and he knew no amount of Advil would ease his discomfort. He was vulnerable and he was livid. He just didn't want to yell anymore, but he was lost without his voice.

Helen lay awake as well. She could feel Henry's body rigid beside her. She knew he was up, but she didn't dare speak. With so much flying around inside, articulation was impossible. Were things just harder now? More difficult for women, for girls? Helen couldn't get her head around what Molly was dealing with. Sure, she and Henry had had their share of problems, moments of isolation, moments of "Is this going to work?" But those issues now seem simple in comparison. Also, before Henry there had been other men. One particular rebel with thick black hair, bell-bottoms, and a knack for undressing her in under a minute. They had a brief scorching affair filled with philosophy and music, and Helen was completely obsessed. She lived and breathed his patchouli smell, scribbled every exchange in her notebook, but she got over it, got over him. Got tired of the hell she endured wondering whether other women may or may not be sharing his bed or holding his lid of weed in her dorm room. Got tired of seeing countless movies alone when he never showed. She got over her obsession with that bad boy, the one her parents warned her about, outgrew him, stopped loving him, starting seeing him for the man he was. Why couldn't her daughter do the same? Find someone steady and sweet and easy most of the time like Henry? Liam was damaged goods no matter how wonderful he could be, a piece of yolk-stained silverware. Molly was an antique set gleaming with the shine of soft-cloth attention. Grand and bright with promise.

What kind of father would a man like Liam be? If and when Molly had her children, could a man like Liam support her, them? Teach them, inspire them? Could Molly make a home with a firm, solid foundation with a man so unsteady? Could she have forever with a man who kills himself slowly? Even if he gets treatment, will he always walk the edge? Live on the precipice of danger? Would he be happy in the simplicity of a normal life? Would he make Molly happy? Helen grabbed the blanket and pulled it tightly around her. She was shivering. She knew she would always have doubts and she hated that. How could she be strong for her daughter when she felt so afraid?

Alex and Renee slept soundly that night wrapped in each other's arms. Despite her burgeoning belly, Alex managed to somehow swallow her in his embrace. Renee breathed in his scent, let the fine hair on his arms tickle her sides. She felt relief. After a long afternoon of yelling and crying and talking to each other, they were centered again. Alex was furious at her for divulging their secrets, yet he knew he couldn't make demands on how Renee needed or wanted to handle the situation. Renee knew he felt ashamed that his sister was well aware of how low he could stoop and it almost made her regret her decision, but she also knew it would never be spoken of again. Maybe everyone, now that all could finally see one another on more human terms, would connect on a more profound level.

Renee snuggled deeper into Alex's embrace. Some days she imagined something bigger, better, something without the baggage they had, but she felt grateful for something reliable. Even after all they had been through she felt blessed with a man who adored her, who never really yelled without good reason. She was lucky to have a man who always bought her small presents and who talked pleasantly to everyone even when reservations were fouled up or parts were missing, broken, or delivered late. She knew she could depend on Alex, always, especially after the storm they weathered. Maybe she was nuts to be grateful for a man who had strayed once, but she was sure that he was the man for her, and that his action was one mistake in what would be a long life of loving moments.

She wished Molly had found someone a little less intense than Liam, less flawed, but Molly was always more optimistic about people, more trusting. She always saw that inner spark no matter the package, and did everything and anything to cultivate it. If someone caught Molly's eye, and Molly believed in him or her, it would be a permanent, direct, and constant stare. If people looked closely into Molly's eyes, they could see their best selves, reflected back. It made people want to be whatever she saw. She carefully peeled away the leaves of self-doubt and deprecation until she unearthed the soft core of who someone was. Like Molly had when Renee was a chubby, awkward teenager who needed someone to tell her she was fine just the way she was, Liam needed Molly's gaze to feel like a man, to feel like he was something worth anything.

Molly loved him because he must do that same thing to her. When you are the one who makes others believe in themselves, it takes a very special person to do the same for yourself. Renee knew that beneath the confident exterior, Molly never felt like enough of anything despite being everything. Renee had seen the vulnerability lurking under the façade of Molly. Somehow Molly had let Liam in and under everything she had once kept tightly locked away. Renee understood now that this was the one man who made Molly view herself in all her glory. He had seen her inside and out, and the gaze was essential—like sun or water or a basket of hot fish-and-chips. Molly would love him and stick by him until there was nothing left. Renee snuggled back into Alex and said a small prayer for her sister, the hopeless romantic who should hopefully never be hopeless again.

Alex felt Renee relax and settle into sleep. Every night, he kissed her hair and twirled a lock in his free hand. It was his ritual. He did it to make sure that Renee was still there because he knew how close he had come to losing her altogether. How could he have been so careless, so stupid? What must his sister think of him? He was scum. He was embarrassed that Molly knew. She had been right this morning. He was not one to judge, but that did not stop him from wanting to. However, how could he deprive someone of the second chance he himself blessedly received? He just wished that the star player in this drama was not his sister.

He looped Renee's hair around his thumb. The blond looked almost blue. He never fell for a blonde before Renee. Small and dark was how he liked them. He always knew Renee and felt completely at ease around her, but never imagined that his sister's best friend and sidekick would evolve into his ideal match. After college and cooking school, he came home to find her the most sparkling woman he had ever met. It's strange how sometimes one can know somebody forever, see her all the time, know her sense of humor, what she likes on her burgers, how she combs her hair, and one day in a flash it is all new. It's as if the most familiar people become perfect strangers in the blink of an eye. One has to relearn every detail and it all seems fresh even though every story, every laugh line, every scar is familiar. When they fell in love everything was novel, yet they had a history. Their webs of connection were so entwined that they got married only one year after they started dating. Why couldn't his sister have found something like this? Something soft like a slipper, warm like hot chocolate, and comfortable like a worn-in pair of boxers? Molly always did things the hard way, always moving, needing change. Alex hoped she would change all this, but he knew deep down he was grasping at straws.

Molly decided the house was too quiet. She longed to scream, shatter the stillness, but that would probably wig her parents out completely. She wanted everything to be out in the open instead of coiled within her like a shiny new Slinky itching for its first flight of stairs. She felt suspended, hovering just outside herself in an alternate reality, one without sound, just the beating of her heart. Molly could almost hear the extra thump of her baby even though she knew that was impossible. Her baby. It was so strange to have those words milling about. She was going to have a baby.

That certainly was not part of any possible plan she had for her immediate future. None of the last few weeks had been a part of her big plan. Not the overdose, nor the store, nor this permanent other priority she was carrying within. Why is it that she could travel along and feel everything was going just the way she imagined them to be and in one rush it all gets flipped on its head? Life can really change completely in an instant. How was she going to have a baby? She slept late, went to bed late, sometimes smoked and drank and cursed and hung out at dive bars with tattooed bartenders and friends with piercings. Wait, she had drunk while pregnant—did she fuck up the baby already? When does fetal alcohol syndrome kick in? There was that doctor's report on TV saying you could have a glass of wine every once in a while that she had watched with Renee. . . .

Molly exhaled. Is it even a baby yet? Just a few cells, right? A fetus, an embryo. Babies were bouncy and buttery and full of powdery smells and tears. Babies were flesh and bone and bedtimes. Babies were responsibility and intense and permanent. Molly was never permanent, even her hair color constantly changed. Molly panicked. She forgets to do laundry, to always clean the toilet. She sometimes lived on cereal. Alone? How? Maybe this wasn't "the" baby, her baby. But it already is a baby. Maybe she could. She can. She would. She was definitely going to have it. It had a face and weight and it already felt like hers. Even an unplanned pregnancy was somehow going to become incorporated into her life. She did always want to have Liam's baby. She was sure of that in the trip up north when she met Elizabeth for the first time. It was the way Liam handled Paige that convinced Molly of how wonderful Liam would be as a father.

Molly had snuck up upon them one morning outside. Elizabeth had set up a mini easel in the garden for Paige, and Liam was sitting next to her on a tiny bench not big enough for a quarter of him. His legs drooped about, sticking out from the nooks and crannies. It couldn't have been very comfortable, but Liam had this big smile on his face, like nothing could take him out of the moment. Paige had in front of her a blank canvas, and the two of them were discussing colors. Even though she was only two, they were speaking a common language of hues. He spoke directly to her, not down to her or around her, and it wasn't as if she was a little girl, she was just a person like any other who had wishes and ideas to express. Liam managed to weave through baby talk and establish a connection. In that moment, Liam was a rainbow, a prism, a disco ball, the towel section at Bed Bath & Beyond. He was a full box of new crayons, One-Eyed Willy's treasure in *The Goonies*. He was everything that twinkled, radiated brilliance, and was on the top of every child's Christmas wish list. It was sweet and simple, a thoroughly magical moment.

Now things weren't quite as simple, but Molly never shook that lightning bolt. The feeling of finding your reproductive match, the one to complement your genes and secure your position in the evolution of the human race was enormous. Inside her, it was growing, more with every passing day, and despite everything, despite the long road ahead, Molly smiled and for the first time said goodnight to their baby.

It was late when Molly finally woke up. The sun shone brightly through her curtains and began to heat up the room. Molly fell out of bed, dressed, brushed, and shuffled downstairs unknowing of what would await her. The house was completely empty. Dishes were drying by the sink, a pot of coffee sat warming, the paper folded neatly on the table. There was no note, no nothing. Everyone must have fled. Molly's family was not a fan of awkward silences. They either were in the thick of it, yelling, dealing, and then trying to find humor in a bad situation or filling the gap with inane conversation about nothing important until they all retreated to their respective corners alone. Molly was grateful for the latter. It gave her more time to prepare. Her parents were going to lose it big time when she told them her news. She almost didn't want to, but it wasn't something like a bad grade that she could hide in her backpack and make up for on the next test.

She went to the fridge, fixed herself some vanilla yogurt and fruit, and picked up the phone. Maybe if she could tell one person who would be happy, the reaction from all the assumed head shakers wouldn't hurt so much when they expressed their disappointment. She dialed Jay's number. On the fifth ring, Jay picked up.

"Screening?" Molly asked.

"No, you know I don't have caller ID. I was peeing." Catching her breath.

"How's the foot?"

"Fine, feels better, but I'm avoiding the whole high heel and liquor combo for a few more weeks."

"Good idea."

"What's up?"

"A lot. Big family blowout last night about Liam."

"Yuck. What did they say?"

"What every good parent would, why be with him, he's not good for you, he's fucked up, you can do better, blah, blah, blah. Nothing new, but it was the first time they found out about the car accident and my wrist and back, and that didn't help matters any."

"I told you, you should have told them about that sooner. It was going to come up."

"It wasn't as big a deal as it got made out to be. We hit a curb for God's sake." Raising her voice a little.

"It was a big deal, Molly, because that curb could have easily been a person or another car. And you couldn't walk properly for more than a month."

"I know, but it wasn't."

"Molly, really, does that matter?"

"No." Quietly. "I just didn't want them to know, and now they do, and now they are certain I should leave him permanently. You probably think the same thing."

"You know I don't. Yes, I'm scared for you. You are becoming a walking patchwork of Liam's induced scars, but I get to see all the other wonderful things and times you share, and I know he loves you. He just really needs to get his shit together big time. How do you feel? That's all that is important."

"I feel like I can't bail the minute he finally admits his problem and goes to get help. That just seems like such a dick move. And especially now with what's going on, I feel like I have to let him try to be better."

"What does that mean? What's going on now?"

"I'm pregnant."

There was a pause on the phone. Molly wanted to reach inside and demand Jay to speak. The pause continued.

"Crazy, huh?" Molly added.

"Beyond." Swallowing. "Are you sure?"

"Yeah, doctor told me yesterday."

"Do they know?"

"Not yet. I figure I would wait till things cooled down before I sprung this new part of the drama on them."

"How do you feel?"

"Weird. Freaked. Scared. My baby's father is in rehab for God's sake." Twirling the phone cord. "But, you know what, despite all that, I feel really happy about it." Starting to smile. "It's like in the midst of all the shit comes this amazingly beautiful gift. I feel blessed. Corny, I know, but all of a sudden everything doesn't feel so heavy and pained. I feel lighter, more free."

"Good, I'm happy for you. I am." With mild enthusiasm. "It's just, Molly, this is intense. A baby?"

"Yup, but I can handle it. It's not just about me anymore."

"What if he and you don't make it? What if he doesn't want it? What if this new sobriety does not stick? What if . . ."

"What if it does and I don't give him an opportunity to fix things, be better, be a father? Then what am I saying about love, about life? That when the going gets tough, I run away? I don't want to keep running, I want to stand still."

"I respect that, Molly, but having a baby with a guy who is still in rehab isn't screaming stable, healthy father to me. It is doing the opposite. Can you start a family with a guy who you don't particularly trust right now?"

"I don't know, but I love him and I have to see if I can trust him again. I have to deal—it's not going to disappear. I know I can. I will. It's not like I am seventeen. I'm almost thirty years old! I have so much more than so many women. A job, family support, and some money. They manage and so will I."

"We, so will we. You do not have to go it alone. I am one hundred percent behind you. Whatever you need with or without him." Giving her support. "We can even add a whole playroom concept to the store."

"Always thinking ahead."

"That's why I get the big bucks." Jay, joking.

"Thanks."

"For what?"

"Being there, here. I love you."

"Me too."

"I should go and prepare for the parental divulging. They're not going to be as easy as you."

"Good luck." Kissing into the phone. "When are you coming home?"

"Couple of days."

"Cool."

Molly hung up with her best friend and smiled again. All the words she had shared with Jay were little surprises she had hidden from herself. Like a twenty you find crunched up in a pocket or a lollipop in the depths of your purse when you are on a diet and at the movies willing yourself away from the chocolate-covered peanuts. The thoughts blossomed and evolved into a new perspective. Suddenly, Molly was hopeful, she was glowing, she felt like the original peach of summer. Turned around, upside down, inside out, and loving the fact that for the first time in days she didn't want to cry when she thought about her future.

Maybe things changed quickly and this epiphany was too fast, but Molly didn't care. The beauty of life is lemonade, and that takes about five minutes to make.

She grabbed her keys and started for the restaurant. In her gut, she knew the crew was there pretending to be busy. Well, they were probably really busy, they were just pretending their minds were on the jobs at hand. Molly parked the car by Sorella and popped her head in. Susan was hanging up a new shipment of Tracy Feith dresses.

"Those are gorgeous." Fingering the colorful silks.

"Aren't they?" Kissing Molly's cheek. "We just got them and I already pulled three for myself. This one would look great on you." Holding up a turquoise spaghetti-strap shift. "Try it." Holding the dress out to her.

"I can't. I have to get to the restaurant. I just came by to see what you had picked out and take the rest off your hands."

"Actually, I have a check for all of them for you. I already sold two." Hanging the dress up and walking to the counter.

"Great!" Following her. "By the way, I may need to pick your brain soon. My friend and I have finally decided to bite the bullet and open a store in LA."

"Very cool. Call me any time. Where are you going to be?"

"On Third by Crescent Heights. I haven't seen the space yet, but my friend tells me it's perfect."

"I'm sure it will be. Good luck." Handing Molly the check.

"Thanks, Susan." Folding it and putting it in her purse. "'Bye."

Molly walked the few blocks to Helen's. She almost felt a slight involuntary skip in her step. She was becoming Mary fucking Poppins! She had herself in a fit of giggles by the time she walked into the restaurant imagining herself flying, holding on to a red umbrella with a big sticker saying BABY ON BOARD pasted to the fabric. Supercalafrajilistic! Helen was behind the bar cleaning glasses when Molly bounded in whistling the catchy tune.

"Hey, Mom." Going around and giving Helen a hug.

"Hi, baby." Setting down her glass and hugging back. "Glad you came by. Everything was such a mess yesterday."

"I know. I had to be alone."

"I don't blame you. Dad and I were . . ."

"Were being parents. You were doing your job."

"Molly, we just love you so much." Tearing up.

"Mom, don't cry. It's all going to be fine."

"Is it?" Staring at her daughter.

"I don't know, but I will be fine. That's the only thing I know for sure."

"I'm scared for you." Pulling Molly closer.

"I am too." Quietly. "Mom, I have to tell you something else."

"What?"

"Where are Dad and Alex? I want to tell you all at once."

"In the back."

Molly and Helen walked into the kitchen. The difference between now and the other night during the party was impossible to ignore. There was no music playing, no jovial joking, or talking at all for that matter. Everyone was sullen and silent, following out their tasks. Henry looked up and saw Molly. His body stiffened. Alex looked up as well and blushed. Molly walked over to her father and put her arms around him. He softened into her embrace and almost choked out a tear. He never wanted to let her go.

"Dad, I'm sorry." Tearing up.

"For what? I am so sorry I yelled at you last night. I didn't sleep at all. I didn't mean to." Rubbing her back. "I love you."

"I know. I love you too." Holding her father.

"I know yesterday I didn't handle things right, but today I will listen to whatever you say."

"And you won't freak out and yell at me?"

"I will try not to."

"Try really hard, Dad, because I have something else to tell all of you."

"What?"

Helen, Alex, and Henry moved closer and leaned in.

"Okay, well, I, huh, okay, just say it, Molly. Guys, I'm pregnant." Spitting out the words.

No one said anything and Molly could almost see her words floating before her tied up with helium balloons. They darted around the stove and huddled together around the back corner by the trash. Without saying a word, Henry walked out the back of the restaurant. Alex looked at his sister, then at his mother, and chased after his father. Helen took a deep breath, closed her eyes, opened them, and walked toward Molly.

"Wow."

"I know."

"Big news."

"The biggest."

"A baby."

"Yeah."

"Wow."

"It's insane."

"Yeah, it is, Molly." Looking at her. "I take it that you're . . ."

"Of course."

"That's a major decision."

"It's the only option. Mom, I think this baby is going to be a good, no, a great thing."

"A baby always is. It's just . . ."

"Mom, I understand and am totally aware of every single thing that is running through your head. I have thought about it all myself. I don't need a rehashing of my situation."

"Okay, then. Wait right here."

Helen walked briskly out the back door and returned a few minutes later with the male half of the family. Henry's face was the shade of a Hawaiian sunburn. Alex immediately scooped his sister up and gave her a bear hug.

"Now our kids will be almost the same age. Cool."

"Yeah. I'm sorry for yesterday."

"Don't apologize—you were right. I just hope that you can forgive me."

"Alex, of all the people in the world, who knows better than I what a shit you can be and still love you despite it all?"

"Thanks." Hugging her again.

"Just don't ever do that again." Glaring at him.

"Trust me, there is no way."

"Good."

Obviously, Helen had said a few words to get Henry to return.

"Daddy?" Molly looked toward him.

"What do you want me to say?"

"Anything, something."

"This is not how I wanted it to be when I heard this."

"Me neither, but here we are." Shrugging. "You have been telling me for the last few years before Renee got pregnant that it was time for me to breed." Trying to lighten things up. "You have finally got your wish."

"I guess you are right." Slightly smiling. "The clock has been ticking."

"Exactly. Now you get two virtually at the same time."

"Molly, do you have any idea what you are doing or getting yourself into?"

"Nope, but with all your help I think I can make a solid go at this."

"I sure hope so." Going to Molly and embracing her. "I do love you."

"I know, Dad." Hugging Henry tightly.

"I think this calls for a toast." Alex, stating.

He went back into the wine cellar and returned with a bottle of champagne and a bottle of apple cider. Alex poured.

"I wonder which is for me," Molly joked.

"To my sister, cheers to getting knocked up!"

"Alex." Helen clucked. "Not funny."

"But it kind of is, Mom," Molly conceded. "To the unplanned pregnancy!" Molly echoed.

"To illegitimate children!" Alex went on.

"To 'Hey, don't bother with that condom!'" Molly kept going.

"To . . ."

"Enough!" Henry yelled over the din.

Molly and Alex quieted down and tried to be serious, but the giggles kept surfacing.

"To my daughter. I love her even when she's crazy and I will, we will," putting his arm around Helen, "always support her because we know she is perfect just the way she is."

Molly swallowed her giggles, and her eyes welled up. She smiled at her dad and they all clinked glasses. She was lucky they all stepped up to the plate with her.

"I've got one more," Alex stated.

"No more," Henry reiterated.

"Please?" Starting to laugh again. "Come on, Dad, we can't end on that bit of mushiness. It's not our style."

"No." Starting to grin.

"Alex." Helen also started to grin.

"To the bastard baby Stern! Hip, hip, hooray!"

"Ouch." Molly winced. "That one stung a little."

"Sorry." Still laughing.

"That was so bad, Alex." Henry shook his head but couldn't help but start laughing. "Really, really bad."

"Really." Helen couldn't help herself either.

"Well, Alex, no one ever said you had class." Molly laughed again.

They all clinked glasses again and dissolved into full bellyaching laughter. Molly had exposed all her secrets, her family had listened, and they all were still standing. They were all still a family. Molly felt stronger, and looking at their compassionate, happy faces, she knew it was time for her to go home. This time the drive would be much easier.

A few days later, Molly sat on the floor of her room packing. Somehow she always went back with more than what she came with. It was a good thing that she drove and had a big car. She could just toss it all in and not worry about claim tickets or misplaced bags. Henry stood in her open door and knocked.

"Hey, Dad."

"Wasn't sure if you were awake yet."

"Wanted a full day."

"Almost done?"

"Yeah."

"Are you sure you want to leave tomorrow? Stay a while longer."

"I can't. Jay and I have to double-time it now on the store, and if I stay any longer I may never leave."

"So?"

"Nice try, Dad." Smiling at him. "What do you have there?" Gesturing to a package in his hand.

"It's for you, from Elizabeth McGuire."

"Really?" Taking the package from her father. "I wonder what Elizabeth sent me."

"Have you told her yet about the baby?"

"No, I want to wait until I tell Liam."

"When does he get back?"

"Soon, I think."

"Are you nervous?"

"Yeah."

Molly opened the plain padded envelope and inside was a tape and a letter. Molly walked to her stereo and put in the cassette. She read the letter while it rewound.

Dear Molly—

I hope you are doing better. It's been a trying time. Liam asked me to send you this and I wish it finds you well. Everything happens for a reason, and sometimes things don't happen as we expect. It's in how we han-

dle the messes that we discover our true strengths. You have many, many more than you even knew.

Love, Elizabeth

"What is it?"

"Just a note and something from Liam."

Molly set down the letter and pressed PLAY. Soon, the room was filled with music and Liam's voice surrounded her.

I'll do anything to change all this
I'm still looking for the right words to say
I'm sorry, I love you, I'll try harder
Have I really pushed you too far away?
It wasn't supposed to hurt
I know this time things were different
How could I lose my nerve?

> **Because**
> **Everyday I hear**
> **Even when I sleep it rings clear**
> **When I wake, when I rise**
> **Even when I close my eyes**
> **Everyday I hear you.**

In the morning the light just doesn't shine
The bed seems rearranged
I still smell your perfume
Even though the sheets have been changed.
I haven't washed in days
I just wonder and wander
I'm lost in every way.

> **Because**
> **Everywhere I see**

Even when I close my eyes to breathe
In my room, in my car
No matter near or far
Everywhere I see you.

Could you forgive all I have done?
Trust I will be better?
I can be the guy on the shiny white horse
I'll be just about anything for another stab at forever.
Please, baby just ask me
Take me again in your arms
Just trust me, believe in me.

Because
Everything reminds me
Even when I try to hide it finds me
In the dark, in the light
Even when I am out of sight
Everything reminds me of you.

Molly let the tape run until it stopped on its own. It was in that moment that Henry finally understood the magic, the pull. He saw the glazed look in Molly's eye, the delicate shadows of adoration flutter across her face. He saw her shoulders relax, her body bloom, her weight shift back and forth on her feet until she appeared to be floating. She was a sponge responding to a bowl of water, expanding and growing in her exposure to her source of nourishment. He walked to her and kissed her cheek.

"Just let me know when you want me to bring the bags down."

"Oh." Startled from her daydream. "Sure, thanks."

Henry left her just as she was, and went downstairs to find his wife. He knew that he had lost her forever, but what a compassionate, loving woman she had become. Molly sat back down on the floor to finish her packing, the song set on REPEAT. Soon enough she had memorized the words and was singing with him. She flashed to his smile, how his clothes were always a little rumpled, how in the summer the bridge of his nose became covered with freckles. She thought about how Liam would leave love notes in random CDs for her to find at later dates, how he would make her macaroni and cheese when she had PMS, how he'd always remember to tape her TV shows. She smiled when she thought about when he was grumpy—his cheeks got mottled and he bit his nails. She exhaled when she remembered how easily she slept next to him despite his *Black Hawk Down* snores. She recalled how he would bitch about how much she shopped, but complimented every new outfit, how they never got bored even in the silences, how he didn't mind her granny underwear or buying her tampons, how he listened when she lost her mind over nothing and threw a fit. Deep down she knew there was always going to be some small drama, some small accident, but hopefully they would be just that—small. They were connected, entwined, and if it meant that Molly was going to have to be the strong one for her, Liam, and the baby, she could and would succeed. Molly kept singing until the sun went down.

After everyone else had gone to sleep, Molly went out to Helen's car to retrieve her blue sweater and a few CDs she didn't want to forget. As she was shutting the door, a hand squeezed her shoulder and Molly screamed. She whipped around ready to fight like every self-respecting, self-defense-trained woman would and found herself going for Liam's eyes with her thumbs.

"Hey, easy." Evading her karate move. "It's me."

"Shit! You just scared the hell out of me." Catching her breath.

The front door flew open, the lights blared, and Henry came running outside.

"Molly! Are you all right?" Rushing to his daughter. "What happened?"

Henry finally caught sight of Liam.

"What on earth?" Looking at them both. "What the hell is going on here?!"

"Henry! Henry, what's going on?" Helen yelled, running out in her white nightgown.

"Relax, Mom. It's all fine."

"Liam." Helen slowed her pace. "What are you doing here? It's the middle of the night!"

"Henry, Helen. I know, I'm sorry." Swallowing. "I'm really sorry for scaring all of you. I just . . ." Liam couldn't finish his sentence. He ran his hands through his hair. He shuffled back and forth on his feet hoping for rescue. There was none.

They all stood there silent, unable to truly register his presence or how they were supposed to handle it. Molly could feel herself shaking. Her body trembled as one large shiver went up and away until even the roots of her hair were alive and kicking. She looked at him and they caught eyes. Her face flushed, she could feel her hands clam up, and her heart felt like it was running the hundred-meter dash. All she could do was swallow and stare. She lost her words, her weight. Helen and Henry glanced at the two of them and then at each other. They were all trapped inside one of those high-definition *Matrix* special-effects shots where the camera does an entire three-sixty around the scene. Helen placed her hand in her daughter's and squeezed gently.

"Why don't we all go inside and straighten this all out?" she suggested.

"Good idea." Henry agreeing.

Molly held tight to her mother and walked through the door with Liam trailing. Liam crossed the door frame with apprehension—he didn't know what lay ahead, but it sure as hell wasn't going to be easy.

All of them settled around the kitchen table as Helen turned on the kettle for some tea. Henry cleared his throat and assumed the helm of this creaky boat.

"Okay, I'm going to just cut to the chase and forgo any polite chitchat. It's late, we are all tired, and we've all had a long few weeks. Sorry, but I'm all out of pleasantries. Let's start from the beginning, and Liam, you can tell me why you are here jumping out of bushes instead of somewhere in California getting clean."

Liam paled, knowing in that one turn of phrase, Henry and Helen knew everything. He felt shame wash over him, and in that instant it all felt real, heavy, devastating. He looked to Molly for some sort of respite, but she just sat there watching. She wanted answers as well.

"I needed to see Molly." Saying tentatively.

"That's pretty clear, but that's just not enough."

"I needed to talk to you. You wouldn't listen on the phone." Looking at Molly. "I wanted to apologize and to try, I don't know, to try and fix things. I have to fix things with you. I had to do it in person and try to make it right. Since we last spoke, all that kept running around in my head was this clear vision of you and us and what we had and how that is what's important. I have to be with you and I wanted you to know that I will do anything for you, anything for another chance."

"That's a real nice sentiment, Liam, but do you think that breaking out of rehab—I can assume you broke out?" Henry, questioning.

"Yes, sir." Answering meekly.

"Okay, so do you think that breaking out of rehab and coming here is going to prove that somehow you are cured and better and trustworthy? You really think that is the way to do this? It looks to me like you are running away and screwing up all over again."

"I know that is what it must look like, Henry, but I have every intention of going back and finishing my program. I just couldn't think of anything else to do to get you, all of you," glancing at Helen, "to realize how much I love Molly. Molly, you wouldn't even talk to me. What else was I supposed to do? Sit in my tiny room and pray you'd be there when I got out? I had no choice."

"You always have a choice. You just have always consistently made the wrong one." Molly stared at him. "It's like you're a criminal sitting here having jumped bail. Am I supposed to hug you and kiss you and pretend we are fine?"

"No, I don't know. Maybe." Letting his head fall. "Why do I keep fucking up?" Liam broke into tears.

Helen nudged her husband as she placed the mugs on the table. As much as she wanted to interject and knew her husband was seriously biting his tongue, this was not their conversation. Henry got up and they left Molly and Liam at the table alone to hash things out. Henry wanted to shake Liam, scream at him, maybe even throw a punch or two, yet he knew that he just couldn't get any more involved.

"Please, stop crying, Liam. I can't take it when you cry because you're going to make me cry, and I have cried enough lately to last a lifetime." Molly choking up. "Fuck, fuck, fuck!"

"Okay." Trying to make a joke. "I'm game if you are."

"Oh, fuck you." Smiling a little despite herself. "How did you get here by the way?"

"I hitchhiked."

"You get smarter by the minute," Molly chided.

"The things one does in the spirit of romance, I guess. Luckily, I found a family on a road trip who were supportive of my 'all for love' mentality. I would have taken a bus but they take all your money when you check in."

"To prevent patients from doing things like this?"

"I guess. You don't see the chivalry at all?"

"Maybe a pinch, but it's a little cliché."

"I think the last time we saw each other, we agreed we were both equally lame." Reaching for her hand.

"Yeah." Feeling his hand on hers.

Molly remembered the bathroom, their romp, and the

words they shared. A tear ran down her face and he brushed it away.

"Don't cry, baby."

"I can't help it." Wiping her face. "Liam, do you know how hard it is for me to love you?"

"I'm beginning to. I'm so sorry. I know that I let you down all the time, and do all the wrong things, but it isn't because I don't love you. I don't blame you at all for hating me and leaving."

"You think I hate you? Are you crazy? I'm totally mad about you and I am just totally mad at you as well. Do you really think that you always let me down?"

"I do. I think that you are this amazing woman whom I constantly screw over unintentionally."

"It's not like that. Most of the time, you are completely present and real and true and totally there for me. I have never been loved like you love me, and ironically you have become better than any drug out there. It is just that when you do blow it, it's with these supremely enormous mistakes."

"Would you expect anything less?" Smiling at her.

"No, but I really need for us to have smaller problems. Do you see how much this disrupts what most of the time is a dream life? We are so blessed. Can you also understand how bad all of this must be for me if I am willing to walk away from you, from my soul mate? You have made me fearful of trusting you, of depending on you. The drugs, the drinking, all clouds who you are and they sweep you away to a place where I don't even exist. I'm afraid of disappearing. I'm afraid you won't come back. You almost died!"

"I'm afraid too. Do you think I want to die? This isn't the life I want to be living. I don't want to be a fuckup. I just have gotten myself into this sick pattern. It's like I can't handle things when they get too good because too good doesn't last, and I would rather ruin it than deal with it ending on its own. That's probably what I have done to you. I push you away and do the things I know you wish I never did so at least I have a reason when you inevitably leave."

"What are you talking about? What is this 'when you inevitably leave' crap? Where the hell do you think I am going?" Getting a little riled.

"Everyone leaves eventually. That's just the way life is. When you love people too much they always seem to leave," Liam whispered.

"So, why ask me to marry you? Why trust in that kind of forever?" Molly pushed.

"Because it's different with you!" Exclaiming. "Everything makes sense with you, which is why it makes no sense that I can't seem to get it right."

"Then what—or really who—are you talking about? Somehow I don't think we are talking about you and me anymore because I have never had any intention of leaving you."

Molly reached across the table and grabbed his hand. Liam looked directly at her.

"Liam, I know that your dad did not leave because of you. He was a grown-up with his own set of issues and problems, and it must have broken his heart to leave you and Teddy."

"Then, why didn't he write or reach out?" Liam cried. "Everyday I waited, waited for him to call me or try to see me. At every big event in my life I would look, hoping to see his face. And then, when he finally did show up, it felt so insincere, so fake. The magic dies and it fucking sucks!"

"I don't know." Going around the table to take him in her arms. "People do fucked up things all the time that we will never figure out. That's where forgiveness comes into play. That's something I have learned in the last few weeks. The heart is infinite in its ability to love and overcome pretty much anything. The only way to move on and live your life is to love and let love in and to forgive when loving lets you down because it will be there for you again. I also remember someone who vaguely resembles the man sitting in front of me who once said that being open and vulnerable and expecting the best from people and really living is the only way you get to the good stuff. Together we are the good stuff."

"I miss the good stuff." Holding her tightly.

"Look, Liam, while I get the romantic gesture of your cross-country escape," pulling away, "you can't do this the easy way. You need to go do the work. If it all were simple, we wouldn't be in this mess."

"And if I do?"

"What? Are you looking for a promise from me?"

"Yeah, I am."

"I think that you need to earn that promise because I want to be able to really mean it and feel it and commit to it when I make it. We have had too many empty ones floating around us lately."

"You're sounding so Oprah." Wiping the tears from his eyes. "I feel like I have just been Doctor Phil'd." Laughing a bit.

"I have been watching a bit too much TV lately." Smiling at him. "But, if I do say so myself, it sounded pretty good."

"Better than the doctors in my program. See, all I need is you. You can be my medicine, my cure."

Liam leaned over and kissed Molly cautiously on the lips. She let them rest there for a second before she turned her head, remembering where they were.

"If only it could be that easy." Unwrapping his arms and sitting back down in the chair next to him.

"I know it's not." Still holding onto the string from her sweatshirt. He did not want to let go. "At least I got a 'when' and not an 'if.' That was a 'when,' wasn't it?"

"For now it's a 'when.' " Brushing her hair out of her eyes. "But if things don't change and you can't or won't get clean, get dependable, and trust me to be there for you and come to me first when you feel disconnected and before doing all this incredibly stupid shit, I'm outta here. It will break my heart forever, but I will leave if I have to. I really need to be able to trust you, especially now."

"Especially now, meaning what?"

"This really wasn't how I wanted this to happen or when, but nothing ever happens how we plan it." Molly took a deep breath. "We're having a baby."

Liam fell silent and looked at Molly. His face drained of what was left of his color.

"A baby? Are you sure?" Not registering.

"Yep. I am pregnant. The doctor confirmed everything." Gazing into his eyes trying to get a read.

"A baby," Liam repeated.

"I'm going to have it. I definitely am having it." Convincing herself.

"What?" Sitting up straighter. "You were even considering . . . ?"

"No, not for more than a second, maybe." Looking at him again. "Even though everything these past few weeks has turned my life on end and freaked me out, this baby is really the one thing that made me smile. This is the only thing I am sure of. I really want it, I'm old enough, I can do it."

"We can do it." Pulling her into his lap. "We are having this together. You're not alone. I promise."

"Don't." Putting her hand to his lips. "Don't make me any more promises. Not now, not yet."

He kissed her slowly and held her the tightest he ever had. She could feel every inch of his body envelop her and soon their hearts were beating in exactly the same rhythm. They sat there for a long time, holding on to each other as the new, fragile web between them began to unfurl and spin about, connecting them with a thin spidery thread.

The next morning around six, the whole gang sat assembled in the kitchen. When Liam and Molly came down to join the group, Alex and Renee looked toward Henry and Helen for some sort of explanation.

"Speak of the devil," Alex said.

"Hey, Alex. How's it going?" Walking toward Renee and giving her a kiss on the cheek of her surprised face. "How are you feeling?"

"Fine." She stuttered. "But, umm, yeah . . ."

"Me too . . ." Alex agreed.

"Shocker, right? I broke out of jail to profess my love and apologize to Molly, which I did, and now, your sister is taking me back to rehab, so I can do my time, reform my evil ways, and be there for our baby," Liam stated.

"You are going to be a great mom." Renee smiled at Molly.

"Thanks." Molly, giving her a hug.

"They'll be about the same age." Liam put his hand on Renee's tummy. "It's really amazing." Keeping his hand there.

"Okay. Has everyone gone insane?" Alex, not really grasping everything. "Mom? Dad?"

"Don't look at me, I just work here." Helen set the pitcher of juice on the table.

"Ditto." Henry flipped some french toast onto a plate.

"Alex, you still look a little bewildered," Molly mused.

"And you aren't?"

"I've had a few hours to digest it all."

"And?" Renee asked.

"And." Molly shrugged. "And we will let you all know what happens."

"That's enough for you, Dad?" Alex pressed. "Have we all retreated to sitcom land when things get resolved after twenty-two minutes?"

"No, but anything I do or say right now would be like beating a dead dog."

"It's a dead horse, Henry," Helen corrected.

"Whatever, you get the idea. Let's just eat, wish them well, and talk about them when they leave."

"Sounds good to me." Molly dug into a plate of food.

She was happy they were all there, but she was never good at good-byes and was beyond tired of explaining everything to everyone. It was time to get back to her life, their life. Who the hell knew what would happen but it was time to start letting it happen. Eager to get on the road, Molly hurried through the meal.

"We all expect phone calls and e-mails often." Alex tried to be normal. "As well as doctors' reports and photos."

"Of course."

"I'll make sure I get some with Molly sitting still," Liam added.

"I can't wait to see you get as huge as me."

"Thanks, Renee." Smirking at her sister-in-law.

"I got you a little good-bye gift." Renee handed her a box.

"It's not like you are never going to see me. What's with all the sentimental mush?"

"I wonder." Renee, gesturing to Liam. "Everything's been a touch dramatic around here lately, wouldn't you say, Liam?"

Liam blushed. It was difficult sitting there knowing everyone knew his business, but he knew he was lucky they didn't toss him out on his ass and he wasn't going to complain about small but well-placed digs.

Molly opened the box and inside was a large pink velour sweatshirt with an even larger yellow cat on the front.

"You know I hate cats."

"Yup." Hugging Molly. "Welcome to the club. Soon enough it will be perfectly placed elastic and station wagons for you as well."

"There is something so wrong in this." Smiling.

"Just desserts," Renee responded.

"You did not just say that?" Alex groaned.

"What?" Renee laughed. "A little pastry humor."

"There's no such thing." Kissing his wife's cheek.

"Thanks, again." Folding the sweatshirt. "I love it!" Handing the box to Liam and whispering, "Hide this please, forever."

"Why? I bet it will look just darling on you."

"Oh, no. Where have all my allies gone?" Molly hung her head.

"We are all here," Helen answered firmly.

Molly looked up and surveyed her family. They all stared back at her. They were all being polite and appropriate, and Molly knew that would always be the case. They even would take Liam back into their family and embrace him and love him, but they would always have her back no matter what. The knowledge and recognition of that made Molly smile.

"Dad and I fixed you some food for the road. It's in a cooler in the backseat, and I want you to call often."

"I will." Looking at her watch. "We should get going. It's a long drive back to the treatment center."

Everyone walked Molly and Liam outside to her car, and after a whirlwind of kisses, hugs, and threatening but graceful last wishes toward Liam, they were off. Once again, Molly was behind the wheel directing her automotive castle through the highways and byways of the road. She was cruising, caught up in the rhythm of lines and green signs, except this time, she wasn't alone and she was heading somewhere without a cloud over her head. All the nicks and scratches had been freshly repainted with a new coat of glossy, bright white number 3. This would be their new color, their second chance to fill the canvas with new memories, mistakes, and magic. She was no longer running from, she was simply driving to. The car wasn't a silent, stifling tomb, encasing Molly in her own gloom. The car was now a ripe pumpkin, revamped, reconditioned, and reconstructed into a shiny chariot bringing them back to the ball.

acknowledgments

There are so many fabulous people to thank. To my agent, Jan Miller, thanks for being a fantastic cheerleader and big voice for a sometimes shy writer. To my editor, Kelli Martin, thanks for tolerating my endless emails and for all the careful notes that tightened the book while keeping it true. To Jill, Elizabeth, and Claire, thanks for spreading the word about my babies, I mean, my books. To my friends, A, A, B, B, L, L, G, J, J, J, J, P, M, L, A, D, D, C, thanks for encouraging me, for laughing with me, and at me, and especially for not getting mad at me when I used you for material . . . or didn't. And finally, to Jake, Ruth, Jason, and the rest of my extended family, thanks for making me the luckiest girl in the world. Your love and guidance is what makes all this possible and I would be nowhere without my refuge, the safe, protected, and honest place all of you have created for me.